THE PROMISE OF THE CLASS OF '64

ALSO BY JOHN GILLOOLY

Pride on the Mount
Friday Night Thunderbolts

THE PROMISE OF THE CLASS OF '64

JOHN GILLOOLY

The Promise of the Class of ’64

Produced and printed by Stillwater River Publications.

Visit our website at
www.StillwaterPress.com
for more information.

First Stillwater River Publications Edition.

ISBN: 978-1-968548-22-3

Library of Congress Control Number: 2026900478

1 2 3 4 5 6 7 8 9 10
Written by John Gillooly.
Cover & interior book design by Matthew St. Jean.
Published by Stillwater River Publications,
West Warwick, RI, USA.

Publisher’s Cataloging-in-Publication
(Provided by Cassidy Cataloguing Services, Inc.)
Names: Gillooly, John, author.
Title: The promise of the Class of ‘64 / John Gillooly.
Description: First Stillwater River Publications edition. | Pawtucket, RI, USA : Stillwater River Publications, [2026]
Identifiers: LCCN: 2026900478 | ISBN: 9781968548223
Subjects: LCSH: High school students--New England. | Coming of age--United States. | Baby boom generation--United States. | Nineteen sixties. | United States--History--1961-1969. | LCGFT: Bildungsromans. | Historical fiction.
Classification: LCC: PS3607.I449 P76 2026 |
DDC: 813/.6--dc23

To Mary K. Gillooly & Ellen (Gillooly) Dacey, my mother and sister—
two strong, intelligent women

The daily New York Times news articles in this book are real.
The story and characters, however, are fictitious.
Any similarities the story and characters have to real life
are purely unintentional.

ONE

> WASHINGTON – I have a dream that one day this nation will rise up and live out the true meaning of its creed: "We hold these truths to be self-evident, that all men are created equal."
>
> *—Martin Luther King, August 28, 1963*

The sun was shining brightly as a 1958 Austin Healey 100-Six with the top down and the radio blasting out the Beach Boys' "Little Surfer Girl" pulled into the parking lot behind the three-story brick high school. The tall, dark-haired driver reached over and turned down the volume knob on the radio.

"Holy shit, what the hell is this? I've never seen so many cars trying to fit into so few spaces," Jay Burke said to his friend Tony Gemma, who was in the passenger seat.

"Welcome to public school, preppy. There are no reserved parking spots here like you had at your little prep school. It's every man for himself here," said Tony.

"Cut the preppy shit. I never went to prep school," said the driver.

"It was a private school where you wore ties and jackets," quipped Tony. "What else would you call it?"

"It was more like a Catholic high school monastery. By the way, why are we starting school on the Thursday before Labor Day? I have never started school before Labor Day." Jay asked.

Tony was busy looking for a parking space, but he offered an explanation.

"It's something about the school department possibly running out of money before the end of the calendar year, and if they do, they might have to close school for a week. So, they want to get in some extra days at the beginning of the school year."

"Hey, over there. You can fit into that spot," Tony suddenly yelled, pointing to a narrow space between two cars."

"No way, I might be able to squeeze into it, but we will never be able to open the doors," Jay offered.

"No problem, we just go out the top. That's why you drive around with the top down, isn't it?"

"I drive with the top down because the top is ripped and I can't afford a new one. Remember, I spent every dollar I earned from my lifeguarding job this summer buying this car because you convinced me, I'm a sports-car type guy," Jay countered.

"You are a sports car type guy—tall, dark hair, and handsome. The girls are always checking you out when we are driving around with the top down. You're a natural sports car type guy," Tony said to his friend.

"Yeah, a sports car type guy on a Volkswagen budget. There, I'm in. Now we just have to get out."

They managed to squeeze out of the top of the car and joined the multitude of teenagers headed for the high school.

"How the hell many kids are in this school anyway?" Jay asked.

"I don't know how many in the whole school, but I've heard we have more than 600 in our senior class. I've heard it's the largest senior class in the history of the school."

"Six hundred in one class. Are you shitting me? We only had 200 in the whole school at Priory. There are three classes here, right? That's 1,800 students in the school."

"Don't worry, you're going to love it. You didn't have anything like that at Priory," Tony said with a big smile as he pointed at three girls walking across the parking lot.

NEW YORK TIMES, AUGUST 28, 1963

> WASHINGTON – More than 200,000 Americans, most of them black, but many of them white, demonstrated here today for a full and speedy program of civil rights and equal job opportunities.
>
> It was the greatest assembly for a redress of grievances that this capital has ever seen.

Jay didn't need to be reminded that he was now in a different educational world, even if he was only five miles from his house and forty miles from his old school. Four months ago, he was at a small, private Catholic all-boys high school. Now he was starting his first day at a massive public high school. It would be the first time he has ever been a public-school student.

It all seemed to have happened so fast.

He never gave much thought to why he had attended Priory for his first two years of high school. It seemed to just happen. He has lived in the same house his entire life. He had grown up attending the Catholic elementary school about a half mile from his house. He was an only child, and his parents were Catholic, so it was only natural that he would go to the Catholic school rather than the public elementary school a few streets from his home. As far as he knew, his life was idyllic. He would walk along tree-lined streets to the school and spend the day being taught by nuns. After school, he would walk home, change his clothes, and head to the field a few streets from his home, where he would play pick-up football games in the fall and baseball games in the spring. In the winter, it was hockey games on the small pond next to the field or basketball games at the church rec hall next to the school. His mother was home when he left for school in the morning, and she was there when he returned in the afternoon. His father would have already left for work before he woke up in the morning, but he was always home for dinner at night, often with some of the dirt and grime of his day's work as a plumber still evident on his hands, a pack of cigarettes in his work-shirt pocket.

He didn't really know much about his parents' lives before he was born. What young boy ever asks questions about his parents? He knew his father had been in World War II, but his father never said much about the War. "I did a job, and I came home" is the way his father would summarize his wartime experiences, the few times Jay remembers him ever talking about it. He knew his parents were both from the same city and had known each other before his father went to war, and they were married as soon as his father returned home. Jay was born on June 15, 1946.

Neither his father nor his mother had gone to college, but his father had started his own plumbing business when Jay was in the fourth or fifth grade, and as his mother said, "they finally had a little money." The Catholic school he attended while growing up was a combined elementary and junior high school, so he was there through the ninth grade. When it came time to start high school in the tenth grade, his parents said they thought the best place for him was Priory, a small Catholic, all-boys school about forty miles from their home. They said something about it giving him opportunities they never had, and he never questioned them.

Most of the students at Priory commuted from their homes every day, but there was also a small dormitory on the hilly campus where a few students lived. Jay's parents told him they felt the eighty-mile round trip every day was too much for him to be a commuter, so he lived in the dorm during the school week. It wasn't bad. He had his own room just like at home, so it wasn't that much different than at home, just a few more people at the dinner table. The school had a football team, which meant Jay could play football in the fall, and when the football season ended, there was basketball in the winter, then baseball in the spring. The school was so close to his home that his parents would come down every weekend and drive him back home after the Saturday football, basketball, and baseball games, then back to school on Sunday night. His short weekend stays at home meant he still could spend time with Tony. The two had grown up together for virtually their entire lives, ever since the Gemma family moved a few houses down the street when Tony was four years old. "They wanted to get out of the city," Jay remembers his parents saying when the Gemmas moved into the neighborhood. Jay and Tony were the same age, born only a few months apart, and they both loved playing sports. So even though Tony attended the nearby public elementary school and then the public junior high, and Jay went to the Catholic school, they were inseparable for their first nine years of school. They were on the same team in the newly organized Little League in their section of the city, and somehow, they always seemed to end up on the same team when sides were chosen for the pick-up football games at the nearby Owen Field in the fall. When they were ten, Tony's father heard of a Pee Wee football team being organized in a nearby town. Tony was short and stocky, so they made him a lineman. Jay was tall, could run fast, and throw a football farther than the other kids their age, so he became one of the team's two quarterbacks. So, the two friends grew up playing sports together and talking about sports. As they moved into their teen years, they started thinking of things other than Y.A. Tittle, the New York Football Giants, and the Red Sox and Yankees, so they shared their other questions about being teenage boys. Jay was now six feet and weighed about 175 pounds. Tony was five-nine and weighed almost 200 pounds.

Not being with Tony almost every afternoon was one of the things Jay didn't like about going to Priory but they spent almost every minute together when Jay was home on weekends. In the summer Tony's parents allow him to stay with Jay and his parents at the summer shack near a beach about forty miles from their neighborhood that Jay's mother had inherited when her parents died a few years after Jay was born.

So, for Jay's first year at Priory, his life hadn't really changed that much. But six months ago, in the middle of his junior year, Jay's idyllic life was shattered.

When he was called to the Priory headmaster's office in the middle of the school day and saw his mother sitting in the office, he knew something was wrong. His father had died from a heart attack that morning, she told him. There was no warning; he hadn't been sick, at least not that his mother knew.

Over the next few weeks, Jay's mother told him his father's death would not change anything. She said he could still attend Priory. But now his mother was home alone, and even though she never admitted it, he knew she was worried about money. Without his father, there was no business, no steady income. His mother was talking about going back to work as a secretary, which she had done before Jay was born.

But even before his father's death, Jay had started having doubts that Priory was the right place for him. There was this sense of sameness. Nothing was ever questioned in a classroom by the students. Plus, on weekends when he spent time with Tony and some of the other guys in the neighborhood, they would talk about how much they enjoyed being at Jefferson High, their city's public high school. How there were kids from all over the city, different kids than the ones they had grown up with in their neighborhood. And of course, there were girls—all day; every day. So, in the spring, a few months after his father's death, Jay told his mother he wanted to transfer to Jefferson for his senior year. She wasn't happy at first, worried about his leaving catholic-school education for the first time in his life. But eventually he convinced her that it was something he really wanted to do, so she agreed.

NEW YORK TIMES, AUGUST 28, 1963

WASHINGTON – The United States reaffirmed today its belief that the South Vietnamese Government had violated pledges on the Buddhist

> crisis and that the Vietnamese military chiefs were innocent of responsibility for assaults on pagodas.

"This is the perfect school for you – girls, football star," Tony said as the duo started walking across the parking lot.

"Football star, that's a joke," said Jay. "I was a backup QB at Priory, and we only had twenty-five guys on the team. This team has at least sixty guys. I have been practicing with the team here for a week, and the head coach doesn't even know my name yet. I will be lucky if I ever step on the field this season. The only position I have ever played is quarterback, and Amore already has a year as the starting quarterback, plus Reall was the backup last year, and that sophomore Belovitch is a really good athlete."

"Don't worry," Tony responded. "You're fast, you're smart, and I know you can throw the ball better than any of those guys. Coach Rowe just needs to get to know you a little better, and you need to learn our system. You ran that crazy "Spread/Opinion" down at Priory, but there's none of that shit here. It's straight T here."

"I noticed, it's all power runs or straight drop back. I'm not that good, dropping straight back," Jay said.

"You can learn," said Tony. "You just need to get some snaps, and even if you don't play the scenery here is a lot better than Priory," Tony added with a laugh as the three girls Tony had pointed out when they were trying to find a parking space approached from the other side of the parking lot.

"Hi Tony," said a blond-haired girl wearing a plaid, pleated skirt that settled on her well-tanned legs at the middle of her knees and a white Oxford blouse with one button open at the neck.

"Did you have a good summer?" the girl asked.

"Hi, Tammy," said Tony. "Yeah, it was good."

"Hello, Tony's friend," the blond offered to Jay while flashing an enchanting smile.

Jay just looked at the girl and didn't say a word as she walked past him along with the two other girls and headed toward the school.

Tony started laughing.

"What the fuck is wrong with you. You look like you just saw a ghost?" Tony said after the three girls were beyond hearing range.

"Who is that girl? Jay questioned.

"Who?" Tony asked with a puzzled look.

"The girl who said hello," Jay said with a disgusted tone that Tony didn't know he was talking about the blond.

"Oh, that's Tammy Clark. Actually, you have seen her before," Tony said.

"I have!" Jay quipped

"Yeah, this summer at the folk festival. She was sitting in the stands a few rows in front of us. But don't waste your time with her."

"Why, does she have a boyfriend?" Jay asked in a disappointed tone.

"Yeah, but he graduated last year, and now he's at some small college in upstate New York. Besides, he was an asshole when he was here. He was a pretty good basketball player, so he thought he was a big shit. I'm not sure how long that relationship is going to last with him not around here anymore. Tammy doesn't stand around idle very long."

"It sounds like you don't like her."

"No, I like her, I guess. I mean, everybody is supposed to like Tammy. Maybe that's the problem. She always seems more interested in being the person everybody is watching; she always has to be the center of attention. Sure, she's pretty, and I guess she's fairly smart, but sometimes it just seems like she thinks she's untouchable. Last year, she was the blond cheerleader who dated the older star athlete. Now, we are seniors. There's nobody older than us. I just wonder what she is going to do."

NEW YORK TIMES, AUGUST 28, 1963

WASHINGTON – The civil rights demonstration that swept more than 200,000 people through the capital today appeared to have left much of Congress untouched physically, emotionally and politically.

Jay stood outside the guidance office wearing khaki, chino pants, white socks, and penny loafers, looking at his schedule. There were six courses in six different classrooms, ranging in numbers from 101 to 330. He started walking the corridor that seemed to go on forever, and there were two more floors just like this one. At Priory, all the classes were held in a building that had two floors and only eight rooms on each floor.

The female guidance counselor had given him some final advice as he left her office.

"You are going to do fine here," she had said. "It's just going to be a little different."

One look at his schedule as he was walking out of the guidance office was all Jay needed to realize he was undertaking a new educational experience. Unlike at Priory, where every class was held at the same time every day, this school worked on a rotating schedule, with every class being held at a different time every day. He figured he had already missed the first class, so he headed for his next class, US History in Room 329.

By the time he walked up three flights of stairs and down the long corridor, the classroom was already filled with students occupying almost all of the thirty-five desks.

"Welcome," the male teacher said to Jay as he timidly walked into the classroom and handed the teacher his slip from the guidance office.

"My name is Mr. Kiley. I see you are new here, so don't believe anything these clowns say about me," said the teacher with a wide semi-circle sweep of his arm toward the students. "Seats are at a premium, but there is an open desk right up front in the third row. Nobody wants to sit near the front."

Jay walked to his seat, a little stunned by the teacher's humorous introduction of himself. At Priory, a teacher would never be so informal when addressing a student. As he made his way down to the empty desk, a little smile came to Jay's face as he looked toward the back of the room and saw Tony sitting at a desk in the back row in the middle of the room. At least he and Tony were in one class together, he thought. When he turned to move into his seat, he noticed the blond he had asked Tony about in the morning was also sitting in the back of the room, two rows over from Tony. He tried to be inconspicuous, but he couldn't help sneaking a look back at her once again when he was in his seat.

"Okay, folks," Kiley continued. "These are your textbooks. The school department requires that I pass them out to you, but take it home today and put it someplace safe because you are never going to use it."

"All right," came a shout from the back of the room. "We are going to watch movies every day."

Jay didn't need to turn and look toward the back of the room. He knew it was Tony interrupting the teacher with his attempt at humor. At Priory, that type of outburst would have had the student immediately heading to the Dean of Men's office, but Kiley just smiled.

"No, you are going to read, just not from this textbook," the teacher said. "The textbook is four years old, which, as textbooks go, isn't that bad. But look at the last chapter. It's all about Dwight Eisenhower being president. The name of this course is Modern U.S. History. You people, are living American history right now. You shouldn't need to wait until somebody writes a book about it."

The teacher then took a few steps back toward his large wooden desk that sat at the front of the classroom, and reached over and picked up a newspaper.

"This is the New York Times," Kiley said, holding up a copy of the August 29th N.Y Times. "This will be your textbook this year. Most of you probably have never seen the Times. Most of you probably read a newspaper, at least the sports section and the comics, but it's probably the local daily. It's a good newspaper, but its main focus is on what's happening in this city and this state. The Times is more expansive. It's about what is happening around this country and the world every day. Look at what's written at the top of the front page every day: 'All the News That's Fit to Print.' That's the Times' slogan.

"I was able to work out a deal with the local distributor for the Times that even the local paper couldn't match. It will cost each of you twenty-five cents a week to get your own copy of the Times every morning. Monday through Friday. They will deliver the papers to the school each morning, and they will be here for you to take every day when you walk into this class. I will collect a nickel from everybody each day, or you can pay a quarter at the end of the week. We will try to work on the honor system. Put your nickel in the jar here on my desk. Don't worry if you didn't have a nickel to spare, I know that's two cartons of milk in the cafeteria. I will put the nickel in for you, but try to find the nickel; remember, I'm a poor teacher. I think you will find it well worth the investment. Every day, there are headlines and stories in the Times that will present multiple accounts about what's happening in this country and the world. We will talk about how those stories relate to you."

The teacher kept describing how the class would be conducted. There was a sense of enthusiasm in his delivery that Jay hadn't seen in any of his teachers at Priory.

"We are going to read the paper, and we are going to talk about what we have read. At the end of each week, you will write a summary report of what we have read during the week. They will not be long, 200, maybe 300 words at the most. You need to learn how to write consciously. The reports will be due every Monday. They can be about the things we will talk about in the class or anything you read in the paper, except sports, Gemma," the teacher said as he looked toward Tony. "I have to give you at least one exam each quarter, but the major part of your mark will come from that weekly report and your classroom participation. Handwrite the reports, type them, whatever you need to do. I just don't want to see ten of the same reports just copying things out of the paper. I want you to summarize, in your own words, what you read in the paper and what we discussed in class. With the rotation schedule, this class doesn't meet tomorrow, so you will not have to do a report for this week. Your assignment for this week will be to take this paper home, read it, and we will discuss it on Tuesday after the holiday."

"Just look at the headlines on the front page of today's paper about what happened yesterday: '200,000 March for Civil Rights;' 'President Sees Gain for Negro;' 'I Have a Dream…'"

"People—Things are happening," Kiley said with a broad smile.

TWO

UNITED PRESS INTERNATIONAL, SEPTEMBER 3, 1963

> MONTGOMERY, Ala. – Gov. George C. Wallace, in his battle against integration in Alabama public schools, ran headlong into the opposition in his own state yesterday, and a showdown loomed at a rural high school today.

"What period is Kiley's class today?" asked the auburn-haired girl wearing the soft mohair sweater and straight black skirt that ran down to just above her knees.

"I think it's fourth," said the blond. "Why are you suddenly so interested in history?" her blond friend asked.

"The eyes, I want to see those eyes again," said the dark-haired girl.

"What are you talking about?" asked Tammy Clark, trying to act nonchalant

"Don't give me that act. You know what I'm talking about," her friend said. "The new kid in Kiley's class. I know you noticed those blueberry eyes when he walked into class the first day of school last week. You got hot, just like I did."

"Burns, you're crude," said the blond.

"I may be crude, but tell me you didn't notice those eyes?" Marty Burns declared.

"I guess so," said the blond. "They are a nice shade of blue."

"I knew you noticed. So, what do you know about him?" Marty asked.

"I know he's Tony's friend and he drives a white sports car, and he went to that little private high school down in Jamestown. But his father died last winter, so he transferred here for his senior year. I think he might play football too," Tammy replied.

"Holy shit, it figures it would only take you a few days to learn everything about a new good-looking boy in school. Do you already have a date with him?" the dark-haired beauty quipped.

"Cut it out," the blond said as she looked at her friend. "I don't know everything about him. I just saw him with Tony in the parking lot on the first day of school last week and said hello to him. Sara was with us, and she told me who he was. They went to that Catholic grammar school on the other side of the city together when they were growing up."

"So, are you going to make a move on him?" Marty Burns asked.

"No, I'm not making a move on him. I have a boyfriend, remember?" the blond replied.

"Speaking of which, did Dave leave for college yet?" Marty inquired.

"Yeah, Sunday. He could check in on either Sunday or Labor Day, but his parents said it was 200 miles to Schenectady, so they wanted to drive up on Sunday and then drive home on Monday."

"Did you go out Saturday night?"

"Yeah, I wanted to go to the movies and see Cleopatra. He wanted to go to the lake."

"So, what did you do?"

"We compromised; we went to the drive-in and saw Tarzan's Three Challenges. It wasn't my idea of a great night at the movies. Of course, he wasn't really interested in watching any movie. I guess he thought he was going to get a going-away present."

"Did he?" the auburn-haired girl asked with a sly smile.

"No, he did not, at least not the present he was hoping for," said the blond. "I was pissed-off at him. He knew I had to stay down at our beach house last weekend because I had to work at the beach concession stand early Saturday and Sunday morning, but he didn't come down any of the weekend nights. He said he didn't want to come down because my parents were there. But I know it was because he wanted to go to some parties up here so he could drink with his buddies. He gave me the 'I'm not going to see these guys until Thanksgiving' line. How about not seeing me? I didn't see him until I came back up from the beach on Wednesday, and we started school on Thursday."

"What time did you get home Saturday night?"

"I was home at 11 o'clock."

"That says a lot," Marty said with a sarcastic laugh. "When is he coming home again?"

"He said he might come home in three or four weeks if he can get a ride, but he wasn't sure."

"How about our homecoming dance in November. Aren't you going with him?"

"I mentioned it to him, but said he's not sure right now. College basketball practice starts on Oct. 15, and the dance is on Nov. 2nd. He called me last night, but he was on a pay phone in his dorm hallway. So, he said he couldn't really talk."

"That stinks. Have you written him yet?"

"I started writing a letter after we talked last night, but I didn't really have anything to say. I'll finish it tonight."

"Well, Dave may be in Schenectady, but blue-eyes is right here, and if you are not interested, I'm going to get to know that young man," Marty declared.

"He's all yours, and God help him," Tammy said with a laugh as the two walked through the big wooden front doors of the high school.

ASSOCIATED PRESS, SEPTEMBER 3, 1963

MEMPHIS, Tenn. – About 500 Negroes protesting crowded school conditions staged the largest racial demonstration in Memphis history

> yesterday and the Negro desegregation drive flared in several other cities across the nation.

They have been friends for two years, ever since they came to Jefferson in the tenth grade from the two different public junior high schools in the city that feed into the one large high school. They were never quite sure what caused them to form a bond. They didn't live all that close to each other, and they certainly didn't look alike. One had auburn hair and freckles on her face; the type of girl people call cute. The other had the type of facial features you see on magazine cover models with blond hair that curled up just before it reached the base of her neck. The blond was an inch or so taller, about five-six, but they both had the type of well-formed bodies that can make a teenage boy's body ache.

And they both were cheerleaders.

The fourteen varsity cheerleaders were Jefferson's female equivalent of the school's star male athletes. With no girls' varsity sports teams at the school, the cheerleaders were the only girls who were constantly in the public eye. Football games, basketball games, hockey games, they were always at the front of the crowd with their short skirts, firm legs, chanting, flashing big smiles, and hearing the cheers from fans when they performed their routines. The celebrity status within the school certainly could be an ego boost, but it also can have a downside. As the only female students who were constantly in the public eye, there definitely was resentment from some other girls.

It probably wasn't surprising that Tammy Clark and Martha "Marty" Burns had become close within the cheerleading group. Some of the cheerleaders seemed to relish the attention and not worry about what other people thought, but it upset both Tammy and Marty that some people thought they were just pretty faces wearing short skirts in front of a big crowd, stealing the attention of the boys. They both had independence streaks, and they were not afraid to voice their opinions, either to the head cheerleader at team meetings or even in the classroom on occasion. While Tammy might have been the blond that people tended to notice first, Marty was the one who tended to push the accepted social limits more often. The hemlines of the skirts of almost every girl at Jefferson High fell to the middle of the girls' knees, but Marty's hemline often came to rest at the top or even an inch or two above her knees.

NEW YORK TIMES, SEPTEMBER 3, 1963

> HYANNISPORT, Mass. – President Kennedy said that the leaders of South Vietnam should realize that the war against the Communist guerrillas was "their war" and that it could not be won unless the Government recovered the popular support it had lost.

"Okay, people, how many looked at last Thursday's Times?" Kiley asked.

His dark, heavy-framed eyeglasses made the teacher appear much older than a man in his late twenties.

He had started teaching at Jefferson a few years ago and almost immediately became a favorite with the students. He was unconventional in his teaching style, tending to spend as much time asking questions about what the students thought about subjects as he did lecturing from the textbook. He had an athletic build, and the word was he had played football at a small New England college, but he didn't seem like a typical jock. He knew about sports, but he seemed more interested in talking about John Kennedy than Sandy Koufax or Y.A. Tittle.

Jay was immediately fascinated with Kiley's plan to use the New York Times as their textbook. He had never been so excited about going to a class.

For several years now, his love for reading that had first been cultivated by reading the fictitious exploits of high school sports stars Chip Hilton and Bronc Burnett had turned toward reading about real people. Sports was still his primary interest, so the first thing he would do when he picked up the local paper every morning would be turn to the sports pages and read about Koufax or Tittle or Bob Cousy. But after he read the sports pages, he would turn to the front page to see if there were any stories about what President Kennedy was doing or some of the other political leaders, both national and local. He liked reading about people, and politicians seemed to be exciting, just like athletes, especially Kennedy. Last Christmas, he had even told his mother that the book "Making of the President" was one of the things he wanted for Christmas, and when he got it, he read it from cover to cover in a few days.

"That's not bad about twenty of you," Kiley said as he did a quick count of the arms that had been raised in response to his question. "Okay, how many of you knew what happened in Washington last Wednesday before you saw Thursday's paper?"

"I saw it on the Huntley-Brinkley report Wednesday night," yelled the stocky boy sitting in one of the back rows.

"I'm impressed you watch the evening news," the teacher said, moving toward the boy.

"Well, it was kind of my parents watching, I happened to notice," the student admitted.

"That's okay," Kiley offered. "Did you understand why they were marching?"

"Equality," the stocky kid quickly answered.

"Equality of what?" Kiley fired back.

There was momentary silence as the boy was searching for an answer, but before he could answer, Tammy Clark spoke out.

"Civil rights," she said.

"That's right. Was that something you ever thought about before you saw the march on TV or read about it in the paper?" Kiley asked the class.

Thirty-two students sat in silence, looking somewhat uncomfortable that the teacher was making them part of the lesson.

Finally, Kiley broke the silence.

"That's not surprising," Kiley quipped. "Ruggieri, how many students are in this class?" the teacher asked the burly football player sitting in the back of the room.

"About thirty," Jimmy Ruggieri answered as he looked around the classroom.

"That's right, and how many of them are Negros?" Kiley retorted.

The students stiffened, but Ruggieri didn't need to look around the class for a second count.

"None, "Ruggieri said sheepishly.

Kiley paused for nearly a minute before giving his reply.

"People, you have to start understanding what's happening outside your own world," the teacher said.

UNITED PRESS INTERNATIONAL, SEPTEMBER 4, 1963

> BIRMINGHAM, Ala. Gov. George Wallace used state troopers to block school integration at Tuskegee again yesterday then rushed them to Birmingham, but encountered the same local opposition here that he had in Tuskegee.

"What's up for the weekend?" Marty asked Tammy as they walked toward the front entrance of the school on Wednesday morning.

"I don't know, we are cheering at the jamboree game Friday night, after that, I haven't given it much thought," Tammy replied.

"Have you heard from Dave?" Marty asked.

"NO," Tammy replied crisply.

"OK," Marty said, knowing not to press the issue any further. "Thank God the football season is starting. Now we have something to do at least one day of the weekend."

UNITED PRESS INTERNATIONAL, SEPTEMBER 4, 1963

> TUSKEGEE, Ala. The county solicitor charged yesterday that state troopers have invaded "Mason County" and said he intended to go to federal court to have school integration orders carried out.

"Who knows what President Kennedy did in June, just about the time you people were getting out of school for the summer?" Mr. Kiley asked at the start of his class on Wednesday.

Almost every one of the thirty-two teenagers in the classroom lowered their heads, hoping the teachers wouldn't call on them for an answer.

Finally, Jay broke the silence.

"Gave a Civil Rights speech," he said.

"That's right. I guess the new kid reads a lot," said Kiley, flashing a smile.

"Okay, people, that's the thing," Kiley continued, "Sometimes you need to know a little recent history to understand what you are reading in today's paper. So, your first major assignment is going to be to write a report on what President Kennedy's civil rights speech was all about. You will need to go to the library and check the Readers' Guide to Periodic Literature for magazine stories about the speech. The good news is that not everybody needs to write the report. We are going to work in teams on projects like this, four or five of you on each team. Clark and Burns, you two are basically joined at the hip, so why don't you team with the new kid, Gemma, Stone, and Miss Snow and work together on this report? Today is Wednesday, and it will be due on Monday."

"Here's something to think about while considering the President's speech," Kiley continued. "I read a comment Martin Luther King made this summer. He said, "Four score after Lincoln's emancipation Proclamation, the Negro is not free."

Before Kiley had a chance to broach another topic, the bell sounded, sending everybody heading for the door.

"Burke," Kiley said as Jay walked past the teacher's desk on his way out of class. "I hope you don't mind me calling you the new kid. I try to give everybody in class an identity."

"No, sir, no problem. I thought it was funny," Jay replied.

"Good, and by the way, I was impressed that you knew about the civil rights speech."

"Thank you, sir. I like President Kennedy, so I pay attention to what he is doing."

"Good, and let me guess. You went to a private school before you came here." Kiley said with a slight laugh.

"Yes, sir, I did," Jay said.

"I figured. Look, I appreciate the respect, but you might want to drop the Sir. It's not something you hear a lot around here. In fact, you will never hear it," Kiley added with a smile.

THREE

ASSOCIATED PRESS, SEPTEMBER 6, 1963

Huntsville, Ala. – Representatives of Gov. George Wallace asked the Huntsville Board of Education yesterday to postpone the opening of desegregated schools. The board refused, opening the way for four Negro pupils to join white children in class today.

"Why are we only playing a twenty-four-minute game tonight?" Jay asked Tony as they drove to school on Friday morning.

"It's not a real game. Two other teams come to our field, and we play each team in a twelve-minute game; then those teams play each other. They call it a jamboree. It doesn't make much sense to me, but at least it's a chance to play some real football."

UNITED PRESS INTERNATIONAL, SEPTEMBER 6, 1963

BOSTON – Four demonstrators vowed last night to remain in Boston School Committee headquarters and eat no food until the committee admits the existence of de facto segregation in the city's public schools.

"Apparently, not all the problems with segregation in education are in Alabama," Kiley said as soon as the Friday afternoon class started. "Here's one story about George Wallace trying to keep a desegregated school from opening, and on the same page is a story about four people demonstrating about another type of segregation in Boston. That's close to home, folks."

"So, can four people influence how the city of Boston runs its schools?" Kiley asked.

"It has to start somewhere," said Tammy Clark. "Somebody has to stand up and refuse to accept it, even if it's only four people."

NEW YORK TIMES, SEPTEMBER. 9, 1963

> WASHINGTON – The Kennedy Administration was privately annoyed but publicly silent about a report that it was continuing to finance the South Vietnamese Special Forces, which recently raided Buddhist pagodas.

"What's the matter? Are you lost?" Jay heard a female voice ask as he stood outside the door of his homeroom, looking down at the class schedule in his hand while a horde of students were moving past him. He looked up and saw the auburn-haired cheerleader everybody called Marty.

"Hi, Marty. I guess I'm still having some problems with my schedule. This is the first class, but it's third period, so I guess I'm in English. You think after a week, I would know where I'm going."

"Don't worry, my first year here, it took me months to figure out where I should be. Let me look at that schedule. Where do you have English?" she asked as she grabbed the schedule out of Jay's hand.

"Ah, 215. I have Spanish next door. I'll walk up there with you."

The two walked together for a few seconds without saying a word until Marty broke the silence.

"I saw you at HoJo's Friday night after the jamboree. Why didn't you come over and talk to us?" Marty asked.

"I don't know. I guess I still feel a little strange around people I don't know that well, so I just hung with Tony and a few guys on the team for a while, then headed home," Jay offered.

"We have to get you introduced to more people. What are you doing Friday night?" the auburn-headed girl asked.

"Nothing special. We have a game in Clinton Saturday afternoon, so I guess I will just stay home and watch 'Route 66.'"

Marty offered an alternative way to spend the evening.

"Well, Jane's parents are going to some dinner Friday night, and they said she could have a few people over to her house. Do you want to go with me?"

The suddenness of the invitation caught Jay by surprise, and without really thinking about it. He said, "Sure."

"Good pick-me-up around seven. This is my address and phone number," Marty said as she scribbled on a piece of paper.

"Yeah, see you then," Jay said, not quite sure how he suddenly had a date for Friday night.

NEW YORK TIMES, SEPTEMBER 10, 1963

> BIRMINGHAM, Ala – Twenty Negro children entered white schools in three Alabama cities today after President Kennedy's federalization of the state's National Guardsmen ended the defiance of Gov. George C. Wallace.

Kiley burst into the classroom, throwing his grade book on the big desk that sat on the two-inch high, four-by-eight-foot wood platform in the front of the room, and immediately broke into conversation.

"Sorry, I'm late, folks. Is everybody here?"

"Yeah, we're all here," yelled Tony.

"Good, then I don't have to waste time taking attendance, just don't tell Mr. Lawson," the teacher quipped about the school principal. "Okay, let's go—team report—Burke, Gemma, Stone, Miss Clark, Miss Burns, and Miss Snow up to the front of the room, please."

"Who is going to do the talking?" the teacher asked.

"I will," said Tammy Clark.

"Why am I not surprised?" Kiley said with a slight laugh. "Go ahead."

She started with the factual information. President Kennedy had delivered a speech to a national TV audience on the night of June 11. He said it followed a series of threats and defiant statements that had forced the Alabama National Guard to carry out a court order that two qualified young Alabama residents who happened to have been born Negro be admitted to the University of Alabama. She went on to say how the president said he hoped every American, regardless of where they live, would stop and examine his conscience about this and other related incidents. She talked about how the President said, while we are committed to the worldwide struggle to promote and protect the rights of all who wish to be free, it ought to be possible for American students of any color to attend any public institution they select without having to be backed up by troops. How it ought to be possible for American consumers of any color to receive equal service in places of public accommodation and for American citizens of any color to register and to vote in a free election.

Jay stood mesmerized, watching Tammy talk. Her blond hair, which lay softly across her forehead, descended from the edge of her scalp on the left side of her face to just along the edge of her right eyebrow before it dropped along the side of her face. She was wearing just a soft cashmere sweater, which accentuated her ample breasts. But his fascination now was more than just the physical features that had caught his attention in the parking lot on the first day of school. She didn't seem to be reciting facts off the neatly handwritten sheets of paper she held in her hands. She seemed to be talking with a passion as she told the class about the Kennedy speech,

"The president said the Negro baby born in America today, regardless of what section of the country he or she is born, has about one-half as much chance of completing high school as a white baby born in the same place on the same day, one-third as much chance of completing college. That doesn't seem right," Tammy said without changing the tempo of her presentation.

Suddenly, Kiley, who was standing against the back wall, spoke up.

"Did the president say that about not being right, Miss Clark?"

"Well, maybe not in those exact words, but it was kind of our opinion that was the way the President felt," Tammy said, looking over at the rest of the team members who were standing off to her left side at the front of the room.

Jay didn't remember talking about it when they were doing the research, but he certainly wasn't going to dispute Tammy. After all, the only time the whole team had gotten together to do some research was one day after school in the school library, and the three boys had only stayed for a few minutes, claiming they "had to go to football practice."

"Good," Kiley said. "I don't want you just parroting what you read. I want you to form some opinions. Okay, sorry to interrupt, keep going."

"The President said we face a moral crisis as a country and a people," the blond said when she resumed.

She went on to read what Kennedy had said.

"This is one country. It has become one country because all of us and all the people who came here had an equal chance to develop our talents. We cannot say to ten percent of the population that you can't have that right; that your children cannot have the chance to develop whatever talents they have. Not everybody has equal talent or ability, but we all should have the same chance to develop those talents," she said, her face beginning to get red with emotion.

"Good," Kiley interrupted from the back of the room. "You don't have to read the whole paper. I think people are getting the idea. But let me ask you a few questions. How does the President think this can be solved?"

"He said it cannot be quieted by token moves or talk that it is time to take action in Congress," Tammy replied.

"Which means what, Miss Clark?" Kiley asked

"He has proposed a bunch of specific laws that, if passed, would end discrimination," Marty chimed in.

"I didn't know you two spoke for each other, too," Kiley said with a laugh, looking at Marty, who suddenly realized she should have waited for Tammy to answer Kiley's question.

"So how quickly does he want to do this?" Kiley said, continuing his questioning.

"In this session of Congress," Tammy quickly responded.

"Which is how long?" the teacher asked.

The question caught the girls off guard, but suddenly Jay found an opportunity to get involved in the conversation, remembering something from a civic class he took in his first year at Priory.

"I think a session of Congress runs from January to near the end of December," Jay offered.

"That's about right," Kiely said. "So, the President wants to get all these laws passed in a few months. Do you think he has a chance?"

"I hope so," said Tammy.

"Well, it might be tough," Kiley injected. "But he is going to be President for at least one more year, so he has some time."

"Okay, good job team, "Kiley said as the six students headed back to their seats.

"We have a few more minutes before the bell, so I just want to talk about something that has been on the front page of the paper a few times over these first two weeks, but we haven't really discussed it because we have been talking about things that are happening in this country. But you should know about Vietnam because I think someday it might affect your lives," the teacher offered before explaining that Vietnam was a small country in Southeast Asia.

UNITED PRESS INTERNATIONAL, SEPT. 11, 1963

> WASHINGTON – President Kennedy yesterday halted the drafting of married men, exempting approximately 340,000 young husbands from military duty.

Most of the students had started pulling their books out from under their desk chairs to be ready for a quick exit once the bell sounded to end the Wednesday class, when Kiley suddenly caught their attention again.

"One other thing," he said. "Every day we look at the front page of the paper, but not everything that might affect your life is on the front page. Here's one back a few pages from the front. It says that yesterday, President Kennedy halted the drafting of married men. That may be important to some of you guys in a few years," said Kiley

"Staying out of the army wouldn't be enough for me to get married," Tony shouted.

"Who would marry you anyway?" Linda King, the tall girl with dark hair who had been going out with Tony since they were sophomores, shouted back to the laughter of the class.

A few minutes later, the bell sounded, and thirty-five teenagers headed into the crowded corridor toward their next class.

"Are you going to Jane's Friday night?" Tammy asked Marty as they walked out of Kiley's class.

"Yeah, I asked Jay to go with me," Marty said with a sly smile.

"Whoa, I have to give you credit, Burns. You didn't waste any time going after blue eyes," Tammy said with a laugh.

UNITED PRESS INTERNATIONAL, SEPT. 16, 1963

> BIRMINGHAM, Ala – A bomb shattered a crowded Negro church yesterday

killing four girls in their Sunday School classes and triggering a reign of violence and terror that left two more persons dead in the streets.

"Why, Mr. Kiley, why would anybody do this? They were little girls," the short, dark-haired girl sitting in the middle of the classroom asked Kiley before the teacher had a chance to utter his first words to the Monday morning class.

Jay had never really noticed the girl. She had always been in the class, but she never spoke up, even in a class where there was a lot of class discussion.

"Let's talk about it," Kiley said. "Why would anybody do something so horrible?"

"They don't like colored people in Alabama," said Russ Lawrence, a running back on the football team.

"It has to be more than just not liking somebody," the teacher replied, "Ruggieri, you don't like that big defensive lineman from Clinton who was pounding the hell out of you every time you carried the ball in the game Saturday, but you didn't drive over to Clinton and throw a bomb at his house, did you?" Kiley said, looking at Jim Ruggieri, the football team's No. 2 running back, who was sitting in the back of the room.

"No," said Ruggieri a little sheepishly.

Kiley kept looking in Ruggieri's direction, hoping for a little more discussion. But the football player obviously wasn't about to expound on his answer, so Kiley looked around the room without calling on any one student. Suddenly, this soft voice came from the other side of the room.

"Hatred," said Tammy Clark.

"What's that, Miss Clark?" Kiley said, quickly moving toward the blond, obviously hoping to further the discussion.

"White people in Alabama hate Negroes," Tammy said a little more forcefully.

Kiley had the interaction he wanted.

"Hate, that is a pretty strong word," the teacher replied. "Do you think every white person in Alabama hates every Negro?"

"Well, maybe not every white person," Tammy said, now feeling a little defensive for her sudden evaluation of the situation.

"So where does this come from? Where does this hatred in some people come from?" Kiley asked.

"I don't know," Tammy said defensively.

But Kiley didn't let it stop there.

"Is that part of the problem? Is not knowing; not caring; part of the problem?" the teacher asked.

The girl had a bewildered look; she didn't know whether Kiley wanted an answer or was just presenting a philosophical conundrum for the entire class. But the teacher quickly took the onus off the student.

"Don't worry, Miss Clark. That's not a question with a simple answer. We know we all care about what happened on Sunday. But is the fact that a lot of people around the country haven't cared what was happening for years one of the reasons this happened? How many people will read this morning about what happened yesterday and think how terrible it is, but then go right to the sports section to see what the Red Sox did? Think about it, people, while you are thinking about how many touchdowns Lombardo is going to score against Brookfield on Saturday."

ASSOCIATED PRESS, SEPT. 16, 1963

BIRMINGHAM, Ala. – "The love that forgives" was the Sunday school lesson yesterday at the 16th Street Baptist Chuck. It never finished.

A bomb exploded there and twisted the lesson into an experience of confusion, terror and death.

Jay spotted the blond walking by herself as they headed down the corridor following Kiley's class. She usually never walked alone, so he quickened his pace and, within a few seconds, he was walking next to her.

"Kiley was a little tough on you in there," Jay said to Tammy Clark.

She looked over at him with a pleasant, soft expression.

"No, it's fine," she said. "He's just trying to get people thinking. I wish he had let me answer. I have a few ideas. I'm not a complete dummy, you know."

"I'm sure nobody thinks that," Jay said.

"Sure, they do because I'm a blond cheerleader, but who cares?" Tammy said with a slight laugh. "Actually, that's what I like about Kiley. He wants girls to say what they think about things that are happening in the country, not just recite a bunch of facts from a book. Sometimes I think most of our male teachers are afraid of what women have to say."

By this time, Jay had stopped in the middle of the corridor and was looking at the blond with that "deer in headlights" expression he had exhibited on the first day of school in the parking lot. He had used the "Kiley was tough on you" opening line strictly as a way of striking up a conversation with a girl he wanted to get to know. Now he was getting a dissertation on the male fear of females having opinions on anything other than how to cook dinner. Tammy looked over at him and sensed maybe she was expressing her feelings a little too strongly.

"Anyway, I heard you went with Marty to Jane's Friday night. Did you have a good time?" she asked, trying to change the direction of the conversation.

"Yeah, it was fun," Jay said as he turned away and stared into space, as the two resumed walking down the corridor.

NEW YORK TIMES, SEPT. 16, 1963

SAIGON, South Vietnam – Bold Communist attacks against two district

> capitals in South Vietnam on Tuesday have underlined basic disagreements on policy between Americans and Vietnamese.

Indeed, Saturday night had been an interesting evening. Jay had enjoyed the evening with Marty at Jane's house.

Jane and her boyfriend, and Sue Williams, another cheerleader, and her boyfriend were there. Jay and Marty left about 10 o'clock so Jay could get home to bed the night before the game, even though he knew he wouldn't be playing. They drove for a few miles, talking about school and some of the kids at the party, before Jay asked.

"How come Tammy wasn't there tonight? I thought you and her were inseparable."

"She was supposed to come, but her boyfriend suddenly came home from college this afternoon," Marty offered.

"Oh," Jay said, trying not to look too interested.

After reaching Marty's house, they sat in front for a few minutes of small talk before Marty moved her face closer to Jay's. He didn't hesitate to respond to her closeness. He reached his arm around her neck, pulled her closer to him, and moved his other hand inside the back of her sweater. He looked down at her face and started kissing her. She was the first to slip her tongue into his mouth, so Jay quickly moved his tongue into her mouth. But something was different. That feeling he usually sensed when he kissed a girl was missing. It wasn't getting hard like it usually did when he French-kissed a girl. Marty sensed it too and began moving away from him.

"I guess I'd better get in the house," she said as she opened the car door, jumped out, and rushed into her house.

So, Jay felt apprehensive when he saw Marty in the school lobby on Monday morning, but she was her usual congenial self when she said "Hi" to Jay while flashing a big smile as she passed through the lobby on the way to her homeroom.

Jay was pleased Marty didn't seem upset about Saturday night. There was something about Marty that made her special. She always seemed to have an inner glow that made you want to be around her. In the few weeks Jay had been at Jefferson, he noticed he wasn't the only person who felt that way. Marty was the person everybody always wanted to be around, even if they weren't cheerleaders or jocks. Marty always had a smile for everybody, always seemed to be the person people wanted to talk to, and she made everybody feel she wanted to talk to them and was interested in what they were saying.

NEW YORK TIMES, SEPT. 17, 1963

> BIRMINGHAM, Ala. – The threat of renewed Negro demonstrations emerged today as this troubled city struggled without apparent success to end its racial crisis.

Jay was walking off the field by himself following practice on Tuesday when one of the young assistant coaches came walking up to him.

"Don't get discouraged, Burke," the coach said.

The statement caught Jay completely by surprise, as if somebody, besides Tony, finally understood how he was feeling. Saturday, the game against Brookfield went as if it were following Rowe's game plan. Jefferson dominated on offense with its powerful ground game, and the defense was great. By halftime, Jefferson was ahead 21-0, and they added another touchdown in the second half en route to a final 28-0 victory. Jay stood in uniform on the sideline, trying to pay attention to how Amore picked the plays he would call.

Jay had only talked to coach Quigley a few times when Jay was serving as the opposing quarterback in the defense drills during practice. Probably because he was the youngest coach on the staff, Quigley didn't say much, but Jay liked him. Unlike Rowe, he didn't yell at players; he seemed to prefer quietly talking to players away from the attention of the rest of the team. Tony had told him Quigley had been at Jefferson for a few years, and he thought he had played football at one of those small New England colleges where most of the students came from New England prep schools.

"You must be a little discouraged not getting any reps here. Didn't you play last year at Priory?" Quigley asked Jay.

"I was one of the backup quarterbacks," Jay answered.

"Is the coach there the guy who runs that 'Option/Spread offense'?" Quigley asked.

"Yes," said Jay sheepishly.

"So, you can run a 'Spread'?" Quigley inquired.

"I didn't play in any games, but I ran it a lot in practice," Jay offered.

"Interesting," Quigley said as he started quickening his pace and moved ahead of Jay.

NEW YORK TIMES, SEPT. 19, 1963

WASHINGTON – President Kennedy has agreed to meet with seven Negro leaders to discuss Birmingham's racial crisis as pressure continued to mount yesterday for action on civil rights legislation.

The sounds of the Angels' "My Boyfriend's Back" blared from the car radio as Jay and Tony headed toward the high school on Thursday morning.

"Is Castle Hill any good?" Jay asked about Jefferson's upcoming opponent on Saturday.

"They're always very fast," Tony replied. "They have this colored kid who is a great running back. He's big and fast and really tough to bring down. We are going to have to work our asses off on the defensive line."

"It should be an interesting game," Jay quipped.

ASSOCIATED PRESS, SEPT. 20, 1963

NEW HAVEN – The acting president of Yale University intervened

> yesterday to persuade a student debating group to cancel an invitation to Gov. George Wallace of Alabama to speak at Yale.

Kiley started talking before he even picked up the Friday Times from his desk.

"Folks, one thing I want to mention before we go over some of the stuff in today's paper. I meant to say something last week when Gemma's team did the report on the President's Civil Rights speech, but it slipped my mind, and with everything that happened on Sunday, I didn't have a chance to bring it up. There was something that happened shortly after the President's speech that I think is part of the story surrounding the civil rights stuff you are reading about right now. Burke, Gemma, Stone, did you happen to come across anything when you were researching for your report?" Kiley said, looking at the three football players.

Jay was desperately trying to think of something that happened last June, but his mind was blank. He looked at Tony, and he knew his friend was also clueless, and Mike Stone didn't look any more informed. Suddenly, Tammy's voice echoed from the other side of the room.

"Medgar Evers was shot and killed the night after the President's speech," she said.

"Good, Miss Clark, and who was Medgar Evers?" Kiley quickly responded.

"He was a civil rights activist from Mississippi," Tammy continued. "He was shot in his own driveway by somebody hiding behind a bush across the street."

"I'm very impressed you knew about Medgar Evers and when he was shot," Kiley said.

Kiley wasn't the only one impressed. Jay's eyes were riveted on the blond.

"To be honest, I heard Bob Dylan singing about it at the Folk Festival this summer," Tammy said. "When we were doing research for the President's speech, I was thinking about it and checked to see when Evers was shot. Then I read some magazine stories about him."

"Well, I'm sure Bob Dylan will be happy to hear he helped you get an A for class participation today," Kiley said with a laugh, looking directly at Tammy.

Jay and Marty were the last two people to leave Kiley's classroom after class ended, so they walked together down the corridor.

"Hey, I meant to thank you last week," Jay said. "You, Tammy, and Jane did all the work on that report, and we got some of the credit."

"It was all Tammy," Marty said. "She asked me and Jane to go to the library with her one night, but we couldn't, so she went by herself. She really is smart, you know. People just don't think of her that way because she's a blond cheerleader."

UNITED PRESS INTERNATIONAL, SEPT. 21, 1963

> WASHINGTON – Demonstrations in a number of U.S. cities yesterday symbolized the mourning and troubled conscience of the nation over the death of four Negro girls in the bombing of a Birmingham, Alabama church a week ago.

Tony certainly was right about Castle Hill. They were fast, but they didn't have much size on the defensive line, so anytime the Jefferson offensive line opened a hole for Lombardo, he raced past the linebackers for big gains. By halftime, he had already run for three touchdowns. The score was 21-0 early in the third quarter when Amore dropped back and tossed a pass to Mike Stone in the flat. As Stone broke into the open and headed toward the end zone, Amore stood watching in the backfield. But one of the Castle Hill defensive linemen still kept coming toward Amore even though the play in the backfield had long ended. Amore didn't even see the charging lineman coming at him from the left side, so the hit sent

Amore flying. Penalty flags flew from the back pockets of two officials, and Rowe immediately raced onto the field screaming about a late hit. Meanwhile, Amore was lying on the ground, obviously in pain. Quigley, the young assistant coach, was the first person to reach the quarterback. "What is it, Ray?" asked Quigley. "My shoulder," Amore said with a groan.

It took a few minutes, but eventually Amore was able to get to his feet and start walking off the field with two coaches wrapping their arms around his waist. But it was obvious from the way his left arm was limp that he was in pain.

"It's dislocated," Jay heard Quigley tell one of the other assistant coaches.

UNITED PRESS INTERNATIONAL, SEPT. 25, 1963

SELMA, Ala – State troopers and local police broke up two anti-segregation demonstrations yesterday and jailed 132 Negroes, most of them students.

"Lombardo is great," Jay said to Tony as they drove to school on Wednesday morning.

"You bet your ass he is. He's the best fucking runner in the state," Tony declared. "Even if Amore can't play as long as Sal stays healthy, nobody is going to beat us."

They drove for a few minutes with the sounds of "Blue Velvet" emanating from the radio when Tony suddenly asked.

"Hey, have you thought what you are going to do your research paper about?"

Jay hesitated before answering, even though he knew exactly what his subject would be.

Finally, he answered the question.

"I think I'm doing it on folk singing," Jay said.

"Folk singing, what the hell kind of research can you do on folk singing. It's music. You can't research music," Tony said with a scowl.

Jay looked at his friend, pretending to be disgusted.

"Are you kidding? Folk singing is more than just music," Jay shot back. "It's about important messages. It's a way of binding people together for a cause. People listen to what you have to say more when you put the message in a song than if you just talk. Music softens people. Music gets people to listen to what you care about. Maybe you can even change some people who are opposed to your cause."

Jay's extensive explanation of why he was writing about folk singing was more information than Tony actually wanted to know.

"If you say so, Tony said with a smirk. "But it seems very coincidental that last week a certain blond said she learned about Medgar Evers from a folk song, and this week you decided you are doing your term paper on folk singing."

"Fuck you," Jay said

ASSOCIATED PRESS, SEPT. 30, 1963

> WASHINGTON – Sen. Barry Goldwater, R-Ariz, said yesterday that President Kennedy cannot win congressional approval of both his civil rights program and an 11-billion-dollar tax cut this year and must decide which he wants.

Jay saw Tammy walking by herself between the second and third period class change, so he quickened his pace and caught up to her while trying to think of an excuse to talk to her. Finally, he thought of his opening line.

"Hey Tammy," he said as he walked up from behind her. "Can I borrow your physics book? I left mine in my locker."

She turned and smiled, almost as if that was a natural reaction any time someone said her name.

"Sorry, Jay," she said, "I think we take different physics classes, so our books are different."

His excuse for talking to her might have been off the mark, but he quickly thought of another way to continue the discussion.

"What physics do you take?' he asked

"Physics II," she said.

"Whoa, you must be one of the smart kids," Jay said with a smile. "I didn't even know they had a Physics II class here."

The compliment brought an even broader smile to Tammy's face, but she tried to act like it was no big deal.

"I'm not smart," she said. "It's just that when I was going into the ninth grade, they had some of us take biology instead of General Science. So, then I took chemistry in my sophomore year, and then had Physics I in my junior year. It's funny when we started in the ninth grade, we had about twenty-five kids in the class, and about ten of them were girls. But every year, it seemed a few of the girls dropped out of the class and took the easier science courses. I don't think their guidance counselors encouraged girls to take the tougher science courses. This year, we have fifteen kids in Physics II, and only three are girls. But I like it. I don't know why, I guess it's just the idea of experimenting."

"Are there any other cheerleaders in the class?" Jay asked

"No, not any football players either," she said with a soft laugh.

FOUR

UNITED PRESS INTERNATIONAL, OCT. 3, 1963

WASHINGTON – The White House said last night that U.S. military commanders in South Vietnam believe they can finish their mission against the Communists by the end of 1965 despite a deeply serious political crisis there.

"Sorry, Mr. Kiley, I guess you were wrong about Vietnam playing a role in our lives. This story says the U.S. will finish its mission there by the end of 1965. We will still be in college," said Paul Lavey, the kid whom Tony had told Jay was the best 135-pound wrestler in the state.

"I hope so. I don't mind being wrong. After all, it will be the first time," Kiley said with a big smile.

NEW YORK TIMES, OCT. 4, 1963

LITTLE ROCK – Gov. Orval E. Faubus of Arkansas sharply criticized federal civil rights programs yesterday while President Kennedy listened from a few feet away. The President chose not to respond.

Jay could hear the sound from where he was standing along the sidelines at the far end of the large group of players watching the action on the field.

Amore wasn't playing, but Reall was doing a good job handling the QB duties, which basically consisted of handing off the ball to Lombardo, who was having his usual outstanding night running. It was late in the third quarter, and he had already scored two first-half touchdowns, and he looked like he might be on his way to another as he circled around the right side of the line. But his right foot slipped on the grass, sending his leg to the right while his upper body was already trying to turn in the other direction. That gave a speedy defensive back the opportunity he needed to send his entire body at the lower part of Lombardo's body. That's when Jay heard the sound. It wasn't just the sound of two padded football players hitting each other. It was the sound of something cracking, like a branch breaking off a tree in a windstorm. Jay could see Lombardo's leg lying at a weird angle from his other leg, and he was in obvious pain as he rolled his upper body on the ground. The coaches rushed onto the field, picked up his head, and removed his helmet. Eventually, two coaches reached under his arms and lifted his body off the ground, carrying him off the field to the far end of the bench. "Tell the cop to call the rescue squad. We need to get him to the hospital," Jay heard Rowe say to one of the assistant coaches.

The Jefferson defense finally gave up a touchdown in the fourth quarter, but otherwise the defense played so well that Lombardo's two early touchdowns were enough for a 14-7 victory. There was a strange silence after the game, not like it had been after the other victories. Rowe stood in the end zone with the team huddled around him.

"Sal is seriously hurt. He's probably out for the season," Rowe said in a grim voice. "It's not going to be easy, but we are a team and a team doesn't quit just because it loses one player, even a player as good as Sal."

NEW YORK TIMES, OCT. 6, 1963

WASHINGTON – The full House Judiciary Committee will begin discussion next week of the most sweeping civil rights legislation ever considered seriously in Congress.

—

"Hey, blue eyes, what are you doing?" the voice said as soon as Jay answered the phone next to his bed.

Even though her words were slurred, Jay recognized it was Marty.

"Hey, Marty, where are you?" he asked.

"We're at a wedding," Marty offered.

"Who got married?" Jay asked.

He was expecting to hear Marty say the bride was some cousin or maybe even an aunt. Instead, she started talking about a former classmate.

"Joyce Storti," Marty replied in a slightly slurred voice. "You don't know her. She was a cheerleader in our sophomore and junior years, but she found out she was pregnant this summer. She and Artie have been going out since she was a sophomore and he was a junior. Artie graduated last year and went right to work. Both their families are Catholic, so Joyce didn't come back to school this year, and they are getting married. It's too bad Joyce was really smart, and she was our sophomore class vice-president. Now, rather than graduating with us in June, she will be taking care of a baby, but at least it's a fun wedding. We're at the K of C Hall."

"Are you drinking?" Jay questioned.

"A little; well, maybe a lot," Marty quipped.

"How did you get served?" Jay asked.

"Joyce's uncle is buying our drinks," Marty answered. "Oh yeah, Tammy said to say hello."

"Has she been drinking as much as you?"

"I don't think anybody has been drinking as much as me," Marty said with pride. "So, what are you doing?" she continued.

"I'm sitting at my desk working on my term paper, why?" he asked.

"Well, Tammy and I were wondering if you could come over

here and give us a ride home. We came with Karen Powers, but she said she had to go home, and we wanted to stay a little longer. I'm staying at Tammy's tonight, so I guess we could call her parents and ask them to come pick us up."

"No, don't do that," Jay quickly interjected. "I don't think you want her parents to see you just yet. I will be there in fifteen minutes. I'll take my mother's Mercury, in case somebody might need to pass out on the backseat."

UNITED PRESS INTERNATIONAL, OCT. 7, 1963

> LOS ANGELES – The Los Angeles Dodgers won the World Series yesterday as a "gift" run and the payoff pitching of Sandy Koufax downed the mighty Yankees, 2-1, and dealt New York its first four-game shutout in 28 trips to the classic.

The Monday morning quarterback meeting was shorter than normal. Rowe ran film of Friday night's game, but he fast-forwarded through the entire third quarter, obviously not wanting to see Lombardo being injured again. Jay knew he had at least fifteen minutes before the home room bell, so he was in no rush as he headed out the door into the corridor that was now starting to fill with students.

"Burke, stick around a minute, will you?" Rowe said to Jay just before he was out the door.

The request caught Jay by surprise. In his four weeks as a member of the team, Rowe had never really spoken to Jay on an individual basis. Rowe didn't waste time letting Jay know why he wanted to talk to him.

"Coach Quigley tells me down at that little prep school where you were last year, they run that 'spread offense'," Rowe said.

"Yes, we did," Jay replied.

"I heard about the 'Spread'," Rowe said, "I think some high school coach from Ohio came up with it about ten years ago. You know, with both Lombardo and Amore out, we might need to add some surprises to our offense, and Coach Quigley thinks you might be able to run an option out of that spread once in a while."

Jay just looked at the Coach without saying a word.

"I'm not saying we are completely changing our offense, but maybe this week we might work on that 'spread' a little at practice. Who knows if we have a big lead on Saturday, maybe we might get you into the game for a few plays."

NEW YORK TIMES, OCT. 8, 1963

> SAIGON, South Vietnam – The United States has quietly suspended commercial exports to South Vietnam while the administration is deciding whether to reduce aid as a possible means of diplomatic pressure.

Jay kept listening Tuesday morning as Kiley talked about what United States diplomatic relations with South Vietnam might mean to the students' lives, but he couldn't help looking over at Tammy and Marty. He was glad to see them back in school after they both had been absent on Monday. He wasn't surprised that the two cheerleaders were not in school on Monday. They both passed out shortly after they got into his car Sunday night after he picked them up from the wedding, so he drove around for about fifteen minutes before stopping at the City Dinner to get coffee.

"Here, have some of this," he said to Marty, who was sitting in the front passenger seat and was awake by the time Jay returned from the dinner carrying two coffees. Marty sipped the coffee before passing the cup to Tammy, who by now had woken up in the back seat. "We need to get you two a little sobered up before Tammy's parents see you," Jay said while holding the other cup of coffee so Marty could gently sip it.

In the back seat, Tammy just drank the coffee without saying a word.

"We love you, you know," Marty uttered.

"Yeah, yeah, and tomorrow morning you won't even know I gave you a ride home," Jay said with an easy laugh.

ASSOCIATED PRESS, OCT. 9, 1963

> WASHINGTON – The Senate commerce committee toned down and then approved yesterday a bill to ban racial discrimination in public accommodations – the heart of President Kennedy's civil rights program.

Jay was sitting in the back row of the auditorium reading the Wednesday N.Y Times while waiting for Tony to come out of the locker room.

"Hey, what are you doing, still reading the paper? Kiley's class was over five hours ago," said a voice from behind the chest-high wall at the back of the auditorium.

Jay quickly turned to see Tammy standing with her arms crossed on the top of the half-wall that separates the auditorium seats from the front entrance. She had quickly walked out of Kiley's class that morning, so it was the first time he had talked to her since he had given her and Marty a ride home from the wedding Sunday night.

"Oh, hi," Jay said, trying to think of something witty to say. He was going to make a joke of her condition Sunday night, but he thought maybe she had avoided him for two days because she was embarrassed about Sunday night, so he skipped the joke and just told the truth about what he was doing.

"I always keep the paper and carry it around. I like to read some of the stuff on the back pages that we don't have a chance to discuss in class."

By this time, Tammy had come around the wall and was standing in the aisle next to Jay's seat, holding some books and the Times. Jay just sat there looking up at the blond.

"You're a real gentleman, aren't you going to ask a lady to sit down?" Tammy asked.

"Oh, yeah, yeah, sorry. Here, sit down," Jay said as he moved into one seat.

"Just kidding," Tammy said. "I have to get going."

But Jay spotted a way to keep talking for a few more minutes.

"Hey, you talk about me. I see you still have the Times. Most of the kids throw them in the waste basket when they walk out of Kiley's class," Jay countered.

The ploy worked as she stopped after taking a few steps down the auditorium aisle and turned back toward Jay.

"I bring it home for my father so he can read the sports section. He likes the Giants football team, and there are more stories about them in the Times than he gets in the newspaper here."

Just then, Tony appeared at the door at the front of the auditorium, which opened onto the corridor leading to the locker room.

"Hey, let's go, I'm starving," Tony shouted without even acknowledging Tammy, who was standing in the aisle about halfway between Jay and Tony.

"Hold your horses, I'm coming," Jay yelled.

"See you at the game tomorrow night," Tammy said as she turned to Jay before she started walking away. "I hear you might get a chance to play."

"Where did you hear that?' Jay asked.

"Sue Allen said her brother was talking at dinner Monday night that the football team was working on some new type of plays at practice, and you might play," Tammy replied.

"The only way I will play is if we are ahead by fifty points," Jay said with a laugh.

"According to Sue, her brother said you know how to run an option," Tammy continued as if she were a football expert.

"What do you know about an option?" Jay said inquisitively.

"My father is a Giants fan, remember," she said with a sly smile as she kept walking down the aisle.

"Yeah, but Y.A. Tittle doesn't run an option," Jay countered.

"Who?" Tammy said with a questioning look as she headed down the aisle and passed by Tony without the burly lineman even acknowledging her presence.

Jay rose from his seat and walked down the aisle toward Tony.

"Let's go," Jay said to Tony when he finally reached the bottom of the aisle. He and Tony started walking toward the back door leading to the parking lot when Jay suddenly challenged Tony.

"Hey, why didn't you even say hello to Tammy. I know she is not one of your favorite people, but at least you could have said hello."

"Don't get all pissed-off," Tony responded. "I was just talking to her this afternoon after Spanish class," Tony said.

"I didn't think you two talked that much," Jay said.

"Usually, we don't. But for some strange reason, she just started talking to me about football and what an option means. I don't know why the hell she wanted to know about the option. Football to her is just a chance to show off her tight ass in that short cheer-leading skirt."

"Be nice," Jay offered with a smile.

NEW YORK TIMES, OCT 11, 1963

WASHINGTON – A "minority" group that is actually in the majority was advised to seek an end to discrimination through the courts. In a report to President Kennedy, the Commission on the Status of Women opposed asking for a constitutional amendment to provide equal rights for women – a suggestion that has often been proposed.

For the second game, Paul Reall had done a good job filling in for Amore at quarterback, so even without Lombardo, Jefferson had more than enough running power to take a 21-7 halftime lead against Ashland. They added two more touchdowns in the third quarter for a commanding 33-7 lead heading into the fourth quarter.

With about five minutes remaining in the fourth quarter, Jefferson got the ball again as Tony recovered an Ashland fumble near midfield.

"Burke," Rowe yelled.

At first, Jay was stunned, but he quickly realized he was finally getting a chance to play and raced toward Rowe.

"Try a few plays out of that spread," Rowe said to Jay as he sent him onto the field.

"You can do this," Tony said to Jay as the two old friends jogged out to the field. "Don't worry, I will make sure the snaps are good."

The Ashland defense was baffled when, instead of standing directly behind Tony at center, Jay lined up about three yards behind Tony. Also, rather than having one halfback lining up to his right side and the other to his left and the fullback directly behind the quarterback, all three running backs were lined up to Jay's left, a few yards behind him, and at various levels on the field.

In the huddle, Jay said the snap would be on three, but just before Tony snapped the ball, Jay moved his right foot back a few inches while keeping his left foot stationary. Jay's move was a signal for the three running backs to start circling a few steps back toward the right side of the field even before the snap. The pressure now was on Tony to deliver the snap a few yards back to Jay before the three running backs started moving forward, and Tony's timing was perfect. Jay grabbed the ball and started running at half-speed to the right. He now had the option of pitching the ball to any of the three running backs; fake a pitch, then tossing a pass to one of the wide receivers breaking down to the field, or fake the pitch, pull the ball back, and run himself.

The first play he pitched to Doug Allen, who raced fifteen yards around the right end before being forced out of bounds.

With a first-and-10 on the Ashford 30, the next play Jay started running to the right again with Allen, Jim Ruggieri, and Bruce Esposito running wide to his right. He made a move as if he was going to pitch the ball to Esposito, but just before he made the pitch, he looked upfield a few yards and saw two Ashford linebackers starting to jump toward where they thought Jay would be making the pitch. So, he faked the pitch, pulled the ball back into his body, broke toward the middle of the field, and raced thirty yards into the end zone. Since the first day of practice, he had been telling himself it really didn't matter if he played. But the reality was that it felt great playing and scoring a touchdown, even if, in the outcome of the game, the six points were meaningless.

NEW YORK TIMES, OCT. 14, 1963

> WASHINGTON – The drive for civil rights legislation is at an extremely precarious point in Congress.
>
> That is the view of the best-informed participants in the campaign. They see a serious danger that all hopes for swift legislation on the racial issue may go down in a political tangle.

"Sorry, I haven't seen you since the first day of school, but it's been a wild first month of school," Jay's guidance counselor said as soon as he walked into her little office on Tuesday morning.

"I understand," Jay said. "It's been hectic for me, too."

"I'm sure it has. How are things going for you here?" she asked.

"Good, I think," Jay said.

"That's wonderful to hear, but I wanted to touch base with you to see if you're thinking about what colleges you are going to apply to," she said.

"I haven't thought too much about it. I figure I still have time," Jay offered.

"Well, in the past that probably would have been true, but this year may be different," the counselor declared. "I have been talking to people at a few colleges, and this year they are seeing a big increase in the number of applicants for next year's freshman class. They are thinking for the first time that the number of applicants may far exceed the opportunities available for admission, especially at the truly selective colleges. Even for good students, there are going to be more students with the same grades applying for the same spots. It sounds like the level of attainment is going to be higher among college applicants. You may need something that distinguishes you from the other people applying. I read something that they are calling the baby boom after the War. You were born in 1946. The story I read said that there were about 600,000 more people born in America in 1946 than in 1945. Most of those people who were born in 1946 are now seniors in high school, like you. I'm trying to make sure all my seniors know it may be different this year. They may not be able to apply to just one college and get accepted. Are you thinking about any colleges in particular?"

"No, not really," Jay replied.

"How about where your parents went to college?"

"My father is dead, but neither he nor my mother went to college."

"Sorry, I should have remembered from our meeting on the first day of school that your dad died last winter," the woman said, her face flush with embarrassment.

"I was looking at your records from your old school, and I see you did well on the standardized tests," the counselor offered. "You scored better on the verbal part than you did on the math. That's unique for a boy. Boys usually score better in math. I just wanted you to realize that if you score like that in the verbal section of your SATs, it may help you get accepted at some colleges. It may give you more options, and this year, people may need options."

ASSOCIATED PRESS, OCT. 18, 1963

SAIGON, Vietnam – Ngo Dinh Nhu, powerful and controversial brother of South Vietnam's President, said yesterday Buddhists under interrogation have identified US Central Intelligence Agency agents and other Americans who constantly prodded them to overthrow the government.

"Did you read Chapter Two yet?" Marty quizzed Tammy as they stood on the sidelines of the football field waiting for the start of the Friday night game.

"Chapter Two of what?" Tammy asked with an inquisitive look.

"The Group," Marty said.

"Oh, yeah, it's interesting," Tammy said.

"Is that what it's like?" Marty asked.

"Why are you asking me?" Tammy said with a defensive smirk.

UNITED PRESS INTERNATIONAL, OCT. 18, 1963

ST. FRANCISVILLE, La – An elderly Baptist preacher yesterday became the first Negro eligible to vote in West Feliciana Parish since 1902.

"Christ, this can't be happening to us,"

Rowe's voice could be heard in the last row of the stands as the fans sat silently, looking at Paul Reall holding his hand after getting up from a pile of players following a tackle midway through the fourth quarter.

Reall had dropped back to pass, but one of the charging St. Paul defensive linemen had caught Reall and spun him around. Apparently, when Reall went to the ground, his hand hit the helmet of another player. When he got up, he signed to Rowe that he was hurting. Rowe stayed on the sidelines for a few minutes as some of the assistant coaches went onto the field to check the hand. After a few minutes, Quigley yelled to the sidelines, "I think it might be broken."

Another injury in a game that wasn't going well for Jefferson. St. Paul's had already lost a game, so most of the Jefferson players weren't expecting a tough test even without Lombardo's running or Amore at quarterback. But the St. Paul defense had done a great job stopping the Jefferson run, keeping the game scoreless in the third quarter. Then, in the final few minutes of the third quarter, one of the St. Paul linebackers intercepted a Reall pass near midfield. It only took three running plays and a completed pass for St. Paul's to get in the end zone, but they missed the conversion kick.

Even though they trailed for the first time all season, nobody seemed too concerned about making up the 6-0 deficit in the fourth quarter, but then on Jefferson's first possession of the fourth quarter, Reall was hurt.

Jay stood on the sideline looking at Rowe. After his touchdown run off the option in the mop-up role in the Ashland game, Jay was expecting Rowe to call him over to discuss what the coach wanted Jay to do when he went into the game.

But Rowe never looked Jay's way. Instead, he told Belovitch, the young sophomore, to go into the game and run the power-right series. It was as if Rowe kept thinking sooner or later something good would finally happen if Jefferson kept pounding the ball on the ground. But it never did. Jay stood looking up at the scoreboard as the final buzzer sounded, Visitor 6, Jefferson 0.

"Shit, we lost," Tony yelled as he walked off the field.

UNITED PRESS INTERNATIONAL, OCT. 21, 1963

> WASHINGTON – Some of President Kennedy's strongest Senate supporters on civil rights complained yesterday that the administration has made a mistake in seeking a toned-down rights bill in the House.

Even before the start of practice, Monday afternoon, it was obvious Friday night's loss had changed how Rowe was going to look at the rest of the season. Before practice, he had called the team together in the middle of the field and talked for at least five minutes. Jay had never heard him talk like that. He said Friday's loss was his fault. That he hadn't reacted quickly enough to make some changes in the offense after Reall was hurt. Then he talked about the rest of the season, how even though the team had lost one game, they still had a chance to win a championship if everybody was willing to work even harder than they had been.

"It will be tough, but we can do it," he had said. As soon as practice started, Rowe told Jay to run the offense.

NEW YORK TIMES, OCT. 22, 1963

> SAIGON, South Vietnam – The United States is reliably reported to have told Col. Le Quang Tung, commander of the politically powerful Vietnamese Special Forces, that from now on it will not pay Special Forces troops used in political and security missions.

By the time Jay finally got out of the locker room after meeting with Rowe, it was virtually dark outside. Tony had already told him he would get a ride home with Linda, who had taken her family car to school. So, Jay walked down the empty corridor leading away from the locker room, daydreaming about how he might finally start seeing some playing time when he heard a voice.

"Hey, handsome, can you give a girl a ride?"

He turned and saw Tammy walking toward him with her plaid skirt, brown knee socks, and mohair sweater.

"My mother was supposed to pick me up after cheerleading practice and take me to the city to buy some winter clothes, but she never showed up," the blond said. "I called home, but she wasn't there. I was going to walk home, but then I saw your car still in the parking lot, so I was hoping you and Tony could fit me between the seats and give me a ride home."

Jay tried to hide the excitement he was feeling about the blond asking for a ride.

"Sure, you can have a ride, and you can even have your own seat. Tony went home with Linda." Jay offered.

As soon as they started driving out of the parking lot, Jay turned on the radio more as an excuse to not have to find something to talk about rather than his love of music. The pair listened to the sounds of Bobby Vinton's "Blue Velvet" as they headed to Tammy's house about a mile from the school.

"Do you want to come in while I wait for my mother?" Tammy asked when they reached her house. "She probably was at one of her women's club meetings and forgot about our shopping date."

Jay didn't hesitate to accept the invitation. They walked through the back door that led into the kitchen, where Tammy immediately spotted the note on the counter.

"That's nice," she said with a sarcastic tone after quickly reading the note. "I guess my mother completely forgot about our shopping day. She went into the city to meet my father for dinner. She left some cold meatloaf for my supper."

"That doesn't sound too appetizing," Jay said.

"No, it's not. What are you doing for supper?" she asked. "I'm going over to Marty's later tonight, but what if I buy you a hamburger at HoJo's?"

The invitation completely caught Jay off guard, but he jumped at the opportunity to be with the blond.

"Yeah, sure, but I don't want you buying my cheeseburger. I will buy," Jay said.

"A girl can pay her own way," Tammy said with a smile. "Why don't you go relax in the living room while I go up and change into jeans—and do a few other things."

Jay was sitting on the living room couch, flipping through some magazines sitting on a coffee table, when he saw it. It was a white envelope that obviously had a handwritten letter folded inside it, but it wasn't sealed. The first thing he noticed was Tammy's name and address written in the top left corner, and then he saw it was addressed to Dave at his college dorm. He knew he shouldn't look at the letter, but he couldn't resist knowing what she and her boyfriend talked about. So, he carefully took the letter out of the envelope and unfolded it.

Dear Dave,

I hope you are fine and school is good and your family is well. I got your letter and you can go screw yourself.

Jay knew he should stop reading right there and put the letter back in the envelope because this wasn't some sweet love letter. But he couldn't stop reading.

> *When are you going to grow up and stop thinking of yourself as a martyr who never does anything wrong but always gets kicked in the ass? Wise up, you bastard. You know damn well what I told Marty was exactly what you said and by Christ if you think I am going to stand around and take shit from you, you're crazy. You told me in your letter that if I'd rather go out with the crowd than you that was all there was to say. I could have the crowd. Well, I'm taking it, don't worry. You know I told you I was going out with Marty and the other girls the first night you were home. Well, up your ass if I can't lead my own life. I have taken so much shit from you – always having to be careful what I say because of your goddam temper. Having you say everything I do is wrong. Giving me all that shit about love and sex. Waiting around for you every time you tell me to screw and when you want to go back with me, I always kiss you and say I'll forget about the language and all the other crap. Do you know how many times that happened? Well, you can go suck ass. I have had it and I don't ever want to go out with you again. Maybe not going out with anybody is what I need. I don't even know what the word love means anymore because of you.*

There were still a few lines remaining in the letter when Jay heard Tammy coming down the stairs, so he quickly folded it back into the envelope, put it on the coffee table, and picked up a magazine.

"Are you ready?" Tammy asked as she walked into the living room wearing a pair of jeans and a cable knit V-neck sweater over a white blouse.

"Oh, I'm ready," said Jay.

ASSOCIATED PRESS – OCT. 25, 1963

WASHINGTON – President Kennedy's efforts to keep from the House floor a civil rights bill he regards as excessive met with little success yesterday.

"Mr. Kiley, why would President Kennedy be trying to keep a civil rights bill from being considered in the House? Isn't he all for getting a civil rights law?" Mike Stone asked as the class was scanning Friday's Times.

"I think it's what you call political strategy," Kiley replied. "We probably are going to see a lot of it between now and when you graduate in June, as President Kennedy tries to get a civil rights bill through Congress. He knows he may have to make compromises to get something passed."

"What do you think, Burke?" Kiley said as he looked at Jay, knowing the quarterback wasn't paying attention to the class discussion. "Will Kennedy use a four or five-man defensive front?"

"What, yeah, that sounds right," Jay said, still somewhat immersed in his daydream.

The class broke into an uproar, and Jay's face turned a bright red.

"That's okay," Kiley said with a smile. "I don't think you are the only one in this classroom, thinking more about the Oxford defense than the Kennedy political strategy. Good luck tomorrow, guys. I know you are going to rebound from last week."

ASSOCIATED PRESS, OCT. 27, 1963

SAIGON – A Buddhist monk jumped off the back of a motorbike in front of a Roman Catholic cathedral doused himself with gasoline and set himself ablaze. This is the seventh Buddhist suicide by fire since June, apparently carried out to point up to a UN team here the Buddhist charges of persecution by the government.

The radio was blasting Ricky Nelson's "Fools Rush In" so loud that Jay didn't hear the phone ringing.

"Jay, it's for you," Jay's mother screamed from the bottom of the stairs.

Jay jumped up from his desk and scrambled a few steps to the phone on the side of his bed.

"Ha, football hero, what are you doing?" the female voice asked.

The call caught Jay completely by surprise. "Who is this?" he questioned.

"It's Marty."

"Oh, hi. But I don't think you have the right number if you're looking for a football hero," Jay said in an effort to offer a funny comeback.

"Don't try playing the modest role with me. You threw three touchdown passes yesterday, didn't you?" Marty declared.

"Yeah, but Doug Allen scored two of them with great runs after he caught the passes, and our defense played great."

"Yeah, yeah, I know all that 'oh, shucks, it's not me, it's the team' crap. But you were the quarterback, and we won the game, so you're now a football hero," Marty offered.

"We will see. We still have four games to play," Jay said, trying not to sound as excited as he actually was.

"So, do you want to take a ride?" Marty asked.

"Yeah, I guess so. I'm trying to do my French homework, but that can always wait. Where do you want to go?" Jay replied.

"The cheerleaders are responsible for the decorations for the homecoming dance this Saturday night," Marty said. "It wasn't my idea, but they decided to go with a Thanksgiving theme, so Tammy and I are going over to one of those farms in Weston to get some corn stalks. Do you want to help us?"

"Sure, who's driving?" Jay said without hesitation.

"Tammy, she has her mother's Plymouth."

"OK, but does Tammy know she has to drive over to the other side of the city to pick me up?"

"I told her I was going to give you a call to see if you wanted to help us, and she said fine. She says she knows where you live."

"She does?"

"Yes, she does. We will see you in thirty minutes."

He hung up the phone and yelled to his mother to forget about making anything for him for Sunday dinner.

"I thought I might get a chance to spend a little time with you," his mother said with a disheartened tone.

Her response made Jay feel bad. He knew the past eight months had been tough for his mother. While he certainly had gone through a lot of changes, his mother had too.

"I know it's just that these kids from school are going to get some decorations for a dance this weekend, and they asked me to help," Jay offered.

"Don't worry about it," his mother said. "I guess your mother doesn't have much of a chance anymore when some blond calls you. Is she blond?"

"Not the one who called," Jay said, trying to protect his privacy.

A few minutes later, Jay sat on his front steps waiting for the girls' arrival, thinking he had been surprised by how easily it happened in Saturday's game against Oxford.

Rowe had come up to him while the team was warming up on the field.

"Get ready," he said to Jay. "If we win the toss, we are going to receive, and you are going to run the first series."

So, Jay didn't really have time to be nervous, and two plays after Jefferson won the toss, he started running wide right with Ruggieri and Esposito circling behind him. But just before he reached the line of scrimmage, he looked downfield and saw Doug Allen running down the left side of the field with no defenders near him. Allen had lined up with Ruggieri and Esposito on the left side in the spread. But rather than circle right behind Jay with the other two running backs, Allen hesitated a few seconds while the play was moving to the right and slowly started running down the field along the left sideline.

When Jay saw Allen alone downfield, without breaking his stride, he fired a cross-field pass to Allen, who pulled down the pass and ran unmolested into the end zone.

Two plays after the ensuing kickoff, Tony recovered a fumble, putting the Jefferson offense on the field again. This time, Jay started running to the right side with Allen to his outside, but he faked the pitch to Allen and, while on the run, tossed a long touchdown pass to Mike Stone, who had broken free down the middle of the field.

By the time the final horn sounded, Jay had thrown another pass to Stone for another touchdown, and he also ran for a touchdown after a faked option pitch to Esposito. Meanwhile, the Jefferson defense was in the process of registering its fourth shutout of the season.

Rowe had given him a chance to show he could play, and Jay proved he could.

Mike Stone had come up to him right after the team had broken from the huddle around Rowe following Rowe's post-game speech.

"Good game, Preppy," Stone said with a big smile on his face.

"You're listening to Tony too much, I'm not a preppy," Jay replied with a laugh.

"I know, just kidding," Mike offered. "But you did play a great game. You throw the ball a lot harder than either Amore or Reall did. I can feel it when I catch the ball, plus your passes get to the receivers much faster than their balls did. A couple of times today, I had barely turned around when the ball was there.

"I have known how hard you throw the ball since the first couple of weeks when you started practicing with us back in August.

One time, I told Coach Quigley how your passes had real zip on them."

Jay looked at Stone and flashed a grin.

"Thanks," he said.

Stone's declaration had brought Jay's mind back to Tony's words on that first day of school. "You can throw the football better than any of those guys. The coaches just need to get to know what you can do," his friend had said that morning in the parking lot.

Now, they knew.

FIVE

UNITED PRESS INTERNATIONAL, NOV. 1, 1963

TOYKO- Gen. Paul D. Harkins, top U.S. military commander in South Vietnam, said yesterday that the fight against the Communist Viet Cong is going so well that some U.S. troops there will be sent home within 60 days.

Jay rushed out of Kiley's class on Friday morning and was quickly heading down the corridor so he could make a stop at his locker before English class when he saw Marty walking toward him.

"Hey, slow down, blue eyes," she said.

"I need to get my copy of Catch-22 before I go to English class," Jay said.

"Here, take mine," Marty said. "Mrs. Weber teaches the same lesson to both of her senior classes, so we're also reading Catch-22. Your luck, I've already underlined all the important passages."

They had only walked a few steps down the corridor together when Marty declared.

"I still can't believe you are not going to the dance tomorrow night," Marty said.

"I just have a lot of other things on my mind," Jay offered. "We have the game tomorrow afternoon, and sometimes I'm not the best person to be with after a game. I probably will just work on my research paper."

"Somebody else isn't going, you know," Marty said.

"Oh yeah, who? Jay asked.

"Your friend and mine," Marty said with a sly look

"What do you mean? Tony is going with Linda," Jay responded.

"No, not Tony, our mutual blond friend."

"Tammy," Jay said, stopping in his tracks.

"Yeah, she told me on Wednesday that she wasn't going. She said Dave called her Tuesday night and said he couldn't get home from college. I think it's more than that, but she didn't want to talk about it."

"You never know," Jay offered.

UNITED PRESS INTERNATIONAL, NOV. 2, 1963

RICHMOND, Va. – A federal appeals court ruled yesterday that the separate-but-equal clause in the Hill-Burton Federal Hospital Act is unconstitutional.

The Saturday morning game against Seymour became one of those games where everything Jefferson did turned up roses.

The Eagles recovered a Seymour fumble on the second play of the game, and it only took a few plays for Jefferson to open the scoring on a thirty-yard touchdown run by Jim Ruggieri after he took an option pitch from Jay.

For two hours, it seemed every time Jay faked a pitch to one of the running backs on an option, the Seymour defense bit and followed the runners. That left some Jefferson receivers wide open downfield. By halftime, Jay had thrown three touchdown passes.

"We shouldn't have given up that touchdown in the fourth quarter," Tony said to Jay as they walked off the field after the game.

"Christ, we won 35-7," Jay said. "Don't get greedy. You guys on defense played a great game," Jay said.

"You weren't too bad yourself, preppy," Tony yelled as the two old friends jogged off the field.

NEW YORK TIMES, NOV. 2, 1963

WASHINGTON – The Kennedy administration was confident last evening that the coup in South Vietnam will greatly improve the chances of victory over Communist-led guerrillas there.

Jay was relieved when the phone rang a few times, and nobody answered. He had been hesitant to make the call, downright scared in fact. But now it looked like fate was going to save him from having to come up with a clever opening line. He was just taking the phone away from his ear when he heard a female voice answer.

"Hello," she said.

He had been trying to think what he was going to say if her mother or father answered, so he was a little stunned to hear Tammy's voice.

"Hi Tammy, it's aw, aw Jay."

"Hey," she said, "You didn't go to the dance?"

"No, I didn't have a date."

"You couldn't have tried too hard. I know a lot of girls who would have loved to go with the star quarterback."

"I don't know about that. Besides, I'm trying to finish my research paper,"

"I know that's what I'm working on too."

"Oh, sorry to bother you," Jay said. "I will let you get back to work."

But she quickly suggested a counteroffer.

"Hey, why don't you bring your research stuff over here, and we can work here?" she said.

He was speechless for a few seconds. The last thing he expected was an invitation to come over to her house. But he quickly gained some confidence.

"Are you sure your parents won't mind? By the time I get there, it will be after 9 o'clock," he replied.

"No, they are in the living room watching the Lawrence Welk

show. After it's finished, they probably will go to bed. We can work at the kitchen table. Just come to the back door. It opens right into the kitchen," she said.

Thirty minutes later, Jay was sitting at the table in Tammy's kitchen.

"It's amazing how Bob Dylan draws you into the message with his music without you even realizing he's delivering a message," Jay said as he read from one of the numerous note cards he had compiled over the past few weeks.

NEW YORK TIMES, NOV. 2, 1963

> AMERICUS, Ga. - A Federal court handed down an injunction today prohibiting the prosecution of four civil rights workers on state insurrection charges.

The ride over to Tammy's house had been filled with self-questioning. Why is she asking him over to her house? Did she ever send that letter to Dave? Has she broken up with her boyfriend?

But he didn't have any answers, and he certainly wasn't going to ask Tammy.

He had walked into Tammy's kitchen trying not to show his nervousness about being alone with the blond at her house, so he headed right to the kitchen table, pulled out his pile of note cards from a large envelope, and immediately started reading from them.

"Listen to this," he said as he read the lines of "Blowin' in the Wind." "War, Civic Rights, it's all there in the first sixteen lines. He gets you thinking every time you hear the song."

In an effort to ease the butterflies in his stomach, he talked about Dylan for three or four minutes without even looking away from the notecards. Finally, he stopped talking, looked up, and realized Tammy wasn't looking at her stack of note cards on the table. She was just watching his face while he was talking.

"Oh, sorry," Jay said. "I didn't mean to go off like that."

But Tammy wasn't looking for an apology.

"You are the quarterback of the football team. You threw three touchdown passes today. Why aren't you talking about today's game or something else involving sports? That's what most guys would do," Tammy declared.

Jay was stunned—and pleased—that she knew he had thrown three touchdown passes in the game that morning, but he tried not to show his glee.

"I don't know, I just get excited about the stuff Dylan sings about. He has this whiny voice, but his message is so powerful," Jay offered while looking straight at Tammy's face, which now was banishing a soft smile.

"I saw him sing this summer," the blond declared.

"I know you did," Jay offered in a soft voice. "I was sitting a few rows behind you."

"How do you know that? We didn't even know each other then?" the blond said with a questioning look.

"I didn't know it that night, but the first day of school, when you said hello to Tony and me in the parking lot, I asked Tony who you were, and he told me I had seen you at the festival."

"Did you remember me?" she asked with a smile.

"Of course, I did," he said.

"Come on, be honest."

"Well, maybe not, but you know Dylan, Joan Baez, Pete Seeger, and Peter, Paul and Mary were on the stage. Plus, Tony told me you were with your boyfriend, so he was probably blocking my view."

"Okay, you're forgiven for lying to me. Now get back to work, I don't want to be the reason you don't get an A on your research paper. I know you prep school boys are accustomed to getting all As."

"Believe me, I didn't get all As at my old school, far from it," Jay said.

"Maybe not, but you think about a lot of things most guys our age never think about. You really like Kennedy, don't you?" she asked.

Tammy's response caught Jay by surprise.

"Yeah, how did you know that?"

"Are you kidding?" she offered in a forceful tone. "In Kiley's class, you're always jumping at an opportunity to talk about Kennedy."

Jay could feel his face turning red with embarrassment. He didn't realize his obsession with President Kennedy was so obvious.

"I guess I like Kennedy's intensity. I just think he's about all the possibilities that our country can be. He takes ideas and puts them into action. He's changing us. It's like when you were talking about his Civil Rights speech a few weeks ago. You talked about how Kennedy said it was a moral issue. Before this year, I went to Catholic schools my entire life, so I just thought a moral issue was about religion; whether something was good or bad according to religious teaching. But even though he's Catholic, to Kennedy, moral issues aren't about religion, they're about what is right for human beings, all humans, not just the people who look like us."

Tammy looked at him for several seconds before speaking. He was flashing an infectious smile that regularly seemed to be on his face. Finally, she broke the silence.

"Like I said, most guys our age don't think about things like that. Now get back to work. You prep school guys are accustom to getting As."

"I'm not a prep school guy," Jay protested

"If you say so," Tammy said with an easy laugh.

ASSOCIATED PRESS, NOV. 3, 1963

SAIGON – A Buddhist-led provisional regime controlled a nervous Saigon today after a bloody coup that brought the downfall and death to President Ngo Dinh Diem and his brother Ngo Dinh Nhu

—

Tammy started pushing on her car horn before the car even came to a stop in front of Marty's house. Marty quickly appeared at the front door but signaled to Tammy to wait a few minutes.

"Hurry up, Tammy yelled I want to get this over with."

It was 10 o'clock Sunday morning, and Tammy wasn't happy that she and the other cheerleaders had to go over to the school and remove all the decorations they had also put up for Saturday night's dance. She felt the cheerleaders had done all the work putting up the decorations, so somebody else should do the clean-up.

Finally, Marty came out, jumped in the car, and Tammy drove off.

"Did you have a good time last night?" Tammy asked.

"Yeah, it was fun. Russ Lawrence may not be Paul Newman, but he is fun, and he's fairly cute."

"Cute enough to go to the lake after the dance?"

"Maybe for a little while," Marty said with a sheepish grin. "Let me tell you, that boy has fast hands. How about you? What did you do?"

"Nothing much, my parents were home watching Lawrence Welk, so I stayed in the kitchen working on my resource paper."

"That's good, at least you got some work done, so it wasn't a wasted night."

They drove for a few minutes without talking when Tammy suddenly broke the silence.

"Oh yeah, Jay came over later in the night, and we worked on our research papers together."

"WHAT," Marty virtually screamed. "What do you mean, he came over? Did you call him?"

"No, I didn't call him. He called me," Tammy offered in her defense. "He said you told him I wasn't going to the dance."

"Well, I did, but I didn't think he was going to call you and ask you on a date."

"It wasn't a date," the blond protested. "He just came over for a few hours, and we worked in my kitchen."

Marty looked over at her friend.

"What are you doing?" Marty said, sounding upset.

"What do you mean?" Tammy replied.

"You know what I mean, Dave can't come home one weekend, so you figure you will play Jay along for a night."

"No, it's not that. I don't have ulterior motives. He just came over for a few hours. It was like we were at the library with everybody working on our research papers. Besides, I think it's all over between Dave and me."

"Why, because he didn't come home one weekend?"

"No, it's more than that. I sent him a letter last week, telling him to go fuck himself because I'm so fed up with his bad temper and all the other shit."

"You have done that before, but then you always make up."

"Not this time," the blond declared.

"So right away you're making a play for Jay. Why, because now, he is the quarterback?" Marty quipped?

"Thanks a lot, friend. I thought you knew me better than that. No, I am not making a play for Jay. I'm not making a play for anyone."

"Yeah, I'm sorry, it's just that I really like Jay. I think he's sweet. I don't want to see him get hurt. Besides, I don't think he's your type."

"Oh yeah, what's my type?" Tammy asked.

"You know. You seem to like guys with a little bit of the bad boy in them. You know, guys who are a little mischievous," her friend offered.

"Yeah, and look where it has gotten me," Tammy said.

Marty looked at her friend with an irritated expression.

"You know he likes you," Marty said.

"Has he told you that?" Tammy asked.

"No, he hasn't said it, but I can tell the way he looks at you."

"Well, don't worry, I'm not looking for a new boyfriend. I'm just trying to get through our senior year and have some fun doing it. I don't want any complications."

UNITED PRESS INTERNATIONAL, NOV. 4, 1963

WASHINGTON – Rep. Richard Bolling of Missouri, a liberal Democrat, said yesterday that congressional failure to pass an effective civil rights bill might "wreck" the United States in bloodshed and harden white prejudice against the Negro.

"Can legislation change people's attitudes?" Kiley asked as soon as everybody settled into their seats and opened their morning New York Times. "What do you think, Aaronson?"

"Yeah, I guess so," said Dan Aaronson, the football team's kicker, and according to Tony, he was a straight-A student.

"So, if Congress passes the Civil Rights Bill this week, next week everybody in Alabama and Mississippi will be fine with Negroes voting and Negro kids going to school with white kids," the teacher asked, continuing the conversation.

"Well, it probably will take some time," Marty interjected from the other side of the room.

"How much time?" Kiley quickly retorted.

"I don't know," Marty said, looking defensive.

"Don't worry, Miss Burns, nobody knows," the teacher said.

"So why is it so important to pass the civil rights bill right now if it is going to take time to change people's attitudes?" Mike Stone asked Kiley.

But before Kiley could even offer an answer, Jay jumped into the conversation.

"It may not immediately change people's attitude, but legislation can immediately change people's behavior because it will be the law," Jay said.

"Interesting point, Burke," Kiley replied without pressing Jay on his answer.

UNITED PRESS INTERNATIONAL, NOV. 5, 1963

> NEW ORLEANS – Police yesterday arrested three Negroes who attempted to eat in the city hall cafeteria and who refused to move on after being ordered to by officers.

"So, what do you think? Is President Kennedy living up to the promises he made about creating job opportunities for Negroes when he was running for the presidency against Nixon in 1960?" Kiley offered as his opening salvo to his Tuesday morning class. But nobody attempted to answer the question, so he directly asked Jay.

"What do you think, Burke?"

Before Jay could even open his mouth, his best friend injected an attempt at good-natured humor.

"Here we go, another half-hour speech about all the wonderful things President Kennedy is doing," Tony quipped from his seat in the back of the room.

A frown came over Marty's face as she looked in Tony's direction, but Jay just smiled at his friend.

"Maybe not everything he promised," Jay said.

"Check that boy's temperature," injected Tony. "He's actually saying Kennedy isn't perfect. Those guys from Seymour must have hit you harder than I thought Saturday."

Kiley was just standing against the wall with a smile on his face as he watched the friendly banter between classmates. But with only a few minutes remaining in the class, he took over the discussion for a closing comment.

"In the past few months, you have seen several stories like this one in today's paper about Negroes in some southern states refusing to accept discriminatory policies. But the past few months are not the first time this country has seen this type of important protest from an individual or a small group of nNegroes. As I have said a few times, sometimes you need to know a little recent history to understand the significance of what we are reading in today's paper. So, if you want a few extra points on your average, check out Rosa Parks, the Greensboro or the Tampa lunch counter sit-ins, and write a few hundred words about one of them," Kiley said.

NEW YORK TIMES, NOV. 9, 1963

WASHINGTON – Secretary of State Dean Rusk said yesterday that South Vietnam's rural war against Communist guerrillas will gain new "impetus" from the coup d'etat which overthrew President Ngo Dinh Diem.

"You're blowing their minds. They don't know which way we're going," Tony yelled to Jay as the two old friends headed to the sidelines with cheers ringing from the stands after Jefferson had scored its second touchdown of the first quarter. That's the way the game went all afternoon. Working out of the spread, Jay was continuing to mix runs with passes off the option.

By the end of the third quarter, Jefferson was leading 28-7, and it was just a matter of playing out the string en route to an eventual 34-7 victory.

"Good job, Gentlemen," Rowe said as he stood in the middle of the team members, who were kneeling in the end zone after the game. "We're 8-1. It's the second week of November, and we are still in the hunt for the title. If we win one more, we'll be playing for at least a co-championship on Thanksgiving morning. We still have a lot of work to do, so don't let anything distract you from our goal."

NEW YORK TIMES, NOV. 10, 1963

SHAKER HEIGHTS, Ohio – The Negro revolution has many battlegrounds,

> but none more surprising than this opulent suburb on the northeast corner of Cleveland.
>
> For generations, the energetic Yankees from New England, then the Irish, the Bohemians, and the Germans have looked on Shaker Heights as the privileged sanctuary of the Rockefellers, the Hannas, the Humphreys and the Boltons. This was the top of the economic ladder, the goal of the ambitious and now it is the middle-class Negro who is knocking at the door.

Usually, Kiley didn't waste any time starting the discussion of the morning Times at the beginning of his Monday class, but this morning, he paused for a personal observation.

"Before we get started talking about what's happening around the rest of the world, I just want to take a minute to congratulate the members of this class who are on the football team," he said. "That was a big victory Saturday, guys. It's great the way you guys have come back after losing a few weeks ago. The success of this school's athletic teams means a lot to the people of this city."

The faces of the five football players in the class were beaming, but Russ Lawrence quickly injected a sense of reality.

"It can't mean that much. After Wednesday night, we might not even have teams," Lawrence declared.

Kiley was stunned by the running back's proclamation.

"What are you talking about?" Kiley inquired.

"Where have you been, Mr. Kiley?" Lawrence asked in a sarcastic tone. "Wednesday night, the school committee is voting whether to cut sports teams as a way to save money."

Before Kiley could even say a word, Joan D'Errico, the petite brunette who sat a few seats from Marty, delivered a declaration.

"That's crazy, they can't cut sports teams. We have to go to that meeting and protest, let people know how important the sports teams are to us," the girl declared.

Joan D'Errico wasn't a girl who normally garners a second

glance from most teenage boys. Her hair was cut into bangs that went straight across her eyebrows, then came straight down the side of her head until it reached the bottom of her neck. She tended to wear jumpers that hid any possible compliment to the physical curves of her body and extended down an inch or so below her knees.

But Jay had noticed she often joined in many of Kiley's classroom discussions, and Marty had said she was a good kid who was president of the Thyrsus club.

Russ Lawrence definitely was startled by the girl's concern for the sports teams.

"Why do you care? Girls don't even have sports teams here," Lawrence asked.

"This isn't just about boys' sports teams," D'Errico declared. "It's about all students having the right to tell the people in charge what's important to us."

NEW YORK TIMES, NOV. 12, 1963

> NEW YORK, NY – Business and industry here in the face of the civil rights revolution have been reassessing their employment policies and hiring Negroes for office and other salaried posts that they rarely held before.

The thirty or so students who had congregated in the parking lot behind City Hall started marching down the street toward the front of the building just after 7 p.m.

They were aligned in rows of four or five students. Russ Lawrence was in the middle of the front row with Marty, Tammy, Joan D'Errico, and Jane Snow on each side of him. Jay, Tony, Jim Ruggieri, and two girls Jay had never seen were in the second row. Most of the students, including Tony and Jay, were carrying a poster-board sign with "Save our Sports" scripted on them that the girls had passed out to the students as they arrived at the parking lot.

"I can't believe the girls made all these signs in only one night," Jay said to Tony while they were waiting for the march to begin.

"I may not know much about women. But one thing I do know is never underestimate what a bunch of women can do in one night," Tony offered with a laugh.

Russ Lawrence had mapped out the plan. They would march along the street that runs next to the city hall. When they reached the sidewalk in front of City Hall, they would ring the walkway leading up to the front entrance of City Hall, so everybody entering City Hall for the school committee meeting would have to pass between students on both sides of the sidewalk. Then, just before the start of the meeting, the students would march into the City Hall, fill the back of the city council meeting room where the meeting was being held, and then start chanting "Save Our Sports" as soon as the school committee chairman started the meeting.

But as the students turned onto the sidewalk in front of city hall. Mr. Lawson, the principal, came walking out of the front door of City Hall and headed down the walkway toward the students.

"It's time to stop this," Lawson said in a loud voice, and his arms raised above his head. "You are blocking traffic. Now break this up and go home."

"We have a right to be heard, Mr. Lawson," Russ Lawrence yelled.

"The school committee doesn't want to hear from you. This is an adult issue."

Lawson said. But the students didn't move. Some were yelling "we have a right" from the back of the crowd. By now, the drivers of some cars who had been driving on the road in front of City Hall had pulled their cars to the side of the road and had gotten out of their cars to get a better look at what was happening. Jay looked over to the side of the street and saw a man with a big camera taking photos of the girls who were carrying signs.

"I think the newspaper is here," he said to Tony.

"Somebody else is also here," Tony said, pointing to six policemen who were walking toward the crowd from the three police cars they had parked at the end of the side street next to City Hall.

"Break it up," the police sergeant said to the students at the front of the crowd.

"We have a right to be here," Russ Lawrence yelled.

But the police weren't in any mood to debate the issue. Four of them grabbed Russ, Jay, Tony, Jim Ruggieri, and Stan Bartkiewicz by their arms and led them to the two police cars. Jay looked back and saw the two other cops, leading Tammy, Marty, Joan D'Errico, and Jane Snow to another police car.

But before the police took another move, another man appeared at the front door of City Hall.

"Who the hell is that?" Jay said as he looked out the side window of the police car.

"It's the mayor," Tony offered.

The mayor was standing at the top of the stairs at the front of City Hall, holding a bullhorn. His voice boomed out of the bullhorn as he spoke. It was obvious he was not happy.

"This is getting out of hand," he declared. "I told the school committee chairman to postpone the meeting to another night. This is something I need to discuss with the city council over the next few weeks. Officers, now let those students out of the police cars, and everybody go home."

The students got out of the police cars and walked back to join the other students on the sidewalk in front of City Hall.

"Did we win?" Marty asked.

"I don't know what you call it, but at least we got the mayor to say he is going to discuss it with the city council. Maybe we will get them to change their mind about cutting sports," Joan D'Errico said.

The students started heading back to the parking lot when Tony noticed the principal standing in front of City Hall talking to a few policemen.

"Look at Mr. Lawson, he doesn't look happy. We could be in some serious shit tomorrow morning," Tony offered.

NEW YORK TIMES, NOV. 13, 1963

WASHINGTON – The United States is sending some of its highest officials to Honolulu Nov. 20 for one-day strategy meeting on South Vietnam

"That was interesting, apparently Mr. Lawson wasn't happy about our little protest last night," Russ Lawrence said as he, Jay, Tony, and Jim Ruggeri started walking down the corridor after leaving the principal's office. "I guess we are lucky we only got one night of detention."

Just then, Marty, Tammy, Joan D'Errico, and Jane Snow came walking out of the Dean of Girls' office.

"Did you get a night of detention like us?" Russ asked the four girls.

"We got two nights," Marty declared.

Jay immediately jumped into the conversation.

"That's not fair. Why did we get one night and you got two?" he asked.

"Because your football players," Tammy offered in a disgusted tone as she was walking away from the group.

NEW YORK TIMES, NOV. 14, 1963

WASHINGTON – A group of national leaders sought yesterday to break the congressional stalemate over medical care for the elderly.

"Hey, do you mind if we stop at the library for a while? I have something I need to check out," Jay said to Tony as they drove away from school following practice Thursday afternoon.

"I guess not," Tony said, "But make it fast, I'm fucking hungry."

As soon as they walked into the library, Tony spotted Tammy sitting with Marty and Jane at one of the long tables in the periodicals section.

"Tell me you didn't know she was here," Tony challenged his friend in an agitated tone.

"Well, maybe I talked to Marty this afternoon and found out the girls were coming here to do some homework."

"Shit, I don't care if you are making a dumb-ass move on a girl, but not when it affects my stomach," Tony said.

But Jay had already started walking toward the girls, so Tony followed.

"Hello, Ladies," Jay said as he reached the table. "Didn't expect to see you here."

"Yes, you did," Tony said, obviously still upset about being late for his dinner.

Marty picked up on Tony's irritation.

"Hey Tony, Jane and I need some help finding a magazine over here," she said as she and Jane got out of their chairs and grabbed Tony by the back of his arms and led him away, leaving just Jay and Tammy at the table.

Jay quickly seized the opportunity to sit alone with the blond.

"Hey, I'm sorry about the detention thing," Jay said.

"What?" Tammy said with a questioning expression.

"It wasn't fair that you girls got two nights of detention and we only got one because we are football players," Jay replied.

"Oh, that. It's no big thing."

"You seemed pretty upset about it yesterday," Jay replied.

"I guess I was, but I got over it. It turns out, it really didn't have anything to do with you being football players. Apparently, Mrs. Harrison was really upset about the way we acted at the protest. She said we didn't act like ladies. I guess she's the one who decided to give us the two nights before she even talked to Mr. Lawson about what he was giving you guys."

"Oh, so we don't have an advantage." Jay quipped, now feeling he had the upper hand in the conversation.

But Tammy quickly regained the initiative.

"Oh, you have an advantage, it's just not because you are football players," the blond declared with a smirk.

"So, what is our advantage?" Jay asked.

"You're men," she quipped as she got out of her seat and started walking toward where Marty and Jane were corralling Tony.

She took a few steps, but suddenly stopped and turned back toward Jay, who was standing at the table with a depressed look on his face.

"We don't have Kiley's class tomorrow, so if I don't see you in school, good luck in the game Saturday," she said.

"Thanks," Jay replied.

Then the blond shocked him with another declaration.

"Give me a call later," she said.

"What," he said about the totally unexpected request for a phone call.

"Give me a call later tonight, and we'll talk," she said.

"About what?" Jay questioned.

"Nothing in particular, we'll just talk. Does there always have to be a reason for you to talk to me?" the blond asked.

"No, no," Jay said as he watched the blond walk away, trying to hide his excitement.

NEW YORK TIMES, NOV. 16, 1963

SAIGON – The withdrawal of 1,000 United States servicemen from South Vietnam will start Dec. 3, Major General Charles J. Timmes announced today. The men are to depart by the end of the year, leaving 15,500 American troops in the country.

Right from the beginning of the game against Dayville, it was obvious this was Doug Allen's day. Athletes have days like this, days when everything they do, every move they make, is in sync with the rest of their body. Allen's running, off option pitches from Jay, accounted for two touchdowns in the first half, then early in the third quarter Jay faked a handoff to Ruggieri and pitched to Allen, who once again broke past several defenders en route to another touchdown. Jay kept the attack in high gear with touchdown passes to Mike Stone and junior wide receiver Ray Hicks early in the fourth quarter.

The final buzzer made it official, the 35-6 victory meant Jefferson would be playing Madison on Thanksgiving morning for a share of the championship.

"We did it," Tony yelled as he grabbed Jay in another bear hug while they headed onto the field to celebrate the victory. "Everybody thought we were dead when we lost to Notre Dame, but now we have a chance to win a co-championship. The Coach said we could do it, and we did. This is the greatest feeling I have ever had, and we're not finished."

UNITED PRESS INTERNATIONAL, NOV. 18, 1963

> SAIGON – A U.S. Army sergeant was killed in an ambush attack by a strong Communist guerrilla force in the central highlands of South Vietnam near the Cambodian border, a U.S. military spokesman said yesterday.

"Okay, let's get going," said Kiley as he burst into class on Monday morning. "I know normally Monday morning we go over the Monday Times because you don't get the weekend papers, but I brought in Saturday's Times because I think there are two interesting pieces in the paper. First, there is this story about President Kennedy speaking at the AFL-CIO convention and saying that providing jobs is the most important issue in the country today, more than civil rights, so what do you think? Didn't Kennedy give a speech in June saying civil rights was critical? Isn't that what we have been reading for three months now? But here he is saying civil rights isn't the most important issue in the country."

He stood in the front of the classroom holding the paper, waiting for somebody to speak.

"It's politics," said Lenny Angelone, a basketball and baseball player.

"What does that mean?" Kiley asked

"I don't know, it's what my father says anytime he hears some politician saying something on TV that he doesn't like," Lenny said with a smile.

The class broke into an uproar.

"Hey, at least I said something," Lenny offered in his defense.

"It's fine," Kiley interjected. "What do you think Angelone's father is talking about when he says it's politics?" Kiley asked the class.

"Politicians say what they think people want to hear," said Karen Powers.

"I thought President Kennedy was supposed to be different," Kiley retorted, trying to elicit involvement from other members of the class.

"You have to get elected before you can get anything accomplished," the girl with dark hair who sat a few seats from the front in the first row, but hardly ever spoke up in class, offered.

Now Kiley had everybody involved in the discussion, not just the usual few, and he was loving it.

"True," the teacher said. "But doesn't there come a time when you say what you believe, even if it might cost you some votes?"

"Maybe that's what President Kennedy is planning to do in his second term," Jay offered. "After he is reelected next year, he will not have to worry about being reelected again, and he could do even more bold things."

"Maybe," Kiley said. "It's something we will look at and talk about as we go into the new year and read about Congress dealing with the President's Civil Rights bill. Are civil rights really that important to Kennedy? We probably will talk about it a lot over the next couple of months."

Kiley was pleased with the extensive class participation. Too often in the first couple of months of school, he felt the class discussion was limited to the same selective group of students, but some different voices were heard this morning.

So, he was flashing a broad smile when he said, "On another issue, it looks like you are not going to have to get married to avoid being drafted, Gemma." Kiley offered, which brought a roar of laughter. He then read an article about the first withdrawal of American personnel in Vietnam, starting in a few weeks in early December.

"The way I read this is if Kennedy gets reelected next fall, the US will be out of Vietnam by the time he is inaugurated next January."

NEW YORK TIMES, NOV. 19, 1963

> WASHINGTON – The Supreme Court asked the Justice Department for its views on whether a state may ever enforce a private owner's decision to exclude Negroes from his place of business. The Justices voted 5 to 4 to put this broad and hotly debated question to the Administration.

"We don't have a game Saturday. So, what are you doing Saturday night?" Marty asked Tammy as they walked down the corridor following Kiley's Tuesday morning class.

"Jimmy Pierce from the beach is home from college. He called and asked me to go out to dinner," Tammy offered

"Where are you going?"

"He said something about going over to Bay Shore."

"Then what?"

"What do you mean?"

"You know what I mean," Marty said. "When a college boy

comes home and asks a high school girl out, he's not just looking for a good meal. I thought you didn't want any complications."

"There's nothing complicated about this," Tammy shot back. "Jimmy is just a friend. You and Jay aren't the only male and female who can be friends, you know."

"I know, but I've never been under a blanket at a beach party with Jay," Marty offered.

UNITED PRESS INTERNATIONAL, NOV. 20, 1963

> WASHINGTON – President Kennedy will make a "non-political" 2 ½-day trip to Texas and during it will deliver at least six speeches. A Democratic fund-raising dinner in Austin Friday night is the only event which the White House said would be strictly political.

Jay spotted Tammy walking on the far side of the empty cafeteria. He knew she was just cutting through the café on the way to the girls' gym for cheerleading practice, and he had a direct route to the door that led to the boys' locker room. But he altered his route so he would need to walk between some of the long tables near the far side of the café. But when the blond just walked past him without looking up on the other side of one of the tables, he could feel his heart drop. His plan for an impromptu meeting now ruined, he questioned whether or not to just let her walk out the exit so that he didn't appear overanxious, but he couldn't.

"Don't you even say hello?" he said in a loud voice.

Tammy was already a few steps past him, but she made a sudden stop and turned around.

"Oh, Jay, I'm sorry. I didn't see you. I wasn't even paying attention to where I was going." She said in an apologetic voice.

"You must be thinking of something really important," Jay said, happy that his plan created the meeting he hoped for.

"I'm just so fucking mad at my guidance counselor," she said emphatically.

The response caught Jay completely by surprise. He knew from her letter to Dave that she was capable of thinking that way; probably every girl was. But you just didn't hear that from a girl, especially not in the high school cafeteria.

"Woah, that's not something I have ever heard from you," he said. "Who is your guidance counselor?"

"Mrs. Lewis," Tammy replied.

"I don't know her, but she must be an idiot," Jay said, trying to show Tammy she had his support.

"No, she's really a nice person," Tammy said.

"So, what's the problem?" he asked.

"She called me down to talk about college. She asked me if I was thinking about where I was going to apply, but before I even had a chance to answer, she started telling me how important it was for women to be educated because educated women have smarter children. All she talked about was going to college, then getting married and having smart kids. Suppose that's not why I want to go to college. I'm decent at math, so why shouldn't I think about becoming an engineer? Or why shouldn't I think about being a lawyer or a U.S senator?"

"I didn't know you were that interested in politics," Jay interjected.

"I'm not really, it's just that some people think the only reason a girl should go to college is so she can become a teacher, then get married and have kids. I don't want to go to college to get a Mrs. Degree."

"A what?" Jay asked with a perplexed look.

"You know a girl who goes to college so she can find a husband," Tammy said, finally having dropped the scowl from her face. "I mean, there's nothing wrong with that for some people, but women can do other things if people would give us a chance."

Jay wasn't quite sure what he should say. It wasn't that he never thought of women as more than being teachers or secretaries. The past few months, a few times, he had thought about how impressed he was with the way his mother had taken over the business after his father's death. She wasn't just doing some bookkeeping like she had done when his father was alive. Now she was running the business, dealing with customers, bidding on projects, and most of the people she had to deal with were men. She didn't talk about it; she just would say things were fine. But she was putting in long hours, usually leaving for work before he left for school in the morning and usually coming home even later than Jay would get home from football practice. Occasionally, when they would be eating dinner, she would make some off-handed remark about how it was tough to work in a man's world, but she never really complained. 'I guess it's just the way it is,' she would say with a little laugh. So, in a way, Jay understood Tammy's frustration, but it wasn't what he was thinking about when he devised his plan to pass by her in the cafeteria. So, he just stood there letting Tammy talk.

"It just pisses me off that the only thing girls are supposed to think about is getting married and having kids," the blond said again. "The idea that women would do something other than produce children isn't ever discussed. My mother was part of the silent generation. They were woman who were taught to keep their chin up and not complain, but that's not the way I want to spend my life."

Suddenly, she noticed Jay seemed to have a stunned look on his face, so she changed her voice to a more mellow tone.

"I'm sorry, I didn't mean to go off on you with my peeve."

He finally thought of something to say.

"That's okay, I like a woman who thinks for herself," he said.

"And you know a lot of women?" She asked with a questioning tone, trying to inject some humor into the moment.

"No, no, not a lot, but apparently I know some interesting ones," Jay said sheepishly.

SIX

UNITED PRESS INTERNATIONAL, NOV. 22, 1963

HOUSTON – President Kennedy toured Texas as a political peacemaker for feuding Democrats yesterday and ran into scattered catcalls and pickets chanting "Cuba" among the hundreds of thousands who greeted him.

It was a typical crisp fall morning as Jay and Tony walked across the parking lot on Friday morning.

"Hey, our last period today is study. Do you want to go over to Sal's and get some dogs before practice?" Tony asked, "There's no problem getting out of the study. We can tell the study room teacher that we are going down to the gym to see Rowe. She will give us a pass."

"I can't. I have to make up a French test that period," Jay said.

"That's shits on Friday afternoon," Tony said.

"I know, but I have to get it done. I will see you in the locker room."

UNITED PRESS INTERNATIONAL, NOV. 22, 1963, 12:39 P.M. (CST) – FLASH

DALLAS, Tex. – Kennedy seriously wounded perhaps fatally by assassin's bullet.

"Did you hear that—President Kennedy has been shot?" the guy with the long white apron standing behind the counter at Sal's yelled as he turned up the volume of the clock radio sitting on top of the glass cabinet that held two rows of pies.

"Holy shit, we have to get back to school," Tony said to the three other football players sitting with him in the booth at Sal's, drinking Cokes and eating hot dogs.

NEW YORK TIMES, NOV. 22, 1963

> DALLAS – President John Fitzgerald Kennedy was shot and killed by an assassin today.
>
> He died of a wound in the brain caused by a rifle bullet that was fired at him as he was riding through downtown Dallas in a motorcade.

Room 24B, where Jay was making up his French test, wasn't even in the actual high school. It was a room that was in a small building just outside one of the back doors of the school. Apparently, at one time it had been used as a storage building, but with the increase in student enrollment this year, it had been turned into a classroom. It was as far away from the main lobby of the school as you could get and still be considered at Jefferson High. To make matters worse, it didn't have an intercom system, and you couldn't even hear the dismissal bell, so it was already several minutes past the 2:30 dismissal time as Jay rushed up the long corridor that led to the stairwell that would take him to the main lobby.

He figured everybody would already be there for their usual afternoon get-together of students before the football players headed off to the locker room to change for practice.

But when he reached the main lobby, hardly anybody was there, and those who were there seemed to have a blank look on their faces. He saw Marty sitting by herself in the chair next to the phone booth, so he started walking toward her when he realized she was crying.

"Hey, what's wrong?" he asked.

She looked up at him with the tears rolling down her cheeks.

"You don't know?" she asked.

"Know what? What is going on here?" Jay said, now starting to get irritated.

"The President has been killed," Marty said, forcing the words out of her mouth.

"What are you talking about?" Jay asked.

Suddenly, she realized he hadn't heard.

"You didn't hear? They announced it on the intercom."

"I was down in 24B making up a test. There's no intercom down there," Jay said, still trying to understand what Marty had just said. "What happened? What did they say? It can't be true," Jay said in rapid fire without giving Marty a chance to answer any of his questions.

Finally, he let Marty talk.

"First, Lawson came on the intercom while class was going on and said the President had been shot while riding in a car in Dallas. Then just before the bell rang, he came back on and said the president was dead. He sounded like he was going to start crying."

"Are they sure it's true?" Jay asked.

"I think so. I was in Mr. Williams' class. He had a radio in his closet. So, we started listening to it. They were saying he had been shot. His wife was with him, but she wasn't shot. How can this happen?" Marty said, looking to Jay for answers he couldn't give.

He just stood there looking into space. All around him, kids were talking, but he didn't seem to hear anything. Suddenly, he realized Marty was still sitting in the chair, crying. He knelt down and pulled her face close to him. There were no words, so he just kept her face buried in his chest. Students walked through the main lobby and headed out the front door, getting on buses in front of the school. There was none of the usual Friday afternoon laughter and yelling of teenagers heading out for a carefree weekend. A few minutes later, Tony appeared in the lobby along with Jim Ruggieri, Vin Rego, and a few other football players.

"Are we practicing?" Jay asked.

"I don't know, we went down to Rowe's classroom, but he wasn't there," Ruggieri said.

"We'd better get down to the locker room," Tony interjected.

"Are you going to be okay?" Jay asked Marty.

"Yeah, I'm okay. I'm going to try to find Tammy."

About half the team was already in the locker room when Jay and Tony walked in; some were sitting on benches still fully dressed, and others were standing in their white jockey shorts in front of their lockers, starting to put on their football pants.

Suddenly, Coach Quigley came into the locker room.

"The Coach wants everybody in the gym," he said.

"Should we put our uniforms on?" Tony asked.

"Come the way you are, just put your pants on," the young assistant coach said, his voice quavering.

Rowe was already standing in the middle of the gym as the players began filling in.

He didn't say a word, but everybody knew to form a circle around him.

His face looked pale, worse than after the Notre Dame loss.

"Guys, we will not practice today," Rowe declared. "Today and tonight is a time you should be with your family, the people you care about, the people who care about you. We will meet here tomorrow at noon. Maybe we will practice, maybe we will just talk. I can't explain what has happened today. I saw men die right next to me in war. It was terrible, and I will never forget it, but somehow, I could explain it. It was war. I can't explain this. I'm not sure if anybody can, but if you need to talk to somebody, the coaches and I are here for you."

Jay walked out of the gym with Tony.

"That's amazing," said Tony, "I have played for that guy for three years, and I never heard him say anything about himself. Never about what it was like in the war or anything."

Jay and Tony walked across the parking lot in silence on their way to Jay's car. They drove down the city's main street toward their side of the city, not saying a word, just listening to the radio. The bank, which normally would be filled with people cashing their Friday paychecks, was virtually empty; the drugstore a little further down the street had already closed and had a hand-written sign on the door. Jay looked up at the passengers sitting in the bus as it drove past on the other side of the street. Nobody seemed to be talking, just blankly staring out the window.

"It just doesn't make any sense," said Tony. "There is a natural order to things, and this isn't natural. Nobody shoots the president in this country; that's what happens in some South American country. Not here."

"Well, Lincoln was assassinated," Jay interjected.

"Yeah, but that was a hundred years ago. I thought this was supposed to be a better place now," Tony said as he just stared out the side window of Jay's car.

Jay kept driving without trying to offer an answer to Tony's question about America, because there didn't seem to be any answers.

"I will call you tonight," Tony said as he exited Jay's car and headed toward his front door.

When he got home, Jay looked at the clock in the kitchen and couldn't believe it was only 4 o'clock. It seemed like it had been days since he first heard Marty declare, "The President has been killed."

He turned on the TV in the living room and started watching Walter Cronkite, but he just didn't feel right sitting there watching TV by himself. His mother still wasn't home from work, so he left a note saying that he would be home later. He got in his car and started driving without a definite destination. Before long, he found himself in front of Marty's house.

"My parents want me to go to church with them," Marty said as they talked at the front door. "Do you want to come with us?"

"Thanks, but you should be with your parents," Jay replied.

"Where are you going to go?" she asked

"I don't know. I'm just going to drive."

"Call me later, we won't be at church that long. Be careful," she pleaded.

He got back in his car and started driving. He thought about going home, but instead he headed the car in the other direction, driving back past the high school, which was now completely closed. A few minutes later, he passed the football field where just six days earlier he had experienced the biggest thrill of his life when he threw the pass that produced the game-winning touchdown. Now that seemed so long ago. He just kept driving until finally he stopped in front of Tammy's house. He was going to drive away because it looked like her parents were home, but he couldn't leave. He sat there trying to work up the courage to go to the door, but he couldn't. He was about to start the car when suddenly the front door of the house opened, and Tammy started walking down the walkway toward his car. He could feel his face blushing.

"I saw your car out here. Why didn't you come up?" She asked.

"I don't know, I was just wondering if you wanted to take a ride, but when I saw your parents were home, I figured I'd better not bother you."

"I'll go," she said without hesitation.

"Are you sure?"

"Yeah, my parents are sitting in the living room watching TV. They seem to be in a state of shock. They're not talking too much. Just come in while I tell them I'm going out and grab a jacket."

He followed the blond into her house and immediately saw her parents sitting next to each other on the couch.

"Mom, Dad, you know Jay," Tammy said.

"Hello Jay," both Mr. and Mrs. Clark said without getting off the couch and hardly taking their eyes off the TV.

"We're going for a ride," Tammy said.

"What about dinner?" her mother asked.

"I'm not hungry. We will be back in a little while."

"Okay, be careful," her mother pleaded.

Then just as the two teenagers were about to head out the front door, Tammy's mother added a suggestion.

"Tammy, maybe you might want to stop by a church and say a prayer for Mrs. Kennedy and the children."

"Maybe Mom," Tammy quipped as she and Jay were walking out the door.

They walked down the front sidewalk without saying a word, but as soon as they were in the car, Tammy rebuked her mother's suggestion about going to church.

"Don't worry, we don't need to do that," Tammy said as they drove away from her house.

"Maybe it's a good idea," Jay said.

NEW YORK TIMES, NOV. 22, 1963

WASHINGTON – Lyndon B. Johnson returned to a stunned capital this evening to assume the duties of the Presidency.

There were only a few dimly lit candles in the church. In the center of the altar railing, they had placed a large photo of President Kennedy on an easel surrounded by black ribbon. Almost half of the pews in the church were occupied. Some people were alone in a pew; others were kneeling with family members. Better than half of the women in the church were holding rosary beads between their fingers. Jay and Tammy, who had fastened a paper Kleenex taken from Jay's car to the top of her head with bobby pins, quietly walked to an empty pew midway up the center aisle. They knelt together in the pew for close to ten minutes, without saying a word. After leaving the church, they drove through the nearby streets. There were lights on in most homes, but nobody seemed to be moving. You could see the light from the TV reflecting in the windows of house after house.

"Do you want to see if HoJo's is open?" Jay asked

"Sure," she said.

But when they arrived at HoJo's, the parking lot was empty, and the lights in the restaurant had been turned off. Like so many other businesses, there was a handwritten note on the door. Jay didn't need to go to the door. He knew what it said—something to the effect of "Closed due to President Kennedy's death."

"I guess I should get you home," he said.

"Why don't we just sit here for a few minutes?" she said.

He was relieved. He didn't want to leave, but he couldn't think of anything to say. He just sat there looking out the side window into the dimly lit, empty parking lot. Finally, Tammy broke the silence.

"Are you alright? I know how much you liked Kennedy," she asked softly. "It's strange. Just this morning, Marty and I were talking about how much you like Kennedy. How you know stuff about him before we even read it in the paper."

"So, you two talk about me," he said, trying to lighten up the moment.

"Girls talk about everything," she said with a smile.

It felt good to laugh, but within a few seconds, Jay drifted back into a melancholy feeling.

"What are we going to do?" he asked without waiting for an answer. "He was our hope for a better world. He made you think that one person can make a difference, and everyone should try. That was the whole idea of the Peace Corps. He came from privilege, but he feels the hurt of other people. Kennedy made us think we have a purpose in life. Not just living, but having a purpose for living. He was our generation's president. Now we go back to our parents' generation with Johnson as President."

"Those are pretty deep thoughts for a football player," Tammy said with a slight laugh.

"Sorry," Jay said. "I didn't mean to get all philosophical."

Tammy quickly interjected, "No, I'm the one who should be sorry. I shouldn't try to make a joke."

She wanted to get Jay back into his self-reflection, so she quickly asked a question. "Have you ever told anybody you felt that way?" she asked.

"Probably not," Jay answered sheepishly.

Tammy continued her probe.

"How long have you liked him?" she asked.

"It seems forever," Jay said. "I remember crying when he lost the nomination for vice-president at the 1956 Democratic convention. I was ten years old; I didn't know anything about politics, but there was something about him. Maybe at first it was because he was Irish and Catholic like me, but the more I heard about him, the more I was excited. I read Profiles in Courage for a book report when I was in the eighth grade. He made you think about how people in public office can make a difference. He made public service seem exciting. He wasn't just with us. He was us. He got people excited about helping others. It wasn't one or two particular things. It was a state of mind. He seemed to have a general empathy for people."

She sat with her back leaning against the passage side door, just listening to him talk without trying to interrupt. Finally, she offered her own feelings.

"I know Mrs. Kennedy did the same thing for girls," Tammy interjected. "She's beautiful and elegant. I know some people just look at her as a beautiful woman, but to me, she's more than just a pretty face. She has a brain, and she isn't afraid to let people know she feels strongly about some things, like how important the arts should be in America. Girls want somebody they can emulate.

Mrs. Eisenhower was just kind of there. Jackie was part of what was happening."

Jay quickly jumped back into the conversation.

"She and Jack changed the way Americans thought of themselves," he said without even looking over at the girl sitting next to him. "They made people think they could accomplish things, not just sit back and wait for things to be done for them."

"The whole 'ask not what your country can do for you, but what you can do for your country' thing," Tammy offered.

"Yeah, I guess so. It's like playing on a football team. You have to think about the guy next to you before you think about yourself. Those guys on the offensive line care about me more than they care about themselves. They give themselves up to make me look good. That's why being on a football team is so different from every other sport. You have eight or nine guys who never touch the ball, but they work their ass off every day."

"I never look at football that way," she said.

Suddenly, Jay caught himself.

"The President has been killed, and I'm talking about football. That's bad," he said.

"I think he would understand. Football was part of his spirit," Tammy quickly offered. "Those touch football games on the lawn in Hyannisport and all that. It was that whole competitive nature of the Kennedy family. It made people think they were like us. He played touch football with his family just like other guys play with their kids in their backyard. It made him seem more accessible. He was a president with vigor."

"Most people probably didn't realize he had a bad back," Jay quickly offered.

"See, I didn't know that. He was always telling people to be active, take fifty-mile walks. He made the counrty think about being active," the blond said as she continued leaning against the passenger's seat door.

"He told us to be the best of what we are. Don't settle for what people might say you are."

"Everything was beautiful," said Jay. "I know nothing is really perfect. But it just seemed unspoiled; it seemed innocent. Now that innocence is gone."

"What could it have been?" Tammy asked.

"I'm not sure, but it wasn't supposed to end this way," Jay declared. "My God, what are we coming to? If the President can be killed by somebody who doesn't like him, then it can happen to anybody. First, it was innocent little girls in a church; now it's the president. Who will be next?"

He was talking without hardly taking a breath, so he paused for a few seconds and looked over at Tammy. She was just sitting there looking at his face, so he continued talking.

"You can't trust anybody. You can't believe in anything," he declared. "I remember the night at the 1960 convention when he was nominated for President. I was the only one still awake in our house when it became official because it was about 11 o'clock. My parents had already gone to bed because it was so late, but I stayed up and watched the voting by myself. I think I cried again that night, but this time it was because I was happy."

"Did you cry today when you heard?" Tammy asked.

Jay hesitated before answering.

"No, I didn't. I was upset. I was shocked, but I didn't cry. What does that say about me?" Jay asked with a puzzling look.

"It says you are maturing," she said.

He had turned from looking at her and was looking straight out the front windshield as he spoke, but now he turned back directly toward her in the passenger seat and realized she had moved as close to him as the stick shift would allow her. He looked into her face, which was partly lit by the dim parking lot spotlights.

"You lost your father less than a year ago," she said as she looked into his eyes. "Now you have lost a man who meant a lot to you. You have learned to deal with tragedy. How to go on with life."

As she spoke, she started to stretch her arms around his neck. He could feel his heart racing, but he didn't know how to react. Her movement had been totally unexpected. Slowly, she moved her face to his and kissed his lips. Now he knew what to do. He reached his arms around her and pulled himself closer to her with the stick shift jamming into the front of his left leg as he turned his body toward hers. Her lips were soft and moist. At first, he hesitated, but then he slowly slipped his tongue into her mouth. She welcomed it and slowly began moving her tongue into his mouth. He could feel her tongue at the back of his throat, and he could feel his dick getting hard.

She moved her hands up to the back of his head and began running her fingers through his closely cut hair. He kept his lips firmly pressed to hers as he slowly started moving his hands down her back inside the ski parka she had unzipped when they first started talking.

His hands moving down her back inside the ski parka were forcing her arms away from him, so he pulled his hands away and moved them inside the front of the parka, never letting his lips separate from hers. He gently moved his hands along her sides inside the parka. Slowly moving his right hand to the front of her body, he gently touched her breast outside her soft sweater. She made no effort to pull away.

They had been in their embrace for several minutes, and he could feel the sweat rolling off his forehead, but he certainly wasn't going to move his hands from the front of her sweater to wipe off the sweat.

Suddenly, they were both startled by the lights of a car moving toward them. There had been some cars that had pulled into the parking lot, but they all just kept on driving by when they saw that HoJo's was closed. But this car was moving in a direct path closer and closer toward their car, which was parked at the far end of the lot.

"Oh shit," Jay said as he finally separated his lips from Tammy's. "It's a cop."

The police were always driving through the HoJo's parking lot, telling the teenagers to "break it" when several cars and a large group of kids had gathered. But theirs was the only car in a dimly lit parking lot, which could be what was drawing the attention of the police. Jay had pulled himself back into an upright position in the driver's seat, and Tammy was fully back in the bucket seat on the passenger side when the cop walked up to their car, directing the beam of his flashlight into the car and telling Jay to roll down the window.

"You are going to have to move this someplace else, kids," he said. "They don't want anybody in the parking lot if the restaurant is closed. In fact, it might be a good idea if you head home. You know the president was killed today, don't you?" the cop asked, obviously upset that Jay and Tammy didn't seem very disturbed by the President's death.

"Yes sir, we know," Jay said. "It's terrible."

Jay started the car, and they drove away while the cop remained in the parking lot.

"Sorry about that," Jay said as they drove down the road.

"It's not your fault," she said.

Jay turned on the radio so that he wouldn't need to talk about what had just happened because he wasn't really sure what had happened. Did she kiss him because she was feeling sad about the president's death? Or was it because she felt bad for him, because she knew how much he liked Kennedy? Or was it something else? He was looking for popular songs, but their regular AM rock station was playing solemn, We Shall Overcome, "Battle Hymn of the Republic" type songs. Fortunately, it was only about a five-minute ride to her house.

He turned off the car, but before he could say a word, she declared.

"I'd better get in," she said. She reached over, gave him a hug, quickly opened the car door, and headed up the walk to her front door.

UNITED PRESS INTERNATIONAL, NOV. 23, 1963

DALLAS, Tex. – A hiding gunman assassinated President Kennedy with a high-powered rifle yesterday.

Three shots reverberated and blood sprang from the President's face. He fell face downward. His wife clutched his head, crying, Oh, no.

"Where were you last night? I called about seven, and your mother said you were out, but she didn't know where," Tony asked as he got into Jay's car for the ride to school for the team meeting on Saturday morning.

"I was driving around. I stopped at Marty's house, then I went to Tammy's. We went to church. When I got home, my mother was already in her bedroom watching TV. I guess she forgot to tell me you called."

"No problem." Tony countered. "I was just watching TV. I was wondering if you wanted to come over. I was up until midnight watching the news on TV."

Tony stopped talking for a few seconds, then suddenly asked a question.

"You went to church with Tammy?"

"Yeah," Jay said without elaborating.

"Okay, it was a strange day for everyone," Tony said without showing any emotion.

UNITED PRESS INTERNATIONAL, NOV. 23, 1963

WASHINGTON – Lyndon B. Johnson assumed the burdens of the presidency last night and immediately won a pledge of bipartisan cooperation from congressional leaders in the dark days following President Kennedy's assassination.

—

"I kissed Jay," Tammy said as she started driving away from Marty's house for the trip to Saturday morning cheerleading meeting.

"WHAT, WHEN? Stop this car!" Marty yelled.

"Last night," Tammy said as she pulled the car to the side of the street about fifty yards from Marty's house.

"Last night? He was at my house last night," Marty said.

"I know then he came to my house, and we went to church. Then we took a ride."

Marty interrupted her in mid-sentence because she wanted more details of the kissing session.

"What kind of kiss, like a good night peck?" Marty asked her friend.

"It was more than a peck. It was several minutes' worth," Tammy offered.

"Any tongue?"

"Yeah, a lot," the blond said.

"How did that happen?" Marty asked

"I don't know. He came over after you went to church with your family, and we went to church to pray for Mrs. Kennedy and the children. Then we went to HoJo's, but it was closed. So, we sat in the parking lot talking. He talked about how much he admired Kennedy because he wanted to make a difference in people's lives. He was so sweet and sad at the same time. I just kept looking into his eyes, and before I knew it, I reached over, put my arms around him, and kissed him."

"You kissed him?"

"Yeah, I started it, but once we started, he was into it. Believe me, I could see him getting excited."

"What else?" Marty asked, wanting to know every detail of the encounter.

"He was getting a good feel outside my sweater," the blond said, unable to look her friend straight in the eye.

"Did you stop him?"

"No, I didn't need to because a cop drove into the parking lot and told us to go home."

"Would you have stopped him if the cop didn't show up?" Marty asked as she continued probing her friend's intentions.

"I don't know," Tammy admitted.

There was a long silence with the two girls just sitting, looking at each other, but not saying a word. Finally, Marty spoke.

"What are you doing? she asked. "I thought after you broke up with Dave, you were just going to have a good time playing around this year, then go off to college and forget all about high school and everybody here. I didn't think you wanted to get involved with anybody this year."

"I don't, I didn't. I don't know what I'm thinking."

NEW YORK TIMES, NOV. 23, 1963

DALLAS- Police officials said they had amassed evidence to convict Lee Harvey Oswald of the assassination of President Kennedy.

"Did you hear they are going to play the pro games tomorrow?" Jay said to Tony as they were driving home from the Saturday practice. "I mean, Harvard and Yale didn't play today, and they have been playing for a hundred years."

"Yeah, I guess it's because they are pros," Tony replied.

"It still doesn't seem right. How can they concentrate enough to play a whole game? I had trouble just practicing today."

The players had walked into the gym on Saturday morning, not knowing what they would be doing the day after President Kennedy's death. Rowe had put a sign on the locker room doors telling everybody to report to the gym before they went into the locker room. Rowe was already there, standing in the middle of the gym as the players filed in. He didn't say a word, just stood there watching the players filing into the gym. By 10:05, the whole team was there, standing in a circle around Rowe.

"Guys, I think we should practice today," the Coach declared. "But if anyone has a problem with us practicing the day after the president was killed, I understand. If you want, we can just talk today rather than practice."

Jay immediately responded to the Coach's question.

"Coach, I think we should practice. President Kennedy's life was all about taking on challenges, and we are going to be facing a big challenge on Thanksgiving. I know I've only been here this season, but this team has become a family to me, and this is a time when people should be with their family."

"Thanks, Burke," Rowe offered. "Okay guys, let's get on the field."

ASSOCIATED PRESS, NOV. 23, 1963

WASHINGTON – A gun will thunder each half hour from dawn to dark Saturday at each Army and Marine Corps base to render honor to the late President Kennedy.

"Do me a favor," Marty said to Tammy as they were driving up to Marty's house following the morning cheerleading meeting.

"Sure, if I can," Tammy replied.

"Don't hurt him."

"Hurt who?" the blond asked.

"Jay," Marty answered.

Tammy looked at her friend with a perplexed expression

"Why do you think I would ever hurt him?" the blond asked.

"Oh, you wouldn't mean to, but you know he is going to fall hard for you."

"How do you know that? Has he ever said anything to you about me?"

"No, he tries not to make it obvious, but anytime you are not with all the cheerleaders, he asks where you are."

"That's not a big thing."

"It's more than that. I see the way he looks at you. You see it too. I know you do. If you just want somebody to play games with and don't really care about him, he is going to be crushed. He's sweet. He's never been involved with somebody like you."

"What do you mean, somebody like me?"

"You are my best friend. I love you, but you know what I mean. You have had more experience with relationships. You have had guys, older guys, tell you they love you. You know how to handle those types of situations. He may be seventeen, but I don't think he has ever told a girl he loves her."

"Why are you so concerned about him? You've only known him for three months," Tammy questioned.

"I know, but he's so sweet. I made a play for him, and he wasn't interested, but he still cares about me. I have never been able to talk to a boy like I can talk to him. I care about him so much."

"Don't worry, you're not the only one who cares about him. Besides, I'm not sure your sweet buddy is all that innocent."

NEW YORK TIMES, NOV. 23, 1963

WASHINGTON – John Fitzgerald Kennedy's two small children were told Friday night that their father was dead.

It was not known what words were used to make them understand or who performed the heart-breaking task. Almost certainly not their mother.

"Want to go to HoJo's tonight?" Tony said as he was getting out of Jay's car after their return from practice. "A bunch of the guys were talking about just going over there and hanging around the parking lot for a while. I'll drive."

"Thanks, but I think I might stay home; try to finish up my

research paper and watch TV with my mother tonight. She has been watching all this stuff about the President by herself. It's tough enough watching it with somebody else to talk to, but it's really tough watching it by yourself."

ASSOCIATED PRESS, NOV. 23, 1963

> NEW YORK – To those working for a better deal for American Negroes, the death of President Kennedy yesterday brought a particular blow. They saw him as a staunch ally in the cause.

Jay was sitting in a chair in his living room, re-reading Profiles in Courage when the phone rang.

"Hey, you're not at HoJo's with the rest of the guys?" the caller asked without identifying herself.

Jay's face broke into a smile, knowing it was Tammy.

"No, I figured I would stay home and finish the research paper. How did you know I wasn't there?" Jay asked.

"I didn't know you weren't there. I just knew everybody was going because Marty had asked if I wanted to take a ride over there, but I'm babysitting. I just figured I would check to see if you were with the crowd and if you're okay."

"I'm okay," Jay said. "Ha, what time are you babysitting to?" Jay asked.

"I'm not sure, but probably not late. It's the couple across the street. They said they were just going out to dinner for a few hours."

"Do you want to take a ride when you finish babysitting? Everybody probably will still be at HoJo's," Jay asked.

"I'd better not, but what are you doing tomorrow?" Tammy asked.

"I think I might go to mass in the morning. It just seems like the thing to do," Jay offered.

"I know I was even thinking about going with my parents," Tammy said.

Jay hesitated, but then asked, "Do you want to go with me?"

"Sure," Tammy said without hesitation.

UNITED PRESS INTERNATIONAL, NOV. 24, 1963

DALLAS – Staff physicians at Parkland Hospital who attended fatally-wounded President Kennedy all agreed yesterday that the late president never knew what hit him.

"Not only was the president killed in Dallas, but also the promise that unless all Americans are free to pursue their dreams, no American is free," the priest declared from the pulpit at Tammy's church Sunday morning.

UNITED PRESS INTERNATIONAL, NOV. 24, 1963

WASHINGTON – President Lyndon B. Johnson declared tomorrow a National Day of Mourning for the late President Kennedy.

"Thanks for coming over to my church," Tammy said as she and Jay walked from the church to Jay's car.

"It was no problem. I like the priests at your church more than the ones at my church. Your priests are young. They said things that make sense. The priests at my church are all old. I mean, every time something bad happens in the world, they talk about how it was God's will. God must be a vicious person if he is always willing for bad things to happen to people."

Tammy stopped and looked at Jay.

"Those are pretty tough words for a Catholic school boy," she said with a big smile.

They got in the car, and Jay reached over to put the key in the ignition, but Tammy grabbed his hand.

"Can we talk for a minute?" she asked.

"Sure, but why is it every time we go to church, we have to talk after?" Jay said, trying to make light of the situation because he was afraid of what she was going to say.

"About Friday night," she said.

It was what Jay was worried might happen. She was going to tell him it was just a momentary thing because she was feeling bad about the President being killed.

"What about it?" he said.

"I just don't want you to get the wrong idea."

Before she could say another word, he jumped into the conversation.

"Don't worry, I know it just happened because of everything that happened that day. I know it didn't mean anything to you." Jay said without looking at her.

"I didn't say that," she said as she reached over, grabbed his face, and turned it toward her.

"It did mean something to you?" he asked now, looking into her eyes.

"Of course it did," she said in a loud voice, "You think I kiss somebody like that if I don't care about him."

"Oh," Jay said, feeling like an idiot because he had interrupted her.

"It's just that I'm a little confused," she said.

"You think you are," Jay said, now flashing a smile

"Can we just take this slow and not worry about where it is going?" Tammy asked.

"That's fine with me," Jay said.

They drove for a few minutes without speaking when Jay asked, "Hey, do you want to go over to Sal's? They serve breakfast late on Sunday morning."

"Why don't we just go over to my house, and I will make some English muffins?"

"What is your mother going to think about you suddenly bringing somebody home for Sunday breakfast?"

"Don't worry, my mother likes you. Yesterday she was saying what a nice boy you seemed to be."

"What did you say?"

"I told her you were."

Jay's face broke into a big smile.

UNITED PRESS INTERNATIONAL, NOV. 24, 1963

NEW YORK – Virtually all stores, banks, schools and theaters in the nation will close tomorrow for the National Day of Mourning for President Kennedy.

"Hello, Mrs. Clark," Jay said as he walked into the kitchen with Tammy.

"Good to see you, Jay. I'm glad you got my daughter to go to church this morning."

"It was her idea," Jay said.

"It was?" Tammy's mother said with a questionable tone as she walked out of the kitchen into the living room, where Tammy's father was already watching TV.

"You are such a suck-up," Tammy said with a smile in a low-tone laugh as soon as her mother was out of hearing range.

"Well, I don't know about the daughter, but at least the mother likes me," Jay retorted.

"You never know," Tammy said with another laugh. "What do you want on your English muffin?"

They had been sitting at the kitchen table for a few minutes, munching on the English muffins without saying much, when they suddenly heard a startled scream from the living room.

"Oh, my God," Tammy's mother screamed.

"Mom, what's wrong? Tammy yelled.

"Somebody shot him," her mother yelled back from the living room.

"Mom, please, they shot the president two days ago. You have to start moving on." Tammy said with a bewildering look as to why her mother was still shocked when somebody talked about Kennedy being shot.

"No, I just saw somebody shoot that man who shot the President," her mother yelled. "I can't believe this is happening."

NEW YORK TIMES, NOV. 25, 1963

WASHINGTON – The strong faces of America paid silent tribute to the dead president in the Capitol rotunda yesterday.

Jay saw Marty, Tammy, Jane, Karen, and a few other girls already standing on the far side of the main lobby when he walked out of the auditorium following the school's memorial service for President Kennedy. The mayor had spoken, and the president of the Jefferson student council gave a speech about how President Kennedy "had inspired our generation." It wasn't anything Jay or any of the other students in the packed auditorium hadn't heard over the previous three days, but it was still emotional for some of the students, while it was obvious that others were there because their parents had told them they had to go to school.

"Do you and Tony want to come over to my house to watch the funeral?" Marty asked.

"I guess so, but we have to go to practice at 2 o'clock," Jay replied.

"That's all right, come over for a little while. Everybody should be together today."

UNITED PRESS INTERNATIONAL, NOV. 25, 1963

NEW YORK – The attendance at seven National Football League games yesterday approached the weekly averages, though many fans protested that the contests should have been postponed out of respect for the late President Kennedy.

Only two of the games produced smaller-than-average crowds, but this was counterbalanced by sellouts at three other stadiums.

—

Jay was already sitting on the couch in Marty's living room when Tammy walked in, so he moved toward the end to make room for her, but she never even looked in his direction. Instead, she headed to the other side of the room where Marty and Jane were sitting on the floor with their backs against the wall.

"Did you know today is John John's birthday?" Marty asked the group.

"The poor kid, he will never be able to celebrate his birthday without thinking it was the day his father was buried. Isn't he adorable in these short pants?" Karen Powers said.

"Did you see Mrs. Kennedy go up with Caroline and kiss the coffin last night?" Jay asked.

"Yeah, and I started crying when Caroline put her hand under the flag on the coffin to be closer to her father," Marty added.

"That was amazing last night, the lines of people waiting in the cold to get in and pass by the casket," Tony offered.

They sat watching the funeral procession on the black and white TV set in Marty's living room. The echo of the horses' hoofs on the road was the only sound emanating from the TV.

"Look at Bobby holding Jackie's hand. He has been next to her all day. At least the kids will have their uncle while they're growing up." Jay said.

NEW YORK TIMES, NOV. 26, 1963

WASHINGTON – The body of John Fitzgerald Kennedy was returned to the American earth yesterday.

The final resting place of the 35th president of the United States was on an open slope among the dead of the nation's wars in Arlington National Cemetery within sight of the Lincoln Memorial.

—

The main lobby of the school had an eerie feeling as Jay walked through it on the way to Rowe's classroom on Tuesday morning. It was only seven o'clock, so there was still at least thirty minutes before the corridors would be filled with students coming back for the first full day of school since President Kennedy had been killed.

Jay had figured the teachers probably would take it easy for the first day back, especially since there were only two days before Thanksgiving.

But the minute he walked into Rowe's classroom, he realized that while some teachers might take it easy for these two days, the football coaches wouldn't.

Rowe was standing at the blackboard on the far side of his classroom, still writing. He had already filled the front of the back-board with writing. After he stared at the boards for a few minutes, Jay realized each line had a number in front of it, followed by six or seven words that described some type of defensive alignment. He looked where Rowe was still writing, and he realized he was working on No. 25.

Jay turned to Quigley, who was standing just inside the door of the classroom.

"It's only 7 o'clock now. What time did he get here to get all this on the board?" Jay asked in a low voice.

"You don't want to know," Quigley quipped.

UNITED PRESS INTERNATIONAL, NOV. 26, 1963

> WASHINGTON – Ever erect, seldom faltering, her head high even in grief, her widow's veil masking her tragedy in her eyes, Mrs. John Kennedy buried her husband yesterday.

"Why don't we put the Times away and just talk. I think some people might still need to talk about what happened since the last time we met on Friday morning," Kiley said to his Tuesday class.

"I feel so bad for Mrs. Kennedy," the brown-haired girl who sat in the middle of the classroom and seldom spoke immediately said. "I don't know how she could be that strong," the girl continued.

"She was strong for her children," said Carolyn Gustafson, the girl who Jay knew was a member of the prep squad and Linda's good friend.

It went on that way for thirty to forty minutes, mainly with the girls talking about Mrs. Kennedy. It was obvious some students had never verbalized their feelings about what they had experienced over the previous four days. When it seemed nobody else wanted to talk, Kiley spoke.

"You will never forget that you were in this school on Friday when you heard President Kennedy had been killed. It will be like most of your parents will always remember where they were and what they were doing that Sunday when they heard Pearl Harbor had been bombed. That action affected your parents' lives in many different ways. It will be different for you; America has not declared war because of President Kennedy's death, but in some ways, I think it could affect your lives. Let's think about that over the next few months as we read every day about what's happening in this country and around the world."

SEVEN

NEW YORK TIMES, NOV. 27, 1963

> NEW YORK – Stock prices soared yesterday in the biggest one-day rally in market history. It was a stunning turnabout from the immediate collapse of prices set off last Friday afternoon with the news that President Kennedy had been shot.

When Rowe sent the team manager to tell the stadium maintenance man to turn on the lights about 4 o'clock Wednesday afternoon, Jay figured they would be practicing for quite a while. Since Tuesday, they had been practicing on the main field in the Stadium so Rowe could have practice go long after it got dark. But only about fifteen minutes after the lights went on and while the sun was still setting, Rowe said that was it and called everybody to the middle of the field.

"Gentlemen, tomorrow will be a day you will remember for a long time, maybe the rest of your life. You're ready for that type of day. You have worked for a day like tomorrow. You had one obstacle after another thrown at you this season, and you have overcome every one of them because you have stuck together. You are a team gentleman, and I just want you to know it has been a pleasure coaching you. Tomorrow morning, there will be a moment of silence for President Kennedy just before the kickoff. We will think about President Kennedy, his wife, and his children when we are standing on the field before the game. Then we will play football for a few hours and not have to think about what has happened over the past week. When the game is over, we will go back to mourning the President, but at least for two hours, the only thing you and everybody in the stands will think about is football. I think it will be good for everybody."

For a moment, it seemed Rowe was choking up with emotion, but he quickly regained his usually stern demeanor.

"Okay," he said, "The coaches will be at school at seven, so you can get into the locker room any time after that. The bus will leave at 8:15. Get a good night's sleep tonight, and I will see you in the morning."

NEW YORK TIMES, NOV. 27, 1963

> WASHINGTON – The Army-Navy football game will be played, but it has been postponed one week to Dec. 7, the Pentagon announced yesterday.
>
> A request by President Kennedy's family that the game be held influenced the decision to postpone rather than cancel the 64th meeting of the service academics. The game draws about 100,000 spectators to Municipal Stadium in Philadelphia every year.

The Thanksgiving game will be played in Madison Thursday morning, so Wednesday's practice was the last time the seniors on the team would be on their home field.

"I can't believe that was the last time I will be on that field as a football player," Tony said as he slowly walked with Jay down the street leading from the stadium back to the high school locker room following the Wednesday practice. "I still remember our first JV game three years ago; it seems like yesterday. I wouldn't want Rowe to hear me say this, but I think I like practices as much as the games. I mean, practice is where you really find out how tough a guy is; it's where you go through hell with guys. Maybe that's why these guys have become such a part of my life. I mean, you have been my friend almost my whole life, and I have an older brother, but a lot of these guys seem like they're part of my family, and I didn't ever know half of them until three years ago. I guess you never think about things like that until it's almost over."

"I kind of know what you mean," Jay said. "I've only been part of this team for three months, but these guys are like the brothers I never had. But hey, it's not over yet. We still have tomorrow morning."

"Yes, we do," said Tony, "And we are going to fucking kill them."

Jay looked at his friend and smiled.

"That's what I love about you," Jay said with a laugh. "You have such an elegant way of expressing your feelings."

"Fuck you, preppy."

NEW YORK TIMES, NOV. 28, 1963

> WASHINGTON – The first Southerner to become President since Woodrow Wilson called for the earliest possible passage" of a civil rights program that would remove "every trace of discrimination and oppression" in the nation.
>
> President Johnson, appearing before a joint session of Congress yesterday, made that the high point of an address that surprised even his admirers with its force, its eloquence, its mood of quiet confidence.

Jefferson warmed up on the field for nearly a half-hour after they piled off the bus, and now Jay was standing along the sideline in front of the Jefferson bench. His arm was feeling great. He thought he was going to be nervous as hell because he had never played in a game like this. But it was only a few minutes into the warm-ups when the butterflies had dissolved. Now he couldn't wait for the opening kickoff.

It wasn't long after the opening kickoff before it became obvious why Madison was undefeated. Their defense was as good as Jefferson had faced all year, and a few guys on their D-line were bigger than anybody on the Jefferson team. But Tony and the other guys on the Jefferson defensive unit were also playing great. So, it wasn't surprising that neither team scored in the first half.

"I can't get the linebackers to bite on the option-pitch," Jay said to Tony as he grabbed some water during the halftime break.

"Don't worry, we will hold them all day, and sooner or later they will fuck-up, and you'll burn them," Tony yelled to Jay as he headed back onto the field to start the third quarter.

Tony must have been psychic because midway through the third quarter, with the ball on the Jefferson 40, Jay saw a Madison linebacker committing early as he was about to pitch to Allen on a right-side option sweep. So, he faked the pitch and started running wide right. He knew he had at least ten open yards before a Madison defender could reach him, but instead of running for a guaranteed first down, he looked downfield and saw Mike Stone running down the left sideline, stride for stride with a Madison defender. Every day in practice, ever since Rowe had given him his first chance "to run some plays," Jay had been working with Stone, not just on passing drills, but also trying to understand Stone's body movements; how Stone looked at the field for open spots. So, while watching Stone running along the sideline with the defender, Jay also looked to the middle of the field, where he saw an open space created by the absence of the Madison linebacker who had bitten on Jay's pitch-out fake. Jay knew Stone would see it too. Sure enough, almost simultaneously, Stone broke out of his race down the left sideline and cut to the inside, and Jay was delivering a perfect spiral toward the open spot in the middle of the field. Stone caught the pass without breaking stride and raced the final fifteen yards into the end zone. Dan Aaronson followed with the conversion boot, giving Jefferson a 7-0 lead with a few minutes to play in the third quarter.

Probably even the most optimistic Jefferson fans didn't think that seven-point lead would hold, but with less than two minutes to play in the fourth quarter, the Eagles were still leading 7-0. Then, with just over a minute to play, the Madison star running back was loose on a sweep around the right side. A great second effort by Vin Rego finally pushed him out of bounds, but not until he reached the Jefferson five-yard line. A touchdown and conversion would give Madsion the tie it needed to win the League championship with a 9-0-1 record, while Jefferson would finish second with an 8-1-1 record.

With one of the best running backs in the state and a huge offensive line, nobody was surprised that Madison tried three straight runs. But each time, the Jefferson defensive line only gave up a yard or so. So, Madison was facing a fourth-and-goal from the one-yard line and only about ten seconds to play in the game when the Madison coach called his final time-out.

Jay stood on the sideline watching as Rowe talked to the defensive unit that had come to the sideline during the time-out. While all eleven members of the defensive unit would be on the field for what could be the final play of the game, in all probability, the responsibility of protecting the lead would rest on the shoulders of the Eagles' seven-man defensive front.

Jay had known Tony most of his life, but the other six members of that defensive front were guys Jay hadn't even known three months ago. Now they would decide if Jay would be part of something he wanted more than anything he could ever remember wanting in his life. He had never been involved in an experience like this. There was Rocky Martinelli, the kid everybody knew Rowe was talking about when he told the School Committee back in October that some students wouldn't be in school if it wasn't for football; Stan Bartkiewicz, the kid Tony said was a math whiz, but who never wanted to talk about anything but football; Walter Tracy the big Irish kid who liked to brag that he could drink two GI Qs in five minutes; Len Angelone, the youngest of five brothers all of who had played football for Jefferson: Herb Fineberg, the six-three, 260-pound Jewish kid who was one of the smartest and most mild-mannered kids in the school during the day, but just plain mean when he stepped onto the football field and Vito Ferraro, the kid with the slicked-back black hair who spent most of his time during the school day around the auto shop.

"Fourth down," the official yelled as he moved his arm in a couple of complete circles, indicating to start the clock. The long hand on the scoreboard clock was so close to zero that it was hard for fans to know exactly how much time was remaining. The players on the field knew because the official, who had the stop watch in his pocket, that was actually the official time, had yelled nine seconds when the other official had started winding his arm as the signal to start the clock. The loud cheering from the Jefferson stands that was deafening after the Eagles had made the stop on third down suddenly went silent. The Madison quarterback didn't waste any time with a long snap count. "Hut one," he yelled, the center snapped the ball, and the Jefferson linemen broke from their stance. The sound of fully-padded bodies smashing into each other could be heard throughout the stadium. The quarterback turned to his right, took one step back, and stuck the ball in the gut of the Madison star halfback coming in from the left side. Once the Madison halfback got the ball, he didn't even take another step on the ground; he immediately left his feet and dove forward in the air, trying to clear the pile of players already on the ground at the goal line. Obviously, he hoped that when he landed from his dive, he would be in the end zone. But Rocky Martinelli, despite fighting off a block from the Madison right guard, saw the halfback leave his feet as soon as he had the ball, and the big Jefferson lineman immediately stood straight up and opened his arms. The helmet of the flying Madison halfback hit square in the middle of Rocky's chest, but Martinelli didn't fall back even an inch. Instead, he stopped the flight of the Madison runner, forcing him to fall straight down to the ground. Everybody on the field tried jumping into the pile of bodies near the goal line. Two officials came running toward the pile.

"No, no," one official yelled, pumping his arm as he pointed to the spot on the ground inches short of the goal line where he said the ball had first touched when the Madison halfback hit the ground. The sounds of the officials' whistles indicating the play was finished, and the horn going off on the scoreboard signaling the end of the game were simultaneous.

UNITED PRESS INTERNATIONAL, NOV. 28, 1963

> ARLINGTON NATIONAL CEMETERY, Va. – Mrs. John F. Kennedy yesterday visited her slain husband's grave for the fourth time since she lit his eternal flame.

"Should we feel this good?" Jay said as he drove home with Tony after they left the locker room following Rowe's post-game speech.

"Of course we should." Why shouldn't we?" Tony answered.

"I don't know. It was just a week ago that the President was killed. I mean, this was only a game. It just doesn't seem right that what happened in a game can make you feel so good after all the terrible things that happened last week."

"Life goes on," Tony said. "Hey, Harvard and Yale are playing Saturday. We can't stop living, and have you ever felt this good about anything else you have ever done?"

Tony was right. Jay had never been as excited as he was the moment that official had picked up the ball, signaling the end of the game.

The bus ride back to Jefferson had been a blur of forty-five ecstatic teenage boys, shouting, singing, and trading good-natured jabs. After they had piled out of the two buses and gone into the locker room, Rowe had addressed the team, telling them how proud he was of them; how they would remember this high school football game for the rest of their lives. After he finished talking to the whole team and while the players were slowly peeling off their pads and heading to the shower, he quietly went around the locker room and sat down on the bench next to a few players and spoke to them individually. Jay was sitting at the far end of one of the benches near the wall in front of the locker he had been assigned that first day he had reported to practice back in August. He was in no rush to change out of his uniform. He had his head down, so he didn't ever notice Rowe moving into a spot next to him on the bench.

"Burke," the Coach said. "It would have been easy for you to have quit when I wasn't even paying attention to you at the start of the season. Lucky for us, you didn't. Thank you."

"Thanks, Coach," was all Jay could say as his throat choked up with emotion.

UNITED PRESS INTERNATIONAL, NOV. 28, 1963

ATLANTA – A sampling of Southern sentiment indicated yesterday that the assassination of John F. Kennedy has done nothing to shake the views of staunch segregationists.

Jay and his mother had only been home for a few minutes after returning from having Thanksgiving dinner at his aunt's house when the phone rang.

"I got it, Mom," Jay yelled.

"Hi," the female voice said. "I'm glad you're finally home. I called a few other times."

The caller didn't identify herself, but Jay knew it was Tammy.

"Sorry, my mother and I were having dinner at my aunt's house," Jay answered pleasantly.

"Anything wrong?" he asked.

"No, I just never got a chance after the game to really tell you what a great job I think you did this season."

Jay could feel the blood rushing to his face. He had received quick congratulations and hugs from Tammy, Marty, and most of the other cheerleaders on the field immediately after the game. And of course, there was the "Thank You" from Rowe in the locker room. It was all very flattering, but nothing compared to the feeling this totally unexpected phone call did for his psyche.

He was literally at a loss for words.

So, he just mumbled a "Ah, Ah, thanks" into the phone.

Fortunately, Tammy quickly picked up the conversation with an invitation.

"Ha, do you want to come over for a little while? All my relatives finally just left. My sister and her husband are here from California, but they just went to a bar to meet some of my sister's old high school friends."

"I forgot you had an older sister," Jay said.

"Ya, she's six years older than me. She went to UConn, where she met her boyfriend. They got married almost immediately after they graduated, and they moved out to California so she doesn't get home too often."

"That's too bad that you don't see her too often," Jay responded.

"Ya, I guess so, but with the six-year age difference, we were never that close, but I do miss her. She actually was very good to her little sister when we were growing up. Anyway, I asked my parents if it was alright if I asked you to come over for a turkey sandwich."

"What did they say?" Jay asked, now feeling more at ease.

"They said sure. Remember, my mother thinks you are a nice young man, and my father said it would be great to have a football hero in the house."

"I'm afraid those days are finished," Jay quipped, "My football hero days ended this morning, but I will still take you up on the offer for a turkey sandwich."

UNITED PRESS INTERNATIONAL, NOV. 29, 1963

WASHINGTON – President Johnston appealed to the American people last night to banish the rancor from our words and the malice from our hearts so that a united nation can face the days ahead.

The phone ringing woke Jay out of a sound sleep on Friday morning.

"Come on," the voice on the phone said, "Everybody is meeting for breakfast at Sal's."

"What time is it?" Jay asked, knowing he was talking to Tony.

"8:30, get your ass moving, everybody is going to be there at 9."

"I suppose I'm driving," said Jay.

"Of course, that's why you have the sports car."

Once Tony got in the car for a ride to Sal's, he didn't hesitate to quiz Jay about his plans for the winter sports season.

"So, what are you going to do now that football is finished?" Tony asked

"I don't know. I haven't really started thinking about it. I think I'm still living in yesterday's game," Jay offered.

"Yeah, I know what you mean, but I know Monday is going to come around and I'm going to have to start getting my weight down for wrestling," Tony replied. "So, what are you going to do?"

"I guess I'll play basketball," Jay said.

"You know the basketball team already started practice last week," Tony declared. "The Coach holds a couple of spots for the guys who played last year, but it will be tough for you, as a senior, to make the team. Anyway, basketball isn't really your sport. Didn't you tell me you only played at Priory because the school requires everybody to play a sport each season?"

"Yeah, pretty much," Jay answered.

"Then why don't you run indoor track? You're fast, and with your long stride, you probably would make a good quarter-miler."

"I didn't know there was an indoor track team. Where do they run?"

"They practice running in the corridors or on the streets outside if there isn't much snow on the ground. Then they run meets in that old armory on Friday night or Saturday morning. It's not like being on the football team, but at least you are competing, and it might help with your speed for football."

Jay looked at Tony.

"What do you mean for football? The season is over."

Tony smiled at his friend.

"Yeah, but now you are thinking about playing in college. Aren't you?" he asked.

"How did you know?" Jay said, "I never said anything."

"No, you didn't, but I know you. I saw how much you enjoyed being part of this team. You took your game to a higher level of competition this year, and you were good. Now you want to know what else you can do."

"You asshole, sometimes I think you know me better than I know myself," Jay said, putting his foot a little harder on the gas pedal.

"So where are you thinking about?" Tony asked.

"I don't know. I know I'm not good enough to play at places like UMass or in the Ivy League, but after the game yesterday, Quigley said he wanted to talk to me Monday. I guess he has sent some letters to the coaches of the schools he played against when he was at Trinity, and some of them called him and said they wanted to see some film. I guess he talked to my guidance counselor, and when she told him what I got on the SATs, he thinks that will interest more coaches."

"So, what did you get? You never told me," Tony asked.

"They were okay, 730 verbal and 700 math."

"Okay? That's fucking great."

Jay kept talking as he drove. It felt good to finally talk to somebody about the idea of playing college football. It still seemed like a dream to him. Three months ago, he was thinking he would be lucky if he even got on the field this season; now he was finally telling his friend he wants to be a college football player.

EIGHT

ASSOCIATED PRESS, DEC. 2, 1963

> SAIGON, South Vietnam – Sixty South Vietnamese civil guards with their wives and children battled a Communist attack early yesterday until every man in the post was dead or wounded.

Jay walked down the long corridor leading toward the locker room about a half-hour after school ended on Monday afternoon. He wasn't quite sure why he was going down to the locker room. He had already turned in all his football equipment in the morning before school.

But for three months, Jay had walked to the locker room every day after school.

So, he instinctively headed toward the corridor that led to the locker room. Even if he didn't have any definite mission, he could head out the side door next to the locker room to go to the parking lot. As he walked along the corridor, he could hear the sounds of a piano coming from one of the music rooms that ran along the corridor. So, he gave a quick glance into the room as he was walking by. He was stunned to see Tammy with her back toward the door, sitting by herself playing what he could tell was the theme from West Side Story. He stopped and quietly walked just inside the door, not wanting to disturb her. He stood there listening for a few minutes, and even when she finished, he didn't say anything immediately. Instead, he just watched her as she sat there looking down at the piano keys. Finally, he broke the silence by clapping his hands.

"That's very good," he said, causing Tammy to turn around with a startled look.

"Oh, hi, I didn't think anybody was down here," she said. "How long have you been standing there?"

"Long enough to realize you are good. I can't believe I didn't know you played the piano?" Jay said.

"There are a lot of things you don't know about me," she said with a slight smile.

"So, I'm learning," Jay said, returning her smile. "Seriously, how did you learn to play like that? Can you play other things?"

"Oh yeah," she said with a laugh, "I can play Chopin till it makes you sick."

"How long have you been playing?" Jay asked, still stunned that he didn't know she could play the piano.

"I started taking piano lessons when I was in kindergarten. Twice a week for ten years. I probably have played in more recitals than you have played football games."

"Why haven't I ever heard you play?"

"I don't know. When I got to high school, I told my mother I didn't want to take any more lessons. Maybe I was just burned out, but when I think back now, some of it probably was that I didn't want to do things people expected me to do."

Jay had slowly been moving further into the room until he was now standing next to the piano, looking down at Tammy sitting on the bench in front of the keyboard.

"Why didn't I see a piano at your house?" he asked.

"We used to have a piano in the living room, but last year my mother said if I wasn't going to play anymore, the piano was taking up too much space, so she sold it. I think it makes her feel bad looking at it all the time."

"Did that bother you?" Jay asked, trying to probe Tammy's inner feeling.

The blond looked up at him and waited a few seconds before answering.

"Yeah, it did. Still does, I guess? But you can't do things because it's what other people want you to do. Not even your parents."

It was the first time Jay had talked to Tammy when she seemed a little vulnerable, a little unsure of what she was doing.

"So why are you in here now playing?" he asked.

"I was just walking by and saw nobody was in the room, and the piano was open, so I figured I would just play a few notes. Then I saw this sheet music for West Side Story, so I figured I would see if I could play it."

"You still like it, don't you?" he asked.

"Of course, I never didn't like playing. It just became more of a chore than a challenge, and for me, that took the fun out of it. Hey, enough of my philosophy on music and life. Let's get out of here. Where are you going?" she asked.

"No place, no more football practice," Jay said.

"Good, can you give me a ride home?" Tammy asked.

"Ya, no problem," Jay said with a big smile.

UNITED PRESS INTERNATIONAL, DEC. 4, 1963

WASHINGTON – President Johnson yesterday threw the full weight of his administration behind an all-out campaign to win the earliest possible passage of the late John F. Kennedy's civil rights bill.

As soon as the bell sounded for the start of the Wednesday class, Kiley took a pile of papers off his desk and put a small stack on the first desk in each row.

"Okay, take one and pass them back," the teacher said. He waited until everyone had a piece of paper before talking again.

"This is a little section of President Kennedy's inauguration speech back in January of 1961. I typed it out and ran off some mimeo copies because I think it's really relevant to what we are studying today. Burke, you seem pretty comfortable with everything-Kennedy. Do you want to read it?"

Jay was caught off guard, but as soon as he looked at the page, he recognized the words.

"All this will not be finished in the first one hundred days, nor will it be finished in the first one thousand days, nor in the life of this Administration, nor even perhaps in our lifetime on this planet. But let us begin." Jay recited almost without looking at the paper as though he knew the words by heart.

"Thanks, Burke," Kiley said. "Let me just interject something here, then we are going to open this up for discussion. What Kennedy was talking about was everything that was included in his inauguration speech, which covered a lot of areas. But for our purpose, let's relate it to what we are reading in the Times today, with President Johnson saying he will throw the full weight of the administration behind getting passage of Kennedy's Civil Rights Bill. It's a little strange to look at Kennedy's words now and realize that the life of Kennedy's administration was just 1,000 days. So, it didn't happen in the first 100 days or the life of Kennedy's administration. But are we going to see the day when this country is truly free because the Negro is completely free during our lifetime on this planet?"

A host of hands suddenly shot up. Kiley's face broke into a big smile. He had his discussion.

"Miss Snow, what do you think?" Kiley said.

"Yes, it will happen. That's why they have to pass the Civil Rights Bill," she said.

"That's what Johnson said he wants to get done at the earliest possible date. Will that do it?" Kiley asked, "I think we talked about this before. Do laws change people's attitudes?"

"Maybe not immediately, but they change people's behavior, and eventually that can change attitudes," Jay shot back, still standing from having read Kennedy's words.

"Okay, good," said the teacher. "Think about that and maybe add your thoughts to your weekly summaries when you hand them in on Friday. I think it is going to be very interesting reading how this develops by the time you people graduate in six months."

NEW YORK TIMES, DEC. 5, 1963

WASHINGTON – The Administration's plan to force the civil rights bill out of the House Rules Committee ran into bitter Republican opposition today. The resentment of the Republicans probably will not endanger final approval of the bill, but it could jeopardize their support for some of its more controversial parts, on which they were already lukewarm.

"I need you to do me a favor," Dan Aaronson said to Jay as the two headed down the corridor after leaving Kiley's class.

"What?" Jay asked.

"I need you to take Sally on a date."

"Wow, I thought you and her were becoming a thing," Jay replied with a surprised look.

"Yeah, we are, and that's the problem," said Dan. "I'm Jewish, and she's Catholic. Her parents aren't happy about her spending all her time with a Jewish boy."

"Did they tell her she couldn't go out with you?" Jay asked.

"No, I think they know she would go ballistic if they said that. But they keep throwing in all these little jabs. So, she wants them to think she is going out with other boys—especially a Catholic boy. I figured you are not going out with anybody, just kind of hanging with the guys, right?"

Jay looked at Dan with a puzzling expression.

"I guess we could go on a date. It will be a little strange, but we could do it."

"No, you're not really going on a date," Dan quickly interjected. "You just go and pick her up at her house Saturday night, then I will meet you two at HoJo's. Then she and I will go out. When we are finished, we will meet you back at the HoJo's, and you can bring her home."

"And what am I supposed to do while you two are parking at the lake?" Jay asked.

"Do what you normally do. Meet the guys at the HoJo's and go cruising around."

UNITED PRESS INTERNATIONAL, DEC. 7, 1963

> WASHINGTON – Mrs. John F. Kennedy and her children moved out of the White House yesterday leaving behind only echoes of the life, laughter and love they brought to it nearly three years ago.

Jay was sitting at the counter in HoJo's with Mike Stone, eating a cheeseburger, when he saw Tammy, Marty, and Jane Snow come through the front entrance. As soon as the girls saw the two boys, they headed over to them.

"What are you doing here? I thought you had a date with Sally tonight," Tammy said to Jay.

Jay's face turned red. He hadn't told Tammy about the arrangement with Dan, figuring it was something Dan and Sally wanted to keep secret. Now Tammy thought he was going on a date with another girl. Not that there was any reason he couldn't. He and Tammy certainly didn't have any type of arrangement, but he felt things had been going well between them. Now she was standing there with a straight face, looking at him, waiting for an answer to why he wasn't on a date, which he never really had. He thought she seemed a little upset. So, he started stumbling as he tried to explain the situation.

"Well, it wasn't really a date," he said.

"What was it?" Tammy quickly retorted with a stern look.

Finally, Marty broke into the exchange.

"Oh, stop it," Marty said with a laugh. "You're killing him. She knows you didn't really have a date. We all know the story, Sally told everybody."

Jay had been afraid to look directly at Tammy, but now he looked up at her and the other girls, who had all broken into laughter. He looked at them for a few seconds, then he too broke into a laugh. The girls started heading for one of the booths, still laughing, but Tammy lagged behind.

"Sorry about that," she said. "I just thought it would be funny, but that wasn't fair to you."

"No problem," Jay quipped. "It was funny."

"Why don't you come sit with us?" Tammy said.

"No thanks, I have to go pick up my date after she's finished parking with another guy."

UNITED PRESS INTERNATIONAL, DEC. 11, 1963

SOUTH BEND, Ind. – Studebaker Corp announced yesterday that it is ending its U.S. auto production 61 years after it entered the car-making business and 103 years after it made its first covered wagon.

"So, have you decided what you are doing this weekend?" Tony asked Jay as they drove toward school on Wednesday morning.

"Yeah, my aunt and uncle are coming over tomorrow morning, and they are going to drive me and my mother up to Amherst just to see the campus and meet the football coach. Quigley sent the coach some film of our last few games, and the coach told him to have me come up. I don't know anything about the place, but I mentioned it to my guidance counselor on Wednesday, and she said it's a great school."

ASSOCIATED PRESS, DEC. 13, 1963

WASHINGTON – The No.1 federal housing official said yesterday the coming year should see the start of significant dispersion of Negro families from "the segregated ghetto into the general community."

—

Jay was walking out of Kiley's class on Monday morning when the teacher waved him over to his desk.

"Coach Quigley told me Amherst is showing some interest," Kiley said.

"Yeah, I'm going up there this weekend to see the campus and meet the coach," Jay replied.

"Good, I played at Williams, and Amherst was our big rival," the teacher said. "It's a school that definitely will challenge you, and that's good. You seem to be interested in politics, history, and how the system can change lives."

"I'm starting to think that way," Jay said.

ASSOCIATED PRESS, DEC. 16, 1963

> NEW YORK – Y.A. Tittle yesterday pitched the New York Giants to the National Football League's Eastern Conference title with three record-breaking touchdown passes in a 33-17 victory over the fired-up Pittsburgh Steelers.

Jay saw Tammy standing with three other girls in the main lobby. He knew there were only a few minutes before the first bell for home room would sound, but he didn't want to seem overly anxious, so he just stood alone pretending he was reading something in one of his textbooks. But as soon as the quartet dispersed, he moved toward her.

"Hey, your father must have been really happy yesterday with the Giants," he yelled to the blond who had already started heading down the corridor to her home room.

She immediately stopped and turned back toward Jay.

"Yeah, my father was happy. But more importantly, how was your trip to Amherst?" she asked.

Jay had caught her attention, so he moved toward the blond who was now standing alone.

"Good, it's an interesting place," he offered. "The coach seemed like a good guy. He has been there for about five years, so I guess he knows what he is doing. But it's an all-boys school. I had two years of that at Priory, I'm not sure if I want to go through that again."

"They are college men, not boys. Amherst is an all-male college, not an all-boys school, Tammy said with a smile. "Plus, it's in the same town as UMass, and there are a lot of college girls there."

The first home room bell had already sounded, but Jay was in no rush to head toward his home room before the second bell sounded.

"So where are you applying?" Jay asked.

"UMass and a few other places," Tammy quickly replied.

"Oh, that's interesting, Tony and I are both applying to UMass."

"I'm also applying to UConn and Wellesley," Tammy said.

"Where is Wellesley?" Jay asked.

"It's a women's college near Boston. I don't think I have much of a chance of getting in, but my mother wants me to apply."

"That doesn't sound like you, applying someplace just because your mother wants you to," Jay said.

"No, it's a good school, but I probably never would have thought of applying unless an old friend of my mother's mentioned it. Apparently, she went to Connecticut College, that women's college down in New London, so she thinks I should apply there too. I don't have much chance of getting into either place, but I guess I will apply to both of them. My mother's friend is really an interesting person. I don't really know her that well, but my mother saw me doing Kiley's weekly report last weekend and asked me what we were studying. When I told her about how we are reading about the Civil Rights Bill, she told me about what her friend does. She lives in Connecticut, just outside New York. Apparently, she and her husband go into some middle-class towns where colored people can't get people to rent them an apartment, and she and her husband take out a lease using the colored people's name. Then the colored people would go in with the lease in their hands and say they are moving in."

"That must piss-off some people," Jay offered.

"I would think it does," Tammy said. "I guess sometimes it works; sometimes it doesn't, but the point is she is really interested in civil rights. She's not who you think of when you think about the people in civil rights marches. I think all her clothes come from Saks Fifth Avenue or those other New York stores. Her husband is big in advertising or something, and they live in a big house, but in her way, she's trying to do her part. When I heard that story, some of this stuff we are reading about the Civil Rights Bill made a lot more sense."

"That's really interesting," Jay said.

"Yeah, but enough about me. Why didn't you call me yesterday and tell me all about Amherst?" the blond asked.

He certainly had thought about calling her, but he didn't want to seem presumptuous that she would be interested in his activities.

"Ah, I went over to Tony's and a few of the guys came over, and we played pool down in his basement."

"Okay, if you would rather spend time playing pool with the boys than talking to me, I get the hint," she said with a laugh as she started running toward her homeroom to beat the second bell.

NEW YORK TIMES, DEC. 17, 1963

NEW YORK – Twenty-five persons, including three ministers, were arrested yesterday for attempting a sit-in at the headquarters of the Board of Education in Brooklyn.

The demonstrators were protesting what they called "the complete failure" of the Board of Education to present a meaningful plan for the elimination of racial imbalance in the city schools.

—

Jay was sitting at the desk next to the phone booth in the main lobby on Tuesday, shortly after the final bell, when he saw Tammy walking down the corridor with Janice Moretti, the tall, raven-haired beauty he knew was the head majorette. He had to admit that early in the football season, when he wasn't playing in any games, he had noticed Janice when she was leading the band on the field during the halftime show. Especially when she and a few of the other majorettes would stand on the wooden platform that was placed in front of the stands and do their high-kicking routines. You couldn't help noticing her. She had perfectly formed long legs that arose from her calf-high white boots and continued until they disappeared under the short red skirt that was part of her majorette uniform. She was a strikingly beautiful girl with long, straight black hair, dark eyes, and perfect facial features.

Jay had heard she went out with John Jordan, the senior who was both the star of the swimming team and a member of the National Honor Society.

"Hey," Tammy said when the pair reached where Jay was sitting. "You know Janice, don't you?"

"Sure," Jay said without hesitation, even though he had never actually talked to the dark-haired beauty who wasn't in any of his classes.

"Janice needs you to do her a favor," Tammy said.

"Sure, if I can," Jay replied.

"You can," Tammy said without hesitation. "Take a walk with Janice. She will explain."

Jay quickly rose from his seat and started walking down the corridor with the majorette.

"Thanks for doing this," the dark-haired girl said. "I have to go up to Mr. Rice's room to go over some make-up work for my Trig class, and I need you to come with me."

Jay was more confused than ever.

"I can't really help with that. I don't have Rice for Trig," he offered.

"I just need you to come into the classroom with me and stay there while I'm going over the work," the girl said.

It all didn't make sense to Jay, but if he could make Tammy happy by doing somebody a favor, he was one hundred percent in.

"Sure, but why?" Jay asked.

"I will explain later," she said. "But please stay in the room even if he tells you to wait outside. Just say you are giving me a ride home, and you will wait in the back of the room."

"Okay, I don't understand it, but I'm in," he said.

Jay couldn't help notice Mr. Rice's surprised look when he walked into the classroom next to Janice.

"Mr. Burke, what are you doing here? You're not in this class," Rice said as Jay followed Janice into the classroom.

The teacher was sitting behind his desk, but Jay never stopped moving, heading right down one of the aisles toward the back of the classroom as he spoke.

"I'm giving Janice a ride home, so I will just sit here in the back of the room until you're finished," Jay said without even looking back at the teacher.

It was obvious from his face that the teacher was perturbed by Jay's presence in the classroom, but there wasn't anything he could do because Jay quickly reached the last row of desks and immediately sat down. Janice stood in front of the teacher's desk as he pointed out the work in a book on his desk, but she never moved very close to the desk.

After about fifteen minutes, Janice abruptly turned away from the teacher and started walking down the aisle toward where Jay was sitting.

"I'm all set. We can go out the back door," she said to Jay.

Without ever looking toward the teacher sitting in the front of the room, Jay jumped to his feet and followed the girl out of the back door of the classroom.

"OK, now can you tell me what that was all about?" Jay asked as they started walking down the stairwell back toward the front lobby.

"It's just that a girl can feel uncomfortable when she is alone with Rice," she said. "Everybody knows it. He likes looking at girls. In his classes, he assigns seats, and the front seat in every row is always a girl. A few weeks ago, I had to go see him after school one day, and he told me to sit on his desk while we went over the work so I could see his textbook better. I didn't think anything of it, so I did. I was wearing knee socks and a skirt like this, and he kept patting my knee as we were going over the work. It felt kind of creepy, so I just wanted somebody to be there with me today. The strange thing is, he's a really good teacher. He knows math better than any math teacher I have ever had."

"That's terrible, I never thought a teacher would do something like that. I guess I'm naïve," Jay offered. "Why didn't you ask John to go with you? Isn't he your boyfriend?"

"Yes, he is, but I would have been embarrassed to tell him about how I felt. It's probably nothing, just me being a little too sensitive. I didn't want to make a big deal about it. Tammy and I have known each other since we were in kindergarten, so I was talking to her in the girls' locker room after gym class this morning, telling her how I was feeling a little strange about going to see Rice. She's the one who suggested we ask you to come with me. She said you're a good guy and would be glad to help. She was right, thanks."

"No problem," Jay quipped.

The pair kept walking down the stairs without saying anything else until Janice broke the silence.

"So, I guess you and Tammy have become good friends," the girl said.

"I guess so," Jay said with a puzzling look.

UNITED PRESS INTERNATIONAL, DEC. 21, 1963

SAIGON, Vietnam – Secretary of Defense Robert S. McNamara was reported yesterday to have made it clear that the war is going so badly in South Vietnam that the United States may be unable to pull out its troops by the target date of 1965.

The dirt kicked up by snowplows had already turned the few inches of snow that had fallen a few days earlier into a light shade of gray as Jay walked along the sidewalk of the shopping center on Saturday afternoon. It was four days before Christmas, and he still hadn't done any shopping for his mother's Christmas present. He didn't have a lot of money, but he still had some money left in his bank account from his summer lifeguarding job, so he went to the bank on Friday afternoon, and now he was window-shopping at the women's clothing store. Suddenly, he was startled by a voice behind him.

"What size are you looking for?" the voice asked.

He turned quickly to find Tammy standing behind him. She was wearing a pair of wool slacks and her power-blue ski parka with a white scarf around her neck. Her blond hair was slightly visible below a white crocheted hat that was tipped to the right side of her head.

"Hey, what are you doing here?" he asked.

"Actually, I'm looking for you," she said. "I was wondering if you wanted to do some Christmas shopping with me, so I called your house and your mother told me she thought you already were doing some shopping here. So, who are you shopping for?"

"You, of course," he said with a smirk.

"You better not be. You know what I said about us," she said with a stern look.

"I know. I was just kidding. I need to buy something for my mother."

"So what size are you looking for?" she asked.

Jay looked at her with a bewildered expression.

"I have no idea. I don't even know how women's sizes go."

"Men are hopeless," she said, trying to act disgusted but obviously pleased she could help Jay with his shopping efforts. "Come on, I saw your mother once. I have an idea of what size she is."

Thirty minutes later, they emerged from the store with Jay carrying one box holding a blouse and another box with a sweater.

"Thanks, I never would have picked out those two things. They are very pretty. I think my mother will like them," Jay said as they walked out of the store.

"I think she will," Tammy said. "So are you going to wrap them?"

Jay looked at the blond with the same bewildered expression he had when she had asked him about his mother's size.

"Yeah, I guess so," he said.

"Do you know how to wrap a package?" she said with a smile.

"Not really," he admitted.

"Hopeless," she said with a phony look of disgust before breaking into a laugh. "Why don't you come over to my house. My mother still has the wrapping paper out on the dining room table. I will wrap them for you. My car is parked over there. I will meet you at my house."

Tammy had already pulled into her driveway and was heading into the house when Jay pulled in front of the house. He immediately noticed her family's other car wasn't at the house.

"Is your mother out shopping?" he yelled as he tried catching up to Tammy before walking into the house.

"No, my mother and father left to visit my aunt in Connecticut this afternoon. They will not be back until later tonight. Why don't you sit down on the couch and watch TV while I wrap these? It won't take long."

"I'll help," Jay offered.

"No, you just sit there. You will just slow down the process. There must be a football game on or something."

Twenty minutes later, two beautifully wrapped packages were sitting on the table.

"They're beautiful, but my mother is going to know I didn't wrap them," Jay said, looking at the packages. "I owe you. How about my buying you a cheeseburger at Ho Jo's?"

"You don't have to buy me dinner. My mother made a meatloaf before she left. I can warm it up if you don't mind meatloaf."

"I love meatloaf," he declared, even though meatloaf wasn't one of his favorite meals.

"Good, just let me go upstairs and change," Tammy said.

Ten minutes later, Tammy came walking back down the stairs dressed in a pair of jeans and an oversized sweatshirt with YALE across the front. The sweatshirt was so big that the neckline stretched a few inches down her chest and along her shoulder line. So much so that Jay couldn't help notice she wasn't wearing anything, not even a T-shirt under the sweatshirt.

"YALE, where did you get that?" Jay asked.

"Oh, my sister went out with a guy from Yale one summer down at the beach. I think they only went out a few times, but she kept his sweatshirt. She didn't take it with her when she moved to California, so now, I own it."

She started walking toward the kitchen, but then changed direction and walked over the couch and sat down with her legs pulled up underneath her.

Jay had been about to get off the couch to head into the kitchen for the meatloaf, but he certainly was much happier sitting on the couch talking with the blond than eating meatloaf.

They sat there on the couch a few feet apart from each other, not saying a word, just looking at the TV. Jay was facing the TV, but he wasn't really paying attention to what Lloyd Bridges was doing on a "Sea Hunt" rerun. Every so often, he would sneak a quick look at Tammy's face. The sun had just set, so her living room was in darkness, except for the light emanating from the TV and from a dining room light that Tammy had put on when she was doing the wrapping. The dining room light was directly behind Tammy's head, creating a back-lighting on the side of her face. Jay looked over at her. He wanted to make a move toward her, but he wasn't sure. There had only been one other kissing session since the night President Kennedy was killed, and it was fairly short in front of her house when he had taken her home after a basketball game. She had ended it quickly, saying it was a school night and she had to get in the house. They hadn't really gone out on an official date on any of the weekend nights since Thanksgiving because one weekend he was visiting Amherst, and the other weekend she was babysitting both Friday and Saturday nights. But he took a chance and moved a little closer to her on the couch. She responded, sliding her legs off the couch and moving her body and her face closer to his. He kissed her and quickly slid his tongue into her mouth as he looked into her green eyes. They embraced, and Jay moved his hands to her back at the bottom of the sweatshirt. He slowly started moving his hand up her back, higher and higher, until he realized his hand's movement up her back was not being interrupted by a bra strap. He then slid both hands up her back, all the way up to the neck of the sweatshirt, and gently moved them to her sides. Her arms were up around his shoulders, so there was nothing stopping his movement toward the front of her body. Suddenly, she lay back on the couch and moved her legs up on the couch with her left leg sliding between Jay and the back of the couch. The move forced Jay to move back momentarily, but he quickly moved back toward her as she was now lying directly below him. Slowly, he moved both of his hands to the bottom of the front of the sweatshirt and moved them up the front of her body. As he moved his hands up her body, the sweatshirt kept rising. Finally, his hands were grasping her firm, naked breasts.

"Merry Christmas, Jay," she said with her eyes wide open and looking into his eyes.

NINE

UNITED PRESS INTERNATIONAL, JAN. 1, 1964

PHILADEPHIA – A court yesterday refused to ban blackface makeup in the traditional New Year's Day Mummers Parade and angry Negroes warned they would form a human chain and block the nationally televised event.

"What's this?" Jay asked his mother as he walked through the living room, where she was sitting watching television on New Year's Day.

"The Rose parade," she said. "I love watching this. The floats are beautiful."

"Too bad we don't have a color TV so you could see what those floats really look like."

"No way," his mother responded. "I just saw an ad in the paper. A floor model like this in color costs $599. I have a lot more important things I could do with $599. The black and white is just fine. That's what your imagination is for. You picture in your mind what the flowers look like."

His mother turned her eyes away from the TV and looked up at her son, who was still standing in the doorway watching the TV.

"Did you have a good time last night? You were home fairly early, considering it was New Year's Eve," she asked.

"You were still awake when I came in," Jay said.

"Yes, I was worried about what you and all your new friends would be doing on New Year's Eve. But it was only about 12:30."

"If I knew you were still awake, I would have come into your room and wished you Happy New Year," Jay said.

"That's fine, I was just happy you were home," she said, offering a soft smile. "Did you feel okay? You must have left whatever party you were at kind of early."

"I didn't go to a party," he said.

"You didn't go to a party on New Year's Eve. Where did you go?"

Jay was starting to feel defensive about his mother's questions. Nobody except Marty and Tony knew the extent of how much he was trying to spend time with Tammy, but he wasn't going to lie to his mother about where he had spent New Year's Eve.

"Tammy was babysitting, so I went over to keep her company. The people she was babysitting for said it was okay for her to have people over."

"That's nice. So how many people were there?" his mother asked.

"It ended up being just her and me."

"Oh," his mother said with a probing look.

ASSOCIATED PRESS, JAN. 1, 1964

TOKYO – President Johnson assured South Vietnam today that the United States would continue to offer that country "the fullest measure of support."

Jay was still surprised that he had spent New Year's Eve alone with Tammy. Ricky Smith, a kid in Kiley's class, had told him last week that he was having a New Year's Eve party at his parents' summer house at the beach. Jay had thought about asking Tammy for a few days, but he couldn't work up the confidence to make the call until December 30.

Jay still wasn't sure exactly where he and Tammy stood. There had only been that one other short kissing session after the night

President Kennedy was killed, when he gave her a ride home after she had cheered at a basketball game.

Of course, there was the episode at her house after they had gone shopping for his mother's Christmas present. But even then, Tammy had quickly cooled the situation after she had given him his "Christmas gift" by saying, "I'd better heat up that meatloaf." And the week before that, Marty had mentioned that she had nothing to do that Saturday night because Tammy had a date with some college guy.

So, he wasn't sure if he should make the call, but he finally decided to do it. He was glad Tammy answered the phone, so he didn't need to exchange pleasantries with her mother before he presented his proposal to Tammy.

"Hey, I know I should have asked you before this, but Ricky Smith is having a party down at his parents' summer house tomorrow night. Do you want to go with me?" he said without taking a breath.

Jay's pulse quickened when there wasn't an immediate response. Finally, Tammy began talking.

"Yes, you should have asked before this. Why didn't you ask on Christmas Eve when we were caroling with everybody?"

"I don't know. Everybody was around us, and I'm still not sure if you want people to know about us. Anyway, I figured you probably already had made plans for New Year's Eve a long time ago," Jay said sheepishly.

Tammy quickly responded in a tart tone.

"Look what people know about us or don't know about us—whatever that is—doesn't make any difference. We are going to do what we do because it's what we want to do. And yes, I had made plans."

Jay's heart skipped a beat, but he tried not to show the disappointment in his voice. "I figured so," he said. "Sorry to bother you. Maybe I'll see you at the basketball game Thursday night," he said, trying to get off the phone quickly so she couldn't detect the disappointment in his voice. But Tammy quickly kept the conversation going.

"Slow down, I said I had plans, past tense. Somebody I know from the beach, who goes to UConn, had called me a few weeks before Christmas and asked if I wanted to go to a party on New Year's Eve, and I said yes. But just before Christmas, I decided I really didn't want to go with him, but I needed a good excuse, so I told him my parents are making me babysit for their friends who are going to a New Year's Eve party at a hotel in the city."

"He believed that you would actually pass up a date because your parents said you had to babysit. He must not know you very well," Jay offered.

"I'm not sure how much he bought it, but I don't care. Besides, I really am babysitting. A couple who live down the street called the other day to ask if, by chance, I was available New Year's Eve because their babysitter has mono or something. I think they were shocked when I said I could do it. So, I guess you are going to be having a wild time at a party down at the beach while I'm babysitting a six-year-old and an eight-year-old."

Jay hesitated, but he figured it was worth a try.

"I don't have to go to the party. I could come over and keep you company. If you want and if you think it would be okay with the people you are babysitting for."

There was a long silence, and Jay's heart dropped again. Finally, Tammy spoke.

"It will be okay with them. In fact, they said if I wanted to ask a couple of friends over, it would be okay."

"I don't know if I can get a couple of people. I think everybody is going to the party," Jay said.

"Just you will do fine," she said.

NEW YORK TIMES, JAN. 2, 1964

WASHINGTON – American youths should receive two more years of free education after high school, leading educators proposed yesterday

"Thanks for giving me a ride home," Tammy said as she reached over and turned down the volume on the car radio Thursday afternoon. "I don't know how Jane and I crossed up our signals. I swore she said she would pick me up in front of the school. You didn't have to do this, you know. I could have walked home."

Jay looked at the blond and shook his head.

"Right, it's twenty degrees out, and I'm going to let you walk almost a mile," he said, looking at Tammy with a smile.

"But now you are going to be late for track practice," Tammy said.

"I have run up and down that hallway in the basement thirty times. The hallway will still be there when I get back."

They drove for a few minutes just listening to the music when Jay suddenly spoke up.

"Hey, I forgot to ask on New Year's Eve. Did you get your Wellesley application in?"

"Yeah, I mailed it last week, and I also finished the one for Connecticut College. But they're both probably a waste of time. I know I don't have much chance of getting accepted at either place."

"Why not? You're as smart as any kid in this school," Jay declared.

"Not quite," Tammy said with a laugh. "My grades and SAT scores are fine for any of the state schools. I shouldn't have any problem with UMass or UConn. But those private schools are more selective, and I don't have a football coach pushing for me."

The statement caught Jay off guard. He felt embarrassed that he had a football coach advocating for him at a college like Amherst, and now, apparently, Quigley also had been talking with the coach at Tufts about him.

"I'm sorry," he said.

"No, don't be sorry. I didn't mean that as a knock on you. I'm really happy for you that your football may get you into a great school," Tammy replied. "It's just that girls don't have that possible advantage. I mean, look at Linda. I know Tony probably has never even noticed this, but she's very athletic. She has three older brothers, so she grew up playing basketball in their driveway with them. You should see her when we play basketball in gym class. Most of us girls can't bounce the ball more than twice without bouncing it off our feet, but she can dribble the ball all day. I know if we had a girls' basketball team that played other schools like the boys' team does, she would be great. Look at Lombardo. Even after he was hurt, he's still going to get a college scholarship. Isn't he?"

"Probably," Jay said defensively.

"So, he is going to be able to go to some big out-of-state college because he's a football player. Linda's family doesn't have a lot of money. They can't afford to send her to some out-of-state college. She's smart, and she's a good athlete, but that doesn't matter when you're a girl."

"I never thought of it that way. That's not fair." Jay said just as he turned the car onto her street.

"No, it's not. But that's the way it is, and it's not going to change—at least not today," Tammy said as the car pulled up in front of her house. She reached over, gave Jay a kiss on the cheek, then quickly got out of the car and headed up the walkway toward her front door.

TIME MAGAZINE, JAN. 3, 1964

Time's Man of the Year has usually been as singular as the first one – 1927's Charles Lindbergh. But there have been groups as well (the 15 top U.S. scientists in 1960) and anonymous symbols (the Hungarian Freedom Fighter and Korea's G.I. Joe). There have been Presidents (every President since FDR, who himself set a record as Man of the Year three times, allies (Churchill, Adenauer DeGaulle, enemies (Hitler); villains

> (Stalin). There have been women too (Wallis Simpson, Queen Elizabeth) But there has never, until this year, been a Negro.
>
> Martin Luther King Jr. has made it as a man-but also as the representative of his people, for whom 1963 was perhaps the most important year in their history.

Surprisingly, everybody was already in their seats when Kiley walked into the Friday afternoon class carrying about eight or nine magazines that he dropped down on his desk.

"Okay, we are going to divert a little from using the newspaper. I stopped at the drugstore down the street and bought all their copies of today's Time magazine. We are going to read the story of Martin Luther King being named the Man of the Year. I think the story is important to what we have been reading since the first day of school. I know most of the time we do team reports, but in this case, I want everybody to read the story about King being named Man of the Year. I think some of the things King says in the story are important to help you understand what we have been reading. You can read it together, talk about it together, but I wanted everybody to think about what the story says about what King brought to the attention of the American people in 1963. Like this paragraph, where it mentions Mr. King talking about how, in 1963, there arose a great Negro disappointment, disillusionment, and discontent. How 1963 was the centennial of the Emancipation Proclamation, and that year, nineteen million Negro citizens forced the nation to take stock of itself. We have been reading about it. Like it says in this story, it's happening everywhere in Congress; in schools; in factories. The story says 1963 was the most decisive year in the Negro's fight for equality. Never before had there been such a coalition of conscience on this issue. We talked about this on the first day of school. The fact is, what you are reading about is happening outside the world you are actually living in, but I hope it's not happening outside the world you are thinking about.

"Look, I think my job is to get you to think about what is happening in the world outside where you are actually living, because pretty soon you are going to be living outside the nice, safe world of this school and this city. I don't care if you're in college or in the Army or who knows what. Your world is going to change a lot faster than mine did when I was your age ten years ago. I mean, just look at what has happened in the past four months: 200,000 people marched on Washington for equality the day before you started school; colored students were admitted to schools in Alabama; President Kennedy was killed. Remember back on that first day of school, I said things are happening. Well, even I didn't think this many things were going to happen by Christmas. I still hope I was wrong when I said back in that first week that a place called Vietnam could play a role in your lives, but the more we read about it, the more I'm worried that I am right.

He kept talking about some other things mentioned in the Time magazine article and a few other things they had read in the Times just before Christmas vacation. But then, suddenly, he changed his tone.

"Okay, I will get off my soapbox now," he said apologetically. "But I just want to remind you that the purpose of this class is to make you aware of things that are happening outside your world when they are happening. Believe me, you are not in this alone. I'm pretty sure there are people your age all over the country in the same type of safe suburban life as you who never thought about these issues before this year. It's a good time to be your age, people. But it's also a little scary."

NEW YORK TIMES, JAN. 4, 1964

The Beatles of Britain were seen in their first complete song on American television last night as Jack Paar presented a film of the mop-headed quartet on his variety show over the National Broadcasting Company.

—

His hand was slightly trembling as Jay rang the front doorbell at Tammy's house on Saturday morning. He was trying to think of what he was going to say if Tammy's mother or father answered the door, but to his relief, Tammy eventually appeared at the door.

"Hi," she said. "What are you doing here? Come in, it's freezing out there."

Jay didn't hesitate to start talking once he stepped inside the door.

"Do you want to go to the movies tonight?" he asked.

Tammy looked at him with a bewildering smile.

"You drove over here to ask me that. There is this new invention called the telephone, you know," she said sarcastically while flashing a little grin.

"I know, but I wanted to ask you in person," he said.

"Why?" she asked.

He hesitated, trying to find the right words.

"Because this is different. It's not our usual meet-up when everybody gets together for something, or even me coming over to your house to work on our research papers or doing some homework, or even you wrapping my Christmas gifts," he said without looking directly at the blond.

"You mean like a Saturday night date?" she said with a slight laugh.

Now Jay was starting to feel embarrassed. Maybe this was a stupid idea, maybe he should have just called her. But he continued.

"Yeah, just you and me," he said.

"It's not like we haven't been alone," she said with a smirk.

"I know, but this is something we will have planned. Not just a meet-up," he countered while still not looking directly into her face.

She stood there not saying a word, looking into space rather than at Jay. Jay could feel his face getting flushed. Then the blond broke into laughter.

"Sorry," she said. "I didn't mean to laugh. But I thought you had been around here long enough now to know things aren't quite as formal as they were in prep school. But I guess once a preppie always a preppie."

Jay stood there looking defensive.

"Sorry," he said.

"No, no, that's what I love about you," she said.

"Love," Jay quickly retorted, regaining his verbal footing.

"Wrong word, Wrong word," the blond said with a smirk.

ASSOCIATED PRESS, JAN.5, 1964

AUBURN, Ala. – A Negro student broke the racial barriers at Auburn University yesterday by registering as a graduate student after first checking into a dormitory where he will live with white male students.

"So, where are you going to apply to college?" Jay asked Tony as soon as his friend got in Jay's car for the Monday morning ride to school.

"I guess just UConn and UMass," Tony offered. "Wardell is trying to convince me I should go to Springfield to wrestle, but I don't love wrestling that much. I've had enough of trying to make weight every week. If I make it to the end of this season, that will be it. So how about you? Have you heard from the Amherst coach recently?"

"No, nothing," Jay said. "But the Tufts coach called the other night. I wasn't home, but he talked to my mother. He wanted to know if my application is in."

"Did you do it?"

"Yeah."

"What do you think?"

"I don't know. It's a long shot. I'm definitely getting my application in to Umass."

NEW YORK TIMES, JAN. 8, 1964

WASHINGTON – The House voted tonight to set up a performing arts center here as a memorial to President Kennedy

"I know some of you saw the movie when it came out last spring, so you might figure you don't need to read the book. But a movie, no matter how good, can never make you understand a situation as well as a book," Mrs. Weber, Jay's English teacher, said as she started the class discussion about "To Kill a Mockingbird" on Monday morning.

"Harper Lee isn't a well-known American author like Hemingway or John Steinbeck," the teacher said. "She's only about thirty-six or thirty-seven, and this is her first book. But I think she's a great writer, and I'm sure she will be writing more great books. "

It was obvious that the author had excited Mrs. Weber's love of literature.

"Her theme is powerful, but her words are soft," the teacher had continued about Lee's writing.

"I want you to read the first ten chapters by next Monday and write 500 words about something you find interesting."

UNITED PRESS INTERNATIONAL, JAN. 9, 1964

WASHINGTON – President Johnson yesterday asked Congress in his State of the Union message to "let this session of Congress be known as the session which did more for civil rights than the last hundred sessions combined."

"You have been reading about this for almost five months now, so what do you think the President's chances are of getting the Civil

Rights bill passed before you graduate?" Kiley asked the Thursday afternoon class.

"From high school or college?" Tony yelled out with a laugh.

"I don't think this is a joking matter, Mr. Gemma," the teacher fired back.

Kiley's stern look made Tony realize it probably wasn't a good time to try being funny.

"Sorry, Mr. Kiley," Tony offered in an apologetic tone just as the bell rang signaling the end of class.

"Saved by the Bell, Gemma," Kiley said, laughing.

A few minutes later, Jay and Tammy were walking alone down the corridor after leaving Kiley's class.

"Do you think even if President Johnson gets the Civil Rights bill passed, it will end racism in this country?" Tammy asked.

"Wow, where did that suddenly come from. I thought that was the type of stuff you only thought about in Kiley's class," he quipped as he looked at the blond while flashing a soft smile.

"I don't know, I guess the way Kiley got so upset at Tony made me realize this is more than just something we should think about when we are in Kiley's class."

"So, what do you think?" she asked.

Jay stopped walking and pulled Tammy over to the wall away from the throng of teenagers walking down the hallway. The smile on his face turned somber as he looked straight into her eyes.

"I hate to say it, but I think racism is everywhere in this country, and it isn't going away easily. But I think it can be overcome, even if it will be a slow walk."

"Thanks," Tammy said, her facial expression now turned to that soft smile Jay had come to know so well over the past few months. "You might be stealing somebody else's line, but you make me feel good about the future."

ASSOCIATED PRESS, JAN. 15, 1964

WASHINGTON – Mrs. John F. Kennedy gave an emotional personal thank-you broadcast yesterday for the nearly 800,000 messages she said have been a source of comfort since the assassination of her husband.

"What are you still doing here?" Jay asked when he saw Marty standing in front of her locker on Wednesday while he was walking out of school after track practice.

"I'm just getting my coat. I have been at the modern dance club practice."

The answer caught Jay by surprise. He didn't want to admit it to Marty, but he didn't even know there was such a thing as a modern dance club at the school.

"How often do you practice?" he asked.

"Everybody practices once a week, but a few of us go twice, sometimes even three times a week," Marty said.

Jay stood looking at her, getting more and more excited with every word she spoke about her passion.

"I guess I'm not a very good friend. I didn't realize you spent so much time dancing," Jay confessed.

"I never say much about it, and most people don't even know we have a dance club. It's not like you playing football, where everybody cheers for you. I spend a lot of time with cheerleading, and everybody sees that. But I love dancing, even if not many people watch high school dancers."

The two friends started walking down the corridor toward the side door, but Jay wanted to know more.

"Is that what you want to do? I mean, professionally someday," he asked.

Marty kept walking, but looked over at him with a little smile.

"I don't know if I'm that good. Besides, if you are really serious about a career in dancing, you need to go to school in New York City, and my parents aren't going to pay for me to go to college in

New York." Marty said as she stopped walking and leaned against the wall.

"Have you ever talked to them about it?" Jay asked.

Marty's expression had turned serious.

"No, that's just kind of my wild dream. I know it's not very realistic. I guess my parents figure I will be a teacher, that's what most girls go to college for. So, I'm just applying to some of the public teachers' colleges in Connecticut and Massachusetts," she said.

"You shouldn't give up on your dream that easily," Jay said.

"Easy for you to say, Mr. Football star. None of the coaches of the Rockettes are calling me."

"God, you two think alike," Jay said softly.

"What?" Marty said.

"Oh, nothing." Jay replied, "Come on, I'll give you a ride home."

NEW YORK TIMES, JAN. 16, 1964

WASHINGTON – President Johnson promised yesterday that "we have just begun to fight" for the program of financing medical care for the aged through Social Security.

Ha, why aren't you heading to track practice? Tammy asked Jay when she spotted him sitting alone in the chair next to the lobby phone booth about fifteen minutes after dismissal on Thursday afternoon.

"No practice today, we have a meet tonight, but the bus doesn't leave until 4 o'clock.

"So, can you give me a ride home?" the blond inquired

"Sure," Jay said without hesitation.

The pair was barely out of the parking lot when Tammy declared.

"I hear Mrs. Weber liked your paper about 'To Kill a Mockingbird' so much that she read it to the whole class."

"How did you hear about that?" Jay inquired.

"I have my sources," Tammy said with a sly smile.

"Yeah, I know those sources. It's called the cheerleader network. Jane is in that class," Jay said with a smirk.

"So, what did you get on the paper?" Tammy asked.

An "A," Jay replied with more of an embarrassed than boisterous tone.

"Why didn't you tell me?" The blond inquired.

"For the same reason, I don't tell you when I get a 'C' on a French test. You have more important things to think about than what mark I got on some English paper."

Tammy gave an exasperated look, but didn't debate Jay's defense. Instead, she asked, "So, what did you write?"

"It was nothing great. I just talked about how in Chapter Three, there's a line where Atticus Finch says, 'You never really understand a person until you consider things from his point of view. Until you climb into someone's skin and walk around in it.'

"I wrote that's essentially what Mr. Kiley has been saying to us for months. That we have to get outside our sheltered lives so that we can better understand what is happening around this country. I guess Mrs. Weber liked the way I brought something we are studying in another class into her class."

Tammy looked at him with her patterned soft smile.

"You like to write, don't you?" she asked.

Jay was still driving, but he didn't need to take his eyes off the road to answer the question.

"Ya, I guess so. I like to tell stories."

The blond, who had been looking straight ahead, now looked over at Jay while he continued driving.

"Sure, everybody likes to tell stories," she said. "But most people like to tell stories about the bad things people do, but you're always talking about the good, positive things people do. Either it's how President Kennedy once did this or that to help people, or how some guys on the football team never get the credit they deserve. Hell, your father died just a year ago, and a President you deeply admired was killed just a few months ago. You have every right to think this world is a shitty place. Yet, you are always talking about the wonderful possibilities that life has to offer. How do you stay so positive?"

By now, Jay had turned the car onto Tammy's Street, but he didn't want to be the subject of her psychoanalysis, so he pulled the car in front of her house and left the engine running.

"It's your influence," he quipped.

"Ya, that's a joke. I am the most negative person in the world, but thank you for always knowing what to say to make me feel good," she said as she reached over, gave him a kiss on the cheek, opened the car door, and started heading up the walkway to her front door.

Jay was about to pull away, but instead he reached over and rolled down the passenger side window.

"Hey," he yelled at the blond, causing her to stop, turn around, and look back at the car.

"That negative person is the old you," he declared and pulled away before the blond could offer a rebuttal.

UNITED PRESS INTERNATIONAL, JAN. 19, 1964.

> WASHINGTON – The government yesterday proposed stiff new rules for cigarette advertising and labeling to remind consumers of "the substantial health hazard of cigarette smoking."

Smoke floated out of the girls' lav as two girls walked out the door, just as Jay and Tammy were walking past on their way down the main corridor, Monday afternoon.

"Have you ever smoked?" Tammy asked.

"No, I haven't," Jay offered. "I guess it's because when I was growing up, I always liked sports, and you always heard if you want to be good in sports, you don't smoke."

"How about you?" Jay countered.

"Yeah, I used to," Tammy said, turning to Jay, who had stopped in his tracks when he heard the answer. "I still have a pack of cigarettes hidden in my bedroom, just in case some time I want to go out in my backyard for a smoke. My parents know I smoked, but they wouldn't let me smoke in the house."

Jay was still having a hard time picturing Tammy with a cigarette in her mouth.

"I mean, I have never seen you smoking," Jay said with a still, somehow stunned look that the blond smoked.

"I know. I probably haven't smoked a cigarette since this summer or at least not since the first few weeks of school," she declared.

"Why did you start in the first place?" he asked.

"I don't know, I guess at the beginning it's doing something that's a little daring; something you know your parents don't want you doing. Maybe I felt pressure because everybody else was doing it," the blond retorted.

"I guess. But why haven't you smoked in the past few months?" Jay asked just as they reached Tammy's locker.

"I don't know. Maybe because I started hearing that it wasn't good for your health, but I think it's more because I used to smoke a lot when I got nervous or was upset about something. The past few months, I haven't been upset about too many things."

NEW YORK TIMES, JAN. 19,1964

NEW YORK – Twin 1,350-foot towers, the world's tallest buildings, will be erected to house the World Trade Center planned downtown. The towers and a cluster of 70-foot-high satellite buildings will form a ring around a five-acre plaza containing reflecting pools.

—

Jay had finished track practice and was heading down the basement corridor toward the locker room late Monday afternoon when he saw Tammy sitting by herself at a table in the otherwise empty cafeteria.

"What are you doing down here by yourself?" he asked the blond.

"I'm trying to finish my paper for Kiley about President Johnson's State of the Union speech. I was upstairs in the library, but the library closes at four, and I wanted to finish writing this before I went home."

Tammy looked at Jay, flashing the smile that had mesmerized him since the first day of school.

"Kiley is a good teacher, isn't he?" she asked.

"I think he is," Jay replied.

"Why?" the blond quickly questioned.

Jay speedily gave his answer.

"I think it's because he makes you think beyond just what he is teaching that day."

"I know that's like Mr. Wadsworth, my Physics I teacher last year," Tammy offered. "He made you want to learn more about what he was teaching. He didn't just teach from the textbook. He was always conducting experiments involving the stuff we were studying that wasn't in the textbook. I guess teachers like him and Mr. Kiley make you realize how important good teachers are," Tammy declared.

"Have you ever thought of being a teacher?" Jay quizzed.

"NO," Tammy declared in a confident tone.

"Why not?" Jay asked.

"Because too many people think the only thing a woman can be is a teacher or a nurse. I like science, but does that mean I can only be a nurse? What if I want to be a doctor?" the blond probed.

"Do you?" Jay asked

Jay looked straight into her eyes, waiting for an answer. But it was obvious Tammy didn't want to get into a long psychological discussion of her future.

"I don't know," Tammy offered without directly looking at Jay. "Maybe someday that will be a dream for a girl in high school, but it's not something I have ever thought about. The only thing I know for sure right now is that I want you to give me a ride home," she said again, flashing her patterned smile.

UNITED PRESS INTERNATIONAL, JAN. 24, 1964

PIERRE, S.D. – The South Dakota legislature, beating-out Georgia legislature in a race to make history yesterday, wrote the anti-poll tax amendment into the U.S. Constitution.

South Dakota became the 38th state to ratify the resolution, ending a practice that had endured since the birth of the republic, when the Senate approved it 34-0. Only five states, all in the South, still have poll taxes.

"Gemma, would you pay to vote?" Kiley asked Tony as the lead-off to his Friday class.

"I'm not old enough to vote," Tony fired back, feeling more comfortable trying for a laugh with a smart-ass answer to Kiley than he would with any other teacher.

"OK, so let's say it's 1968 and you are old enough to vote in a presidential election for the first time, but they say if you want to vote, you have to pay a $10 tax. Would you pay?"

"No, you shouldn't have to pay to vote," Tony declared in a loud voice.

Kiley smiled as he took a copy of the morning paper off his desk and pointed to a front-page story.

"Well, it has taken almost two hundred years, but that's now what the Constitution says, too." Kiley offered.

UNITED PRESS INTERNATIONAL, JAN. 28, 1964

> WASHINGTON – Sen. Margaret Chase Smith, tired of being told that "this is a man's world and that it should be kept that way," announced yesterday that she will campaign to become the nation's first woman president.

Kiley walked into the classroom a few minutes after the bell sounded and looked around to take his usual informal attendance.

"OK, looks like everybody is here," the teacher declared.

"So can a woman be President of the United States?" he asked while displaying his copy of the Times with the story of Sen. Margaret Chase Smith announcing she would campaign to become the nation's first woman president.

For some reason, Vin Rego, who normally didn't have much to say in the class, jumped into the conversation.

"No way, there never has been a woman President," the running back offered.

"True," said Kiley, "But does that mean there never can be one?"

Rego just kept coming back, not realizing he was like a quarterback about to be hit with a blind-side tackle.

"No, a woman can't be President," he said without giving much thought to his answer.

"So, every young American boy can grow up thinking one day he might be President, but a girl can't have that dream?" Kiley said.

Rego started backing off a little after looking at the faces of some of the girls sitting around him. But it was too late.

"Does anybody want to offer a rebuttal to Mr. Rego's philosophy?" Kiley asked with a sinister smile.

Tammy's hand immediately shot up.

"Why am I not surprised?" Kiley said, now chuckling about the verbal battle he knew was about to ensue. "Go ahead, Miss Clark, have at him."

Tammy didn't hesitate to blitz Rego.

"Why can't girls dream about becoming President, because we don't play football?" she quickly offered as her opening salvo in the impromptu debate.

Jay was trying to hide his laughter as he slid down in his chair. This is going to be funny, he thought to himself. Vin has no idea what's about to hit him.

NEW YORK TIMES, JAN. 30, 1964

> WASHINGTON – The United States government made no official comment last night on the latest coup d'etat in South Vietnam. Officials here were obviously embarrassed that the government they helped bring to power only last November had been overthrown.

"You know what I don't like about the N.Y. Times? Tammy said as she, Marty, Jay, and Mike Stone walked four abreast in the corridor heading for the cafeteria after Kiley's Thursday afternoon class.

"They don't write enough about the New York Giants?" Jay said with a laugh.

"No, that's my father's complaint," Tammy offered with a smile. "I hate that they don't have comics."

"I never thought of you being a big comic reader," Mike interjected.

"Are you kidding me? When I was in junior high school, I grabbed my father's paper every night to see what the Jackson Twins were doing."

"How about you, Marty? Did you follow the Jackson Twins?" Jay asked.

"I sure did," said Marty.

"Now you two are living the part—without the twin thing," Jay said. "Two cute, popular high school girls who do everything together."

"Isn't he nice calling us cute?" said Marty.

"He's a suck-up," Tammy said with a sly smile.

"So do you still read them?" Jay asked, trying to deflect the conversation from his transparent attempt to flatter the girls.

"No, not that much anymore," said Tammy. "I have too many other things to do, and besides, they don't seem that realistic to me anymore. Nothing seems to change in their town or their lives. Look at how many things have changed in the three years we have been here, especially this year. Nothing ever seems to change in their lives. They just seem oblivious to everything that is happening around the county. But I still read Peanuts. That Lucy is my type of girl."

TEN

ASSOCIATED PRESS, FEB. 4, 1964

WASHINGTON – Opponents launched a series of attacks on the administration-backed civil rights bill yesterday in an unsuccessful drive to narrow its scope.

The usual post-dismissal gathering of students in the front lobby was breaking up, so Jay started heading toward the locker room to change for track practice. But suddenly, Tammy interrupted his departure with a question.

"Hey, do you have time to give me a ride home before practice?" she asked.

"Sure," Jay said, jumping at the opportunity to spend time alone with the blond, even though he knew he would be late for practice by the time he drove her home, then drove back to school.

A few minutes later, the pair was driving out of the school parking lot with the radio blasting the mellow sound of "Dawn," but Tammy reached over and turned down the volume.

"Do you ever think of what you want to do with the rest of your life?" she asked.

"Where did that suddenly come from? Jay replied as he looked over at the blond, yet continued driving.

"I don't know. I guess with all this talk about college, it just got me thinking about the future beyond the last few months of our senior year. So, have you ever thought about it?"

Jay hesitated for several seconds before answering, but finally offered a response.

"You know it's funny. Growing up, I was pretty good at math, and I heard that if you are good at math, you should become an engineer. But over the past year, I have been thinking that I want to be involved in public service. I don't know, maybe it's the Kennedy thing. You know, 'Ask not what your country can do for you, but ask what you can do for your country,'" Jay said.

"You mean you want to be a politician, run for political office like Kennedy did at a young age?" Tammy asked.

"I don't know. I'm not sure if I could ever get people to vote for me. But you don't have to be an elected official to be in public service. There are a lot of other ways to be in public service. Public service is a way to make a difference in people's lives," Jay declared.

"You heard Kennedy say that, didn't you?" Tammy questioned.

"I guess so," Jay admitted.

A smile suddenly flashed across Tammy's face.

"I can see people voting for you someday," she offered.

"Why do you think that?" Jay asked as he turned his car into Tammy's Street and pulled the Healey in front of her house.

"Because you're smart, you're a good person, and you genuinely care about people." She took a long pause, then said, while flashing a broad smile on her way out of the car, "And you're handsome."

NEW YORK TIMES, FEB. 5, 1964

WASHINGTON –The civil rights bill's section on discrimination in public accommodations survived all major attacks today as tentatively approved by the House of Representatives.

"So, who went to the movies last weekend?" Kiley asked as his opening salvo for his Wednesday morning class, the first period of the day.

A scattering of six or seven hands timidly rose, not exactly sure why their teacher would want to know about their weekend social activities.

"Good, so what did you see, Miss Slocum? Kiley asked the petite red-haired girl who sat in the seat in front of Jay, but rarely spoke up in class.

"Tom Jones," she said.

"Was it good? The teacher asked.

"Yes, I like it," she said, puzzled about the teacher's questions.

"So did you go with a date or with some other girls?" Kiley asked, continuing his strange line of questioning.

Now the girl was really starting to wonder about the teacher's questions, but she gave him an answer.

"I had a date," the girl said sheepishly.

"I hope he paid for your ticket," Kiley said with a slight laugh.

"He did," the girl replied with a smile.

"Good, but how would you have felt if, when your date went to buy the tickets, the cashier said she wouldn't sell him tickets because he was with a girl who had red hair. Or even if she sold him tickets, she said the only place in the theater a girl with red hair could sit was way up in the back of the balcony, even though there were plenty of empty seats up front?"

The girl's expression suddenly changed to a look of confusion, and she didn't reply. But Kiley kept looking at her for an answer. Finally, she squeezed out a reply.

"I guess I would have been embarrassed, but that's not going to happen, Mr. Kiley," she offered.

"No, it's not. But what's the difference between you and your date not being able to sit in the front row of a theater because you have red hair and a girl your age in Mississippi not being able to sit in the front row of a theater with her boyfriend because they are colored?"

The girl hesitated, thinking about what the teacher had just asked her.

"I guess there is no difference," the girl said with a perplexed look.

"Alright, I think you get the idea," Kiley said, finally turning his attention away from the red-headed girl and directing it toward the entire class.

"You see in today's paper where the section of the civil rights bill on discrimination in public accommodations seems to have survived some major attacks. I know that may not be a big thing to you because you can walk into any theater or any restaurant and sit wherever you want and feel comfortable doing it. But not every teenager in this country can do that. People, just because something doesn't directly affect you, doesn't mean it's not part of your life. I know you are getting a little tired of me saying this, but I firmly believe the things you are reading in this class are going to affect your life for a long time to come. At least I hope so. OK, you have a few minutes before the bell, so Gemma, you can check out the sports and everybody else, check the whole paper to see if there is something you didn't know about before you came to school this morning."

He turned his back on the students and headed toward the chair behind his desk, but he suddenly turned back toward the class.

"Oh, Miss Burns, there's a slip here for you," he said. "Mrs. Harrison wants to see you in the Dean of Girls' office before the next class."

NEW YORK TIMES, FEB. 5, 1964

LONDON – A multi-million-dollar industry, the Beatles, returned from Paris today to prepare for an American debut.

Jay was heading for a meeting with his guidance counselor midway through the second period when he spotted Marty walking down the corridor toward him, wearing her ski parka.

"Where are you going with your coat on? Shouldn't you be in class?" he said, trying to create some humor.

But when Marty turned toward him, he could tell she wasn't in any mood to laugh.

"I have to walk home and change my skirt," she said with a disgusted look.

"Why, I think it looks nice," Jay said

"I guess that's what Mrs. Harrison is afraid of. She thinks too many boys are looking at it. She saw me in the main lobby this morning before school, so she sent that note to Kiley's room in the first period. When I went into her office, she told me my skirt was too short. She had a ruler right there, and she measured it. She said the bottom of my skirt was more than an inch above my knees. She knows where I live, so she said I could either walk home and change it or I could spend the rest of the day in the nurse's office. I didn't want to sit around the nurses' office all day, so I'm going home."

"Holy shit, "Jay offered. "That skirt is not that short. I can barely see your knees. Hell, it's not like people here haven't seen your legs. They see a lot more of your legs when you are cheering at football and basketball games."

"I know it's stupid, but what am I going to do?" Marty offered.

"Do you want to take my car?" Jay asked.

"Thanks, but I can't drive a stick shift. I'll just walk home. It only takes about ten or fifteen minutes, but by the time I walk home, change, and walk back, I'm going to miss lunch. I'm really starting to get tired of this high school bullshit."

NEW YORK TIMES, FEB. 7, 1964

SAIGON – Communist guerrillas, whose activity has been increasing, have imposed a sharp new defeat of government forces in a battle in the Mekong Delta about 85 miles southeast of Saigon, military sources reported yesterday.

—

"Party at my house Sunday night to watch the Beatles," Dan Aaronson announced to a group of mostly football players sitting at the first table in the café at Friday lunch. "My parents are going out for the night."

NEW YORK TIMES, FEB. 8, 1964

NEW YORK - Multiply Elvis Presley by four, subtract six years from his age, add British accents and a sharp sense of humor. The answer: It's the Beatles (Yeah, Yeah, Yeah)

The rock'n'roll group, which may become Britain's most successful export since the bowler, arrived at Kennedy International Airport yesterday and more than 3,000 teenagers stood four deep on the upper arcade at the International Arrivals Building to greet them.

"Did I wake you up?" Jay said when Tammy answered the phone.

"Kind of, it's only 9 o'clock. Why are you calling this early? I was babysitting until 1 o'clock this morning," the blond said, her voice barely audible on the phone.

"Sorry, but I have a track meet at eleven, and I have to be at school at 9:30 to catch the bus," Jay offered in an apologetic tone.

"Okay, you're forgiven. What's up?" she asked.

"Dan's parents are going out tomorrow night, and they said he could have some people over to watch the Beatles on the Ed Sullivan show. Do you want to go with me?"

"Sorry, somebody else already asked me to go?"

"Who?" Jay said with a tone of disappointment, mixed with anger, that some other boy had asked Tammy to go to Dan's.

Maybe because she still wasn't really awake, or maybe she realized he was upset, but fortunately for Jay's nervous system, Tammy didn't keep him in suspense with some of her usual teasing.

"Who do you think—Marty," she quickly responded. "Dan

asked her to come over, but she got the feeling it was going to be mostly guys. So, she didn't want to walk in there by herself."

His blood pressure having returned to normal, Jay responded.

"She's probably right about that. I know Tony is going, but he's not taking Linda. So, I'll see you there."

"Yeah, I'll be there. Marty is trying to find at least one other girl to go with us."

NEW YORK TIMES, FEB. 9, 1964

> WASHINGTON – The House failed to complete action on the civil rights bill last night after bogging down in a morass of amendments to the section outlawing discrimination by employers and labor unions.

"Hurry up, it's almost eight o'clock, and I heard they are going to be on at the start of the show," Tony yelled.

Dan's parents' den had shelves of books lining walls on three sides, a leather couch, two big easy chairs, and a big Motorola black and white TV. The room was already filled with teenagers when Jay arrived, so he took a spot sitting on the floor with his back against the wall across the room from the couch where Tammy, Marty, and Jane Snow were sitting.

When the show started, there wasn't an empty space on the couch, the three chairs, or even on the floor.

"Good evening, ladies and gentlemen, tonight live from New York, the Ed Sullivan Show," the off-camera announcer proclaimed as the screen projected a stage curtain backdrop opening with the 'Ed Sullivan Show 'scripted across it. After declaring that tonight, the Ed Sullivan Show is brought to you by Anacin and Pillsbury, the voice declared, "Now here he is—Ed Sullivan."

Sullivan came walking onto the stage to loud applause. He mouthed a thank you that was barely audible and raised his arms with the palms of his hands out to quiet the audience.

"This particular season we have had many exciting nights on

the stage," Sullivan said, going on to describe several entertainers, including Sammy Davis Jr. and Ella Fitzgerald. "Now, tonight the whole country has been waiting to hear England's Beatles, and you are going to hear them—they are a tremendous ambassador to goodwill—after this commercial."

"Shit, I don't need to see a commercial for Aero Shave," shouted Tony.

But they all sat patiently for thirty seconds watching the Aero Shave commercial, and even for another thirty seconds watching a Griffin liquid shoe polish ad.

Finally, Sullivan was back on camera and immediately started talking about his guests.

"Now, yesterday and today our theater has been jammed with newspaper men and hundreds of photographers from all over the nation, and these veterans agree with me that the city has never witnessed the excitement generated by these youngsters from Liverpool who call themselves the Beatles. Now tonight you are going to be twice entertained by them, right now and in the second half of our show."

"Ladies and gentlemen...... the Beatles," Sullivan declared as he swung his right arm out toward the audience, then back to the stage.

The first image was of the audience, filled with screaming and clapping young women and teenage girls. Then, after a few seconds of watching the audience's ecstatic reaction, the four young men from England appeared on the screen. They were all dressed in—what on the black and white TV were—identical black suits with skinny lapels, and they were wearing white shirts and thin black ties. They were in the center of the stage with twelve large arrows on the floor of the stage forming a complete circle that pointed to the quartet in the middle. George, Paul, and John stood side by side in the front playing guitars, and behind them was Ringo sitting on the second level of a double-level circular raised platform playing the drums. A small "the" and a large "BEATLES" were scripted across the front of his bass drum. Their hair was evenly cut across the front of their faces. George's was almost a straight cut across his forehead at his eyebrows. Paul's and John's had a little wave, and Ringo's was completely over his eyebrows, down almost into his eyes. The closely-cut hair was tight to their heads, so most of their ears were visible, but around the back of their heads, the hair ran down so it lay just on top of the collar of their white shirts.

> *"Close your eyes and I'll kiss you*
> *Tomorrow, I'll miss you"*

Paul was blasting out the words, standing in front of one microphone while George and John played their guitars in front of another mike. It wasn't the swiveling hip movements or snarling expressions of Elvis Presley. They stood firm and upright, their feet never leaving their original footprints. Their facial expressions were sweet smiles. The American cameramen had done their homework. They understood that it was their faces and their heads, along with their music, that had won the hearts of girls in England. The camera switched between close-ups of Paul and Ringo, then switched to a close-up of a girl in the audience. She had dark hair running straight down until curling underneath just before the base of her neck, just like the hairdos of the three girls sitting in the room. The girl's hand was touching the side of her open mouth as she screamed. She was in a state of ecstasy.

Jay looked away from the TV over toward the three girls on the couch. Each girl had her face locked onto the images on the TV. They weren't screaming like the girls in the audience in New York, but all three had smiles on their faces as they bent forward to get a closer look with their elbows on their knees and their chins resting in their hands.

"God, they are so cute," Jane declared. "I love their hair, but if a boy came to my house with his hair like that, my father would kick him out."

"They are flirting with us," Marty said in a soft tone. "They are singing that to me."

"They are singing to a couple of million people," Tony said with a laugh.

"You're a guy. You wouldn't understand," Marty retorted.

The song ended, the camera switched back to the audience, where just about every female member, which was virtually the entire audience, was bouncing up and down in their seats. The quartet took simultaneous bows, with the three in front bowing from the waist and Ringo bowing his head over his drums. Then they immediately broke into a second song.

"There were bells on a hill
But I never heard them ringing"

The camera moved in for individual facial close-ups of each Beatle with just their first name written across the bottom of the screen. Not that any American female between the ages of twelve and twenty-one needed them to be identified. First it was Paul, then Ringo, then George. When John appeared, under this name was the message: 'Sorry, girls, he's married.'

There was a close-up of Ringo just looking out with his doe eyes and a smile, mouthing something to the audience.

"Ringo is adorable. He has that little puppy-dog look," said Marty.

They finished singing "Till There was You," took a bow, then broke right into a third song.

"She loves you, yeah, yeah, yeah"

There were continual close-ups of the four mixed with shots of ecstatic females in the audience. They finished the third song and bowed again. The camera went to an audience shot, then switched to Sullivan standing alone on another part of the stage, clapping.

"They will be back," Sullivan declared. "But right now, a word about Anacin."

Shit, another commercial, yelled Tony.

But there was ample teenage chatter to pass the few minutes before Sullivan was back on stage, declaring:

"Ladies and Gentlemen, once again ……," He never even got "The Beatles" out of his mouth before the roar from the audience drowned out his voice. Even Sullivan's normal straight-faced expression turned to a smile as he again swung his arm in the direction of the group. The full stage image of the four came on the screen.

"Well, she was just 17
You know what I mean"

"See, I told you they were singing to me. I'm seventeen," Marty yelled out while the Beatles were still singing.

"Yeah, you and two million other girls in America," Tony yelled back with a laugh.

The room full of teenagers watched in awe as the quartet sang. They went on for two and a half minutes, interrupting the singing a few times for thirty seconds or so of strictly instrumental play. They finished the final words of "I Saw Her Standing There." The camera immediately switched to the screaming audience for a few seconds, then back to the four who broke right into another song.

"Oh yeah, I'll tell you somethin'
I think you'll understand"

John was singing solo when the camera flashed to the audience and zoomed in on a girl with dark glasses dressed in a jumper and blouse. Her dark hair was pulled behind her ears, and she was smiling so all her teeth were visible, screaming sounds of delight. The camera kept moving back and forth from the stage to the audience. There was a woman, at least ten years older than the teenagers in the audience, but she had the same expression of near-hysteria that was on the face of every teenage girl in the audience.

The four young Englishmen finished the song and took a bow. Paul, George, and John left their guitars on the stage, and Ringo came down off his platform, and the four headed off the stage. Suddenly, there was a shot of the four walking up behind a smiling Sullivan, at least Sullivan's version of a smile, and shaking hands. They stood on the stage for about thirty seconds, saying something to Sullivan, who was in the middle. Sullivan pointed up to the audience, and the four waved as screams rained down. Then they quickly headed off the stage, weaving and within a few seconds were out of camera range, leaving Sullivan alone on the stage. Sullivan again raised his hands, trying to quiet the audience. Finally, he spoke.

"All of us on the show want to express our deep appreciation to the New York Police Dept. for its superb handling of thousands of youngsters who were at Broadway and 53rd Street ready to greet the Beatles," Sullivan said.

He also added a "deep appreciation to newspaper and magazine writers who have been so kind to the Beatles and us." Sullivan then introduced another act, but nobody moved from their spots in the den for the two minutes or so of some jumping and spin circus-type act, hoping they might get another glimpse of the quartet.

But the Beatles never appeared again.

Finally, Sullivan appeared back on the stage.

"First of all, I want to congratulate you. You have been a fine audience," he said to the audience with his usual stern smile.

"I know the Beatles have been deeply thrilled by their reception on their first appearance. Now get home safely, Good Night," Sullivan said as the TV faded to another shot of the theater curtain backdrop with The Ed Sullivan Show scripted in front of it.

The teenagers in the den sat motionless and speechless for several seconds. Finally, Marty broke the silence.

"That was amazing," she declared.

NEW YORK TIMES, FEB. 10, 1964

> WASHINGTON – The House of Representatives passed the most far-reaching civil rights bill ever considered by Congress on Sunday night.
>
> The measure will be sent to the Senate on Monday.

"Good morning, and I hope everybody isn't too tired after watching the Beatles last night," Kiley said as he opened his Monday morning class. "So, Miss Burns, who is the cutest one? Is it Paul or Ringo?" the teacher said with a smile.

Marty just looked at the teacher, not knowing whether he really wanted an answer or was just trying to be funny, but she quickly joined in the banter.

"Paul," she said. "He's adorable."

Kiley looked at some of the other girls in the class.

"Agree, ladies?" he asked.

A few girls shook their heads in agreement.

"Good, well, at least we have that important issue settled. So let's get on with what happened in Washington this weekend, because apparently not everybody was watching the Beatles Sunday night. Today's paper talks about how the House finally passed the Civil Rights Bill last night, which is a significant achievement even though it still has to get through the Senate, which is the tough part.

"But before we get to that, I want to go back to something

that was in Sunday's paper. I know I don't require you to read the Sunday Times, but there was something in the Sunday paper that I think could have an effect on the lives of some of you young ladies."

Suddenly, some girls who were probably still daydreaming about John, Paul, George, and Ringo turned their attention toward the teacher.

"You people are all doing a great job keeping up with reading about all the action on the Civil Rights bill," Kiley said. "But I know there probably are times when some of you are thinking, sure, it's important to know this stuff, but the Civil Rights Bill doesn't really affect me. But something happened Saturday night that I think could be a monumental step for women, even if it's not the main emphasis of the story in the paper."

Kiley held up the entire front page of the Sunday Times to show the story to the class.

"Up here in the left-hand corner," he said, "You see this headline that says Jobs Issue Blocks Attempt in House to Vote on Rights. The first paragraph described how the House failed to complete action on the civil rights bill Sunday night after bogging down in a morass of amendments to the section outlawing discrimination by employers and labor unions. When you read this, it would be easy to think it was just another case of a southern congressman trying to delay voting on the Civil Rights Bill, like we have been reading about for a month. I think that probably was their intent, and what usually happens is they take all sorts of time discussing these amendments, then they are voted down. It's just a way to stall a vote on a piece of legislation. But you need to read more of the story to see how this story is a little different.

This Congressman from Virginia, named Smith, offered an amendment with the proposal of prohibiting discrimination on the basis of sex. I'm not sure if he's really trying to improve the Civil Rights or was just trying to make his wife happy because he said,

'This bill is so imperfect, what harm will this little amendment do?' He said it would 'help an important minority.'"

Apparently, Kiley felt some females of the class were drifting back to daydreaming about the Beatles because suddenly he stopped talking and took a long, silent pause. The thirty-second or so pause caught the attention of the entire class. Finally, Kiley, knowing he now had the class's attention, resumed talking.

"Ladies," he said, focusing his eyes on the girls in the class.

"That minority is you—females," he declared, elevating the tone of his voice.

Kiley went on to tell that the story said how several times last week similar amendments to other sections were defeated, but now every congresswoman, but one, suddenly rose to the amendments' defense. One congresswoman said that if the Civil Rights Bill passed without the protection of this amendment, white women would be at the bottom of the list in hiring after white men and Negro men and women. Another Congresswoman said we want this crumb of equality.

"The bill passed 168 to 133." Kiley declared.

"So, ladies, you now have a stake in this Civil Rights Bill we are reading about almost every day," Kiley summarized. "If this bill becomes law in a few years, when you are looking for a job, legally nobody will be able to tell you they are not hiring you because you are a woman."

Tammy, who was listening intently to Kiley's account of the story, spoke up before the teacher even asked if there were any questions.

"Mr. Kiley, do you think it is going to be that easy. Just pass this law, and immediately a woman is going to have the same chance at a job as a man?" she asked.

Kiley smiled; he had the type of class discussion he loved.

"No, probably not, Miss Clark. It will take time," Kiley admitted.

"But it will be the law, and sooner or later it will help women like you."

"Or our daughters," Marty yelled out with a sarcastic laugh.

"Well, that may be, Miss Burns," Kiley continued. "But this is a case of how sometimes something that is done for one purpose might benefit some other people."

ASSOCIATED PRESS, FEB. 10, 1964

> CLEVELAND – The Cleveland Board of Education approved a resolution today calling for the immediate integration of Negro pupils transported by bus to three East Side schools with predominantly white enrollments.

"What do you like about Jay?" Marty asked Tammy as the two girls walked through the Junior Miss section of the department store after school on Monday in search of some winter sale bargains

Tammy stopped suddenly and looked at her friend.

"What is this, another test to determine whether I really care about your friend?" the blond said with a smirk, but didn't hesitate to give Marty an answer.

"It's a lot of things, but I think what I like the most is the way he is always encouraging me to do things that sometimes even I'm not sure I can do. He's always telling me I'm smart and I can do things. After all the shit I got from Dave, that's different."

"Oh," Marty said as she turned her attention toward some blouses on a table with a sign proclaiming 50% off.

Tammy had sufficiently answered her friend's question, and it seemed Marty was satisfied, but the blond didn't stop talking.

"He has this strange sense of kindness that I have never seen in a guy. At least any guys I've ever known."

The blond kept talking.

"His face always lights up when he sees me. Sometimes he tries to hide it. I guess boys don't want you to think that they get all emotional about just seeing you, but I can tell. It's nice to know somebody feels that way about you."

Marty stopped looking at the clothes and turned to her friend. "Do you ever tell him that?" she asked.

"Of course not," Tammy said, flashing a sinister smile.

NEW YORK TIMES, FEB. 11, 1964

WASHINGTON – President Johnson renewed today his appeal to Congress for a program of hospital and nursing home care for the aged to be financed through Social Security.

Marty and Jane Snow were already sitting in a booth at HoJo's in their cheerleading uniforms when Jay walked in with Tammy after he drove her from the wrestling match on Tuesday night, where the girls had cheered.

"Do you have room for us?" Tammy said as she sat next to Jane without even waiting for an answer. Marty moved farther into the booth, making room for Jay to sit down on the other side, facing Tammy.

They sat for several minutes with Jay just listening as the girls monopolized the conversation with talk about how some girl Jay didn't even know had a fight with her boyfriend, whose name Jay also had never heard. Just then, three boys walked past the table.

"Hey, Jay," John Albanese, a junior back-up lineman on the football team, said without stopping as he walked past the table with two other juniors on the football team.

"Hey, guys," Jay said casually to his football teammates, who already were beyond the booth by the time Jay responded.

Jane watched the trio slide into a booth at the back of the restaurant, then spoke up.

"He doesn't wear underwear, you know," Jane said.

"Who?" Marty inquired.

"Albanese," Jane said.

"How the hell do you know that?" Jay asked with a stunned look.

"Judy Potter told me. She said Elaine Pezzi went out on a few dates with him, and she told Judy he didn't wear any underwear."

Jay started laughing.

"Is that what you girls do all the time? Talk about guys and whether they wear underwear," he said, continuing his laugh.

"Not just whether they wear underwear," Jane said with a sly smile.

"That's terrible," Jay said, trying to look serious.

"Yeah, right, and you guys never talk about us girls," Jane fired back. "Come on, I know guys talk as much about what they got off their date down at the lake as they do about football in the locker room," Jane countered.

Jay sat there with a defensive look on his face, with all three girls looking at him. Finally, he spoke.

"I guess some guys talk about that," Jay offered.

"And you don't?" Jane said.

"No," Jay said firmly without hesitation.

Jane looked at Jay and realized he was serious.

"Where did you find this guy?" she said, looking at Tammy.

"In the parking lot the first day of school," Tammy said with a laugh.

UNITED PRESS INTERNATIONAL, FEB. 14, 1964

NOTASULGA, Ala – Six Negroes were admitted to another empty Alabama school house today, but Gov. George C. Wallace hinted that the school might be closed, like another that was desegregated.

"Stan Williams called last night," Tammy said to Marty as they headed down the corridor after Kiley's Friday class.

"What did he want?" Marty asked about the guy who had graduated from Jefferson last year and was now a freshman at Brown.

"He said he heard I wasn't going out with Dave anymore, so he asked if I wanted to go to dinner tomorrow night."

"What did you say?" Marty asked.

"I said no." Tammy offered without showing any emotion.

"What did you use as an excuse?" Marty said, getting more and more curious about her friend's reason for not wanting to go out on a date with a college guy.

"I didn't really give him an excuse, I just said I didn't want to."

"You not wanting to go out with an Ivy League college guy. I mean, he must have found that a little strange. Didn't he push for a reason?"

"Yeah, kind of," Tammy said softly,

"What did you say to him?"

"I told him I was kind of going out with somebody and I didn't want him to feel bad."

"Wow, so is this thing with Jay officially serious now?"

"I don't know. I just enjoy being with him, and I know if I go out with somebody else, he's going to feel hurt."

"Is it that or are you afraid you might lose somebody who makes you feel comfortable?" Marty asked.

"Believe me, he doesn't make me feel comfortable," Tammy offered with a stern look at her friend.

UNITED PRESS INTERNATIONAL, FEB. 16, 1964

BOSTON – The National Association for the Advancement of Colored People pledged its full resources yesterday to defending any person prosecuted for participation in the Feb. 26 boycott of the city's public schools.

"What the hell is this?" Tony yelled out from the other side of the room. "I thought the Ed Sullivan Show was on at eight."

Tony wasn't even finished yelling when the voice came on while horses were still running down a race track.

"Good evening, ladies and Gentlemen. Tonight, live from Miami Beach, the Ed Sullivan Show." While the announcer was talking, The Ed Sullivan Show was being scripted over the front of the horse racing backdrop. "Now, from the stage of the Deauville Hotel, here he is .... Ed Sullivan," the announcer proclaimed. In a few seconds, Sullivan was on the screen, standing on a stage. Unlike in New York the previous Sunday, where it was a theater with a balcony, the first camera shot was from behind the audience, who were sitting on one level of chairs in what obviously was set up in a large room with a stage in front.

"Now this has happened again," Sullivan immediately declared. "Last Sunday on our show in New York, the Beatles played to the greatest TV audience that has ever been assembled in the history of American TV. Now tonight, here in Miami Beach, again the Beatles face a record-busting audience."

After a commercial, Sullivan was back on stage, and he didn't waste any time making the announcement everybody was waiting to hear: "Ladies and gentlemen, here are four of the nicest youngsters we have ever had on our stage.... The Beatles—Bring'em on."

The curtain opened, and there were Paul, George, and John in front with their guitars and Ringo in the back on a raised platform with his drums. They immediately started singing

> "*She loves you, yeah, yeah, yeah*
> *She loves you, yeah, yeah, yeah*"

While the New York audience had been virtually all older teenage girls, this was more of a mixed audience with older women, some very young girls, and several men. The Miami audience might not have been in a constant frenzy like the New York audience had been a week earlier, but the three girls in Dan's den still were mesmerized by the quartet. They sat with their eyes steadfast on the TV, Tammy and Marty on the couch, Jane on the floor with her back against the wall.

"I love his British accent," Marty injected into what was an amazingly quiet room considering there were eight teenagers scattered around it.

The quartet finished "She Loves You" and then sang "This Boy" followed by "All My Loving." When they finished the third song, they took a bow, and the camera immediately switched to Sullivan standing by himself on another part of the stage.

"Ladies and gentlemen, out in our audience tonight, the heavyweight champion of the World, Sonny Liston," Sullivan announced.

"Shit, he's big," Dan offered, "Cassius Clay is going to get killed."

Finally, after singer Mitzi Gaynor performed "It's Too Darn Hot" and a few other guests performed various actions and several commercials consumed about thirty minutes, the Beatles appeared back on the stage and sang "I Saw Her Standing There," "From Me to You," and "I Want to Hold Your Hand."

After they finished, they headed off the stage.

"That's it," said Tony while Sullivan was still on the screen. "I don't need to see any more commercials or hear Ed Sullivan telling everybody how much he appreciates their help."

On the TV, the show was ending with flamingos flying around at Hialeah Park as Marty raised herself off the couch and Tammy followed. Suddenly, she turned, looked up at Jay, and gave him a momentary kiss on the lips almost simultaneously with her getting up from the couch.

"See you tomorrow," she said as she stood in front of him. "I have to drive Marty and Jane home." Then she walked out of the room without saying another word.

Jay just sat back on the couch, not believing what had just happened. She actually showed a sign of affection without worrying if anybody would see it.

"Let's go. What the hell are you doing just sitting there?" Tony yelled as he looked back into the room from the hallway.

NEW YORK TIMES, FEB. 17, 1964

> WASHINGTON – Senator Everett McKinley Dirksen said today that the public accommodations section of the civil rights bill passed by the House last week was "much more acceptable" to him than the original version.

"Mr. Kiley. Does this mean the Civil Rights Bill is going to pass?" the dark-haired girl with the short cut hair that settled tightly around her ears, who sat at the desk in front of Jay, asked when Kiley began discussing the story about Dirksen saying the public accommodations section was more acceptable.

"It's a step in the right direction. But I think there's still a long way to go," Kiley offered.

NEW YORK TIMES, FEB. 18, 1964

> WASHINGTON – Secretary of Defense Robert S. McNamara has told members of Congress that the United States still hopes to withdraw most of its troops from South Vietnam before the end of 1965.

"Happy birthday," Jay said as Tony eased his way into Jay's car for the ride to school on Wednesday morning.

"How did you remember it was my birthday?" Tony said with a surprised look.

"Come on, I went to too many of your birthday parties when we were growing up to ever forget your birthday."

"Do you believe it? I'm eighteen. I have to register for the draft," Tony declared.

"Ya, but you're not going to have to worry about the draft. You're going to college. In yesterday's Times, McNamara said all this Vietnam shit will be over by the time we get out of college," Jay said as he drove off.

ASSOCIATED PRESS, FEB. 20, 1964

WASHINGTON – Sen. Richard Russell, D-GA, threw down the Southern gauntlet yesterday on the forthcoming civil rights battle saying, "We intend to fight this bill with all the vigor at our command.

"So, what do you think? Is President Johnson going to win this, or is Senator Russell?" Kiely asked his Thursday afternoon class.

Mike Stone jumped at the question.

"He's only a senator. A senator can't beat the President."

Kiley just smiled.

"Never underestimate the power of a U.S. Senator, especially somebody who has been around as long as Russell has," the teacher said.

UNITED PRESS INTERNATIONAL, FEB. 23, 1964

SAIGON – American and South Vietnamese military men believe they cannot win the war against the Communist Viet Cong until they extend the war to Communist North Vietnam, authoritative sources said yesterday.

Jay was pleasantly surprised when he answered the phone on Sunday morning, and it was Tammy.

"Hi, Marty called and asked if, rather than going to Dan's, we want to just come over to her house to watch the Beatles tonight."

"Sounds good to me," he said. "Besides, it's not a live show. It was taped two weeks ago in New York before they left on Friday to go back to England."

UNITED PRESS INTERNATIONAL, FEB 24, 1964

WASHINGTON – Sen. Jacob Javits, R-NY, said yesterday that with President Johnson's pressure, the Senate can produce the votes to halt a filibuster against the civil rights bill

—

Without even taking attendance, Kiley quickly opened his Monday morning class with a question.

"Did anybody read the story in the local paper about the girl from Greenvale being arrested down in Atlanta because she was demonstrating with some other students at a restaurant against segregation?" he asked.

A few hands up.

"Good, at least a few people were able to function this weekend, even if the Beatles were back in England. I think this brings what we've been reading about a little closer to home. I know sometimes the things we have been reading every day still seem a long way from our city, but this girl is just like you. She's a white girl from a suburban town, which is a lot like this city. Heck, her home is only about twenty miles from here, and she is eighteen years old. Some of you are already eighteen, and most of you will be eighteen sometime this year, so she's basically your age. She goes to Connecticut College for Women. It's a small private college in New London. Maybe one of you has even applied to it."

Jay immediately looked over to the other side of the room toward Tammy and pointed his finger in her direction as if to say, "You." He didn't think anybody had noticed his little gesture, but Kiley picked up on it.

"Who are you pointing at, Burke?" he asked.

Jay hesitated answering because he wasn't sure if Tammy had told anybody else that she had applied to Connecticut College. But Kiley was waiting for an answer, so he turned toward the front of the class, lowered his head, and quietly said, "Tammy."

Despite his low tone, Kiley heard the answer.

"You have applied to Connecticut College, Miss Clark?" Kiley asked, looking toward Tammy.

Jay was afraid to look toward Tammy, not sure if he would see a face raging with anger because he had revealed something she didn't want people to know. Or maybe she might be embarrassed because she was being singled out, and Jay was the reason she had suddenly become the center of unwanted attention. Either way, Jay figured she wasn't going to be happy. But when he finally looked over at her, she didn't seem angry or embarrassed.

"Yes, I have," she said without showing any emotion.

"Great and good luck with your application. It's a very good school," Kiley said, then went back to discussing the young woman from the nearby town.

"This girl was down in Atlanta for a college exchange program and saw how colored people are treated differently there," Kiley said. "She didn't think it was right, so she joined in the protest, knowing she could be arrested. A year from now, when most of you are her age, are you going to be willing to be arrested for something you think is unfair?

"Will you be willing to do something like this girl did? Her life in Greenvale wasn't being affected by colored people being refused service in a restaurant in Atlanta, yet she was willing to be arrested for something she felt was unfair."

"On the first day of school, I told you we are going to be studying the things that are happening now; things that might directly affect your lives more than stuff in the history textbooks. We have been reading the paper for six months now. We only have a few months left. I don't know what you think, but it seems some of the things we have been reading about are closer to your life now than they were on that first day of school in August."

NEW YORK TIMES, FEB. 25, 1964

MIAMI BEACH – Incredibly, the loud-mouthed, bragging, insulting youngster had been telling the truth all along. Cassius Clay won the world heavyweight title tonight when a bleeding Sonny Liston, his left shoulder injured, was unable to answer the bell for the seventh round.

Tony came bouncing down the front walk of his house while still trying to put on his ski parka before getting in Jay's car.

"Let's go," Jay yelled. "We are going to be late. If we get another late slip, we are going to get detention for a week."

"Sorry, I was talking to my father," Tony offered. "He went to that closed-circuit broadcast of the fight last night. He said it was amazing. Clay was so fast. He just floated around the ring. Nobody could believe Liston just sat there and didn't come out for the seventh round. My father said Clay just kept dancing around, hitting Liston with quick punches and never giving Liston a chance to hit him."

"Yeah, I've liked him since I saw him fighting in the 1960 Olympics," Jay said as he quickly drove away from Tony's house. "He's exciting. He's a big guy, but he doesn't look like the other heavyweights. He's something like six-three, and he's young. I think he's not that much older than us."

"Yeah, I think I read he's only twenty-two," Tony said.

"It's going to be fun watching him," Jay offered.

They drove for a few minutes without saying anything when Jay suddenly broke the silence.

"Oh, the Tufts coach called the other night," he said.

"For what?" Tony asked.

"Just checking on how I was doing and if I was still interested in Tufts?"

"What did you tell him?"

"I told him I'm still interested." Jay offered.

NEW YORK TIMES, FEB. 27, 1964

BOSTON – The Boston School Department said 20,571 pupils were absent yesterday in a boycott called by Negro leaders to protest alleged racial imbalance.

In a similar demonstration last June 18, 8,250 pupils had stayed out.

—

Kiley was on a roll, from the minute the bell sounded signaling the start of Thursday morning class. Like normal, he didn't bother taking any attendance and jumped right into the conversation.

"So why are people protesting against discrimination in education everywhere in the country? It wasn't Alabama or Mississippi this weekend; it was Boston. That's kind of close to home. Look at how quickly the situation has changed. In just eight months, the number of students involved in a boycott against an imbalance of education opportunities in Boston has more than doubled. Why does education stir emotions so much?" he asked.

Kiley looked around the room for somebody to respond. He looked at all the usual people who would start a discussion—Tammy, Marty, Jay, Russ Lawrence, Mike Stone—but nobody was offering anything.

Then, suddenly, a voice came from the back of the room.

"Because education is the ticket to a better future," Tony yelled. "Rich or poor, it doesn't matter. If you get a good education, you have a chance to go somewhere, to do something with your life. So, until everybody has the same education opportunities, there's no equality."

"Where did that come from?" Kiley asked, somewhat surprised that Tony would offer a thought-provoking response. "I am very impressed, Gemma."

"I didn't know, it probably wasn't those exact words, but it was something I read and started thinking about this year," Tony proclaimed.

"That twenty-five cents a week may be the best investment of your life, Gemma," Kiley said with a smile.

ELEVEN

UNITED PRESS INTERNATIONAL, MARCH 2, 1964

NEW YORK – The Rev. Martin Luther King Jr. said yesterday civil rights forces in the Senate should force continuous sessions if necessary to overcome the expected Southern filibuster against the pending bill.

Tammy and Jay were sitting on her living room couch watching "Arrest & Trial" in what, for a few weeks, had been a regular Sunday night session of watching TV and making out while Tammy's parents were participating in a Sunday night mixed bowling league. His right hand had been working its way down to her lower back. When it reached the waistband of her jeans, he moved his hand around to the front of her body, unsnapped the jeans, edged his fingers inside the top of her silk panties, and was working them down the front of her body. He hesitated for a second when he touched her pubic hair, but his fingers quickly continued their downward exploration.

Suddenly, Tammy pulled away from his embrace and moved to the far side of the couch.

"So do you think the Civil Rights forces can stop a Senate filibuster?" she asked.

"WHAT?" Jay declared in an aggravated tone.

"Do you think the civil rights forces can stop a filibuster?" she repeated.

"I know what you said, I just don't know why you said it now," Jay offered.

Tammy just smiled.

Jay looked at the blond with a stunned and dejected expression and tried to move back in close to her. But Tammy moved farther away from him. Suddenly, a smile came over his face.

"Oh, I see. Is this sudden interest in the Civil Rights Bill your way of telling me to cool down?" he asked.

"Maybe," she said

"Sorry, I won't try that again," Jay offered in an apologetic tone.

She looked at him with a smile firmly planted on her face.

"Yes, you will," she declared.

UNITED PRESS INTERNATIONAL, MARCH 4, 1964

WASHINGTON – Secretary of State Dean Rusk said yesterday that the administration believes the anti-communist war in South Vietnam can be won even though it is "a mean, frustrating and difficult struggle."

Before Kiley could even offer his usual, "Good morning," to start his Wednesday class, Mike Stone blurted out a question.

"Mr. Kiley, sometimes I don't think they know what they are doing in Vietnam. Three months ago, some general said that by 1965, all the troops would be out of Vietnam. Then, about a month later, McNamara says the war is going so badly that the US may not be able to pull out its troops by 1965. Now, Rush said the administration believes the war can be won, but it's a difficult struggle. What are they trying to say? Do they know what they are doing?"

"I think a lot of people are starting to ask that same question," Kiley responded.

NEW YORK TIMES, MARCH 9, 1964

WASHINGTON – The Supreme Court held today that a public official cannot recover libel damages for criticism of his official performance unless he proves that the statement was made with deliberate malice.

—

Kiley didn't hesitate to let the Tuesday morning class know what he felt was the most important item in the Times on this day.

"Alright, let's get going," he declared, not even taking time to offer his usual jovial class warm-up banter. "Take a look at this story here on the right-hand side of the front page," Kiley said, pointing to the one-column story with the headline "High Court Curbs Public Officials in Libel Actions."

"This story is about freedom of the press, and that's basically what this course is all about," Kiley declared.

He then dedicated the entire fifty-minute class to a discussion of why it was important that the Supreme Court ruled the New York Times did not have to pay libel damages for accurately reporting the actions of some Alabama officials.

"I think this ruling will widen press freedom in covering the segregation issues in the South, and that's important," Kiley offered.

NEW YORK TIMES, MARCH 9, 1964

HOA HAO, South Vietnam – Secretary of Defense Robert S. McNamara barnstormed the countryside today to dramatize America's commitment to support Maj. Gen. Nguyen Khanh and his new Government in their anti-Communist war effort.

Jay purposely waited in his seat, fiddling with his copy of the Times after the bell sounded, ending Kiley's class, and watched Tammy, Marty, and Jane Snow head into the corridor together. Finally, he left the classroom by himself and followed a few yards behind the three girls as they walked down the corridor. But when the other two girls broke away from the blond, Jay quickened his pace to move closer to Tammy.

"Hey, do you have a minute?" he said as he came up behind her.

She stopped and turned.

"Do I have a minute? Is that all the time you want to spend with me?" she said with her typical easy laugh.

Jay fashioned a slight laugh, but it was obvious he had something on his mind that he needed to say.

"Will you go to the prom with me?" he blurted out without wasting time with small talk as a lead-up to his question.

She stared at him with a questioning look, causing Jay's heart to skip a beat. It wasn't the immediate acceptance he had hoped for. Finally, she spoke while flashing a soft smile.

"The prom, God, that's three months away. I hadn't really thought about it," she said.

Jay could feel the palms of his hands sweating.

"I know it's a long way away, and who knows what will happen between now and then. But I heard a few guys saying their girlfriends were already talking about it. So, I figured I would ask you before somebody else did," he said.

Tammy just broadened her smile, "Who else is going to ask me?" she said.

Jay stood with that lost puppy-dog look he gets every so often when he doesn't have an immediate answer to one of Tammy's questions.

"I don't know. There probably are a lot of guys who would want to go to the prom with you."

"Not really," she said. "But, it's sweet of you to think so. Sure, I will go with you."

NEW YORK TIMES, MARCH 13, 1964

NEW YORK – Thousands of demonstrators, many of them homeowners from Brooklyn, the Bronx and Queens marched on the Board of Education and city hall yesterday, shouting that they wanted to preserve the tradition of neighborhood schools.

—

"Most of the demonstrations we have been reading about have been people demonstrating to bring about equality in education," Kiley offered as his opening salvo for his Friday afternoon class. "They have a plan in New York that will solve some of the racial imbalance in the schools, but these people are demonstrating against it. Why do you think that's happening?"

Usually, Kiley waited for somebody to offer a response, but this time he immediately turned toward Tammy on the left side of the room.

"Miss Clark, what do you think?"

Tammy didn't hesitate to offer her opinion.

"It is going to inconvenience their lives," she said. "It would be an inconvenience for their kids to go to a school outside their neighborhoods. A lot of people are all for change, until the change makes their life more difficult."

"That might be a little cynical, Miss Clark, but I can't say you're wrong," Kiley offered.

UNITED PRESS INTERNATIONAL, MARCH 14, 1964

SAIGON – The United States and South Vietnam were reported yesterday to have reached an agreement in principle for carrying the war against Communist rebels into North Vietnam with clandestine sabotage and guerrilla attacks.

"Jay, it's for you," his mother yelled from downstairs about the Saturday morning phone call. Jay reached over and picked up the extension phone on the side of his bed.

"I'm going to New York City to study dance," the voice on the phone shouted out without even identifying herself. Jay, however, immediately knew it was Marty.

"Hey, Marty, what are you talking about? When are you going to New York?"

"Next year," she shouted.

"You mean, for college?" Jay asked, now fully engrossed in the conversation.

"Yeah, I'm going to Hunter College," she said, still talking in an elevated, fast-paced tone.

"When did all this happen?" Jay inquired. "You never told me you applied to a school in New York City. I thought you told me your parents would never pay for you to go to college in New York."

"I know I didn't want to say anything because I figured it would never happen," Marty continued, her voice now starting to return to a normal tone. "But after we talked that day about New York and you said I shouldn't give up on my dream that easily, I went home and just casually mentioned it to my parents. They said if that's what I wanted to do, I should find out about it. I was shocked that they would even let me think about it. So, I talked to my guidance counselor, and she looked into it. She found out they just started a new dance company at Hunter College, so I applied. My acceptance came in this morning's mail. When I showed it to my parents, they said, 'If that's what you want, somehow, we will find a way to pay for it.' My father said he would work more overtime. I never thought they would understand how much this means to me."

Jay could sense she was suddenly having a problem talking.

"Are you crying?" he asked.

"Yeah, kind of," Marty admitted.

"I can't believe you didn't tell me about this. Did Tammy know you applied?"

"Yeah, but she was the only one besides my parents. Don't be mad at her for not telling you. I told her not to tell anybody, even you. I never figured I would get in, and I didn't want to feel like a fool when everybody knew I was rejected.

"Don't worry, I'm not mad at her, I'm happy for you," Jay replied. "Did you call Tammy and tell her you have been accepted?"

"No, you're the first person I called," she answered.

UNITED PRESS INTERNATIONAL, MARCH 16, 1964

> SAIGON – Six more Americans were killed in combat against Communist guerrillas yesterday and Saturday when Viet Cong gunners shot down two U.S. Army aircraft. The casualties brought the number of Americans killed in South Vietnam to 199 since the United States began taking an active part in the anti-Communist war in 1961.

Jay finally found Tammy sitting by herself in the front row of the otherwise empty auditorium about thirty minutes after the final bell on Monday afternoon.

"Hey, where have you been? I've been looking for you," he said while walking down the aisle toward the front row.

She turned toward Jay as he approached, and he immediately could see she had been crying.

"Wow, what's wrong?" he said, quickly moving into the seat next to her.

"It's really not a big thing," she said, trying to regain her composure. "When we were standing in the hall after school, Karen Powers told me there was a piece in the local paper about Joe Fuller being killed in some stupid accident down in Cuba."

Jay had no idea who Tammy was talking about.

"Who is he and what was he doing in Cuba?" Jay asked.

Tammy whipped a few tears from her eyes and turned toward Jay.

"He graduated from here two years ago. He was a hockey player, and he went out with Joyce Baker. She was a cheerleader who graduated last year. Joe was wild. He always seemed to be getting in trouble, but Joyce told me he really was a good guy. I think his family had money because they lived in one of those big houses near the water over on your side of the city. His parents wanted him to go to college, but he didn't want to have anything to do with college, so he joined the Navy right after he graduated. Joyce told me last year that she thought it was his way of rebelling against his family. Officially, they broke up when Joe went into the

Navy, but I know Joyce still loved him. She's beautiful, but last year she never really went out with anybody. She is in college this year, but I heard she still wasn't going out with anybody. I guess Joe was stationed at that Navy base down in Cuba. I didn't really know him that well, but I feel so bad for Joyce. I just needed to get away from everybody for a few minutes, so I came down here."

Jay was amazed by the story.

"So, what happened?" Jay asked, caring more about consoling Tammy than finding out the details of the death of somebody he didn't know.

"I don't know for sure. Karen said the story in the paper said something about Joe and some other guys wandered into a mine field that's near the base, and a mine exploded. I guess it killed Joe and another guy."

"That's terrible," Jay said as he moved his position in the wooden auditorium chair so that he could look straight at Tammy.

But she continued just facing forward, looking at an empty stage without saying a word. So, Jay picked up the conversation.

"When you think a guy who was sitting here just two years ago was killed thousands of miles away from here. It's a little scary," Jay continued. "You know it's strange. I stopped in to see Mr. Kiley after the last period. He was reading the Times, and just off the top of his head, he said, 'You know someday a member of your class could be killed in this stupid war.' What happened to this guy had nothing to do with Vietnam, but it makes you think it can be a dangerous world out there. I don't want to grow up. I just want to stay here. It's nice and safe here."

Suddenly, Tammy turned her head and looked straight into Jay's eyes.

"No, you don't," she said, her expression having changed from a look of sorrow to her soft smile. "There are no more challenges for you here," she added. "You're ready to meet new people and take on new challenges a long way from here."

NEW YORK TIMES, MARCH 18, 1964

WASHINGTON – The White House announced plans to provide additional military and economic assistance to a new South Vietnamese plan to combat the Communist Viet Cong guerrilla insurgency.

"The Tuft's coach called last night and said it's not official yet, but it looks like I'm getting in," Jay said to Tammy as they walked toward their homerooms Wednesday morning.

"That's great," Tammy said without breaking a stride or even turning her head toward Jay.

She didn't seem all that interested in talking about college, so Jay tried to push the issue by asking about the status of her applications.

"How about you? Heard anything?" he asked.

"The UMass acceptance came last week," she said in a matter-of-fact tone while still walking.

"Why didn't you tell me?" Jay said, stopping and turning completely in Tammy's direction. He gently grabbed her left arm and slowly moved her out of the middle of the corridor to the wall a few yards down from the door to her home room.

"It's no big thing, I knew I was getting in," she said, finally looking into Jay's eyes.

"When do the Wellesley and Connecticut College acceptances come out?" Jay asked.

"I don't know, sometime in the next few weeks. But I don't have any chance of getting into either of them. I'll see you," she said as she broke away from Jay's gentle grip on her arm and began walking into her homeroom.

NEW YORK TIMES, MARCH 21

WASHINGTON – A Southern spokesman accused New York's two Senators today of trying to force the racial integration of schools in the South while preserving "de facto" segregation in New York City schools.

Senator James O. Eastland, a Democrat of Mississippi, made the charge in debating the civil rights bill with Senators Jacob K. Javits and Kenneth B. Keating, New York Republicans.

Jay was only partially awake when he heard the phone. He let it ring a few times, figuring his mother would answer it downstairs. But after a few more rings, he figured she had gone out to do some Saturday morning shopping, so he reached across his bed and answered.

"Want to take me to breakfast?" the voice said as soon as Jay said hello.

"Wow, this is a pleasant way to wake up on Saturday morning. I'll be there in twenty minutes," he said to Tammy.

NEW YORK TIMES, MARCH 21

WASHINGTON – Some Senators are becoming increasingly restive over Communist gains in South Vietnam and are pressing for radical changes in United States policy

Tammy didn't even give Jay a chance to get out of his car before she was out the front door of her house and sitting in the passenger seat of Jay's car. Jay looked at her and knew something was bothering her.

"Are you okay?" he asked.

"Yeah, I'm fine. Let's just go," she snapped.

"Where do you want to eat?" he asked.

"I don't care, just go," she snapped again.

Jay knew enough to stop asking questions or even try to initiate a conversation. So, he just drove down Tammy's Street out onto the main street that leads toward the high school. He didn't say a word, just watched her fiddling with the knobs on the radio, changing stations. Finally, she broke the silence.

"I'm not getting into Wellesley," she proclaimed

"How do you know? I thought the acceptances didn't come out for another week," Jay said in rebuttal.

Tammy didn't look at him as she answered the question.

"The official word isn't sent out until then, but they send out these letters that tell you what your prospect is of being admitted, and mine isn't good."

"That shits," Jay yelled as he pulled the car over to the side of the road and sat there banging on the steering wheel.

"You're more upset about this than I am," Tammy said, looking at him. "It's no big thing; I knew I didn't have much chance of getting in."

Jay sat there still seething.

"I know that's what you said, but I thought once they realized how special you are, you would be a cinch to get in," he declared. "They don't know who they are missing."

"They know," she said while flashing her soft smile.

She sat there just looking at him for a few seconds, then reached her arms around his neck, pulled her face close to his, and gave him a kiss on his lips.

"Thank you," she said after her lips parted from his.

The kiss certainly was a welcome surprise, but Jay was even more interested in keeping Tammy in an optimistic mood.

"You still have to hear from Conn College," he said.

"That's going to be the same thing," the blond said, trying to foster a smile. "Come on, get this car moving, I'm hungry."

NEW YORK TIMES, MARCH 23, 1964

WASHINGTON – Senate leaders hope to reach the first milestone this week in the long march toward the passage of civil rights legislation. Southerners who have held the floor for 13 days have indicated that they may ease up on the talk and permit a preliminary vote.

—

"So, do you think the Senate is finally going to pass some of the civil rights legislation?" Kiley asked as the opening salvo for his Monday morning class.

"I think it's still a long shot, but at least they may end the filibuster," Tony offered from the back of the room.

Kiley flashed a smile.

"Gemma, you amaze me more and more every week," the teacher offered about Tony's assessment of the critical Senate action.

NEW YORK TIMES, MARCH 26, 1964

WASHINGTON – The Senate finally got squared away today for the formal civil rights battle as the bipartisan managers of the bill closed two and a half weeks of preliminary skirmishing with two easy victories.

Jay and Tammy were sitting by themselves in a booth at HoJo's on Friday night after having seen "Cleopatra" at a movie theater in the city.

"I can't believe nobody is here," Jay said as he looked around and didn't see any of their Jefferson classmates.

"It's GOOD FRIDAY," Tammy declared, "Everybody is probably at church. In fact, I was a little surprised when you asked me to go to the movies rather than going to church tonight."

"I had enough years of Stations of the Cross on Good Friday," Jay declared. "I will go to Mass with my mother on Easter. That will be enough church for me."

Tammy sensed Jay didn't want to discuss his Catholic upbringing, so she changed the subject.

"How is baseball practice going?" she asked.

"Okay, but I know I'm not going to play in many of the real games," he offered.

"I don't understand, "Why aren't you going to play in the games?" she asked with a puzzling look.

He looked at her and smiled. He knew he could try explaining that he is a pitcher and this year's Jefferson baseball team was loaded with pitching depth. But he knew, with her limited understanding of sports in general, she probably wouldn't know what pitching depth meant, so he simply stated.

"I'm really not that good at baseball," he declared.

"Then why even be on the baseball team and spend all this time going to practice every day?" she asked.

Jay's answer puzzled the blond.

"I don't know," he offered. "I guess I'm starting to realize that for me, playing sports is about more than just winning games. I mean, winning a championship in football was amazing, and now football might help me get into a great college. But I also enjoy just being part of a team. Even if it's not in my best sport I can still do my part to help the team."

Tammy sat there and didn't say a word for several minutes, just looking at Jay's face as he ate his ice cream sundae. Finally, she broke the silence.

"You really like the pressure of knowing people are depending on you, don't you?" Tammy asked.

Jay took the spoon away from his mouth and looked at the blond.

"I've never thought about it, but I guess so," he concluded.

"Another benefit of playing sports that girls don't have," Tammy said while flashing a sarcastic smile.

"Maybe someday" was the only response Jay could offer. He looked over at Tammy's face, his eyes gazing directly into her eyes. He was feeling guilty of the advantages his masculinity was giving him, but he still asked the question.

"You probably don't want to go to the lake?" he probed.

She looked at him with her soft smile.

"Yes, I do," she professed.

NEW YORK TIMES, MARCH 30, 1964

> Washington – Secretary of Defense Robert S. McNamara said yesterday that the United States will pay nearly a million dollars a week to help support a program under which South Vietnam will draft up to 50,000 men for its armed forces.

"Just let me tell my parents we are going to Ho Jo's," Tammy said to Jay as they walked into her house early Monday night. "I'm sure they're in the living room watching the news."

Like Tammy expected, her parents were sitting on the living room couch, watching Walter Cronkite on the CBS Evening News when the two teenagers walked into the room.

"Mom, you don't have to worry about me for dinner, Jay and I are going to HoJo's," Tammy said to her mother after she and Jay had barely taken a few steps into her living room.

"Have fun," Mrs. Clark offered without taking her eyes off the TV screen.

Jay and Tammy were headed back out of the room when Tammy suddenly stopped and looked back at the TV.

"Do you think there ever will be a woman broadcasting the national evening news?" she asked Jay.

"I have never thought about it," Jay offered.

"WHY NOT?" Tammy shot back.

Her angry retort threw him on the defensive. So much for the hassle-free trip to HoJo's for a cheeseburger, he thought to himself, but then offered a reply.

"I don't know, all we ever see are guys," he said. "There's Cronkite on CBS; Huntley and Brinkley on NBC, and that guy Cochran on ABC."

"I know." Tammy agreed, "But does that mean there can't be a woman. I mean, if a woman can be president someday, why can't a woman be on the Evening News?"

"Well, you did a great job arguing with Vinny about why a

woman could be President," Jay offered. "Maybe you should bring it up in Kiley's class tomorrow."

"Maybe I will," she proclaimed.

"Good luck, Mr. Kiley," Jay whispered.

"WHAT!!" She spoke.

"Nothing, Nothing," Jay responded, trying to get out of the house without any further discussion.

TWELVE

NEW YORK TIMES, APRIL 1, 1964

> WASHINGTON – The Senate's bipartisan supporters of the civil rights bill began today their promised title-by-title analysis of the measure with an attack on discrimination in voting.

Jay immediately saw the envelope lying with the rest of the mail when he walked in his front door on Wednesday. It was almost six o'clock by the time he had taken a shower after baseball practice and driven home. Sometimes his mother was home by six, but obviously tonight she was working late. In a way, he had hoped she would be the first one home so she could pick up the envelope. It was a big white envelope with a Tufts University logo on the upper left corner. He had shown her the UMass acceptance and told her that when a big envelope came from a college, it was good news because it also contained all the information about a student's acceptance at the college. Rejection letters, he had told her, came in small envelopes. So, if she had come in the door first, she would have seen the big envelope, and Jay figured that would have made her happy, knowing her son had been accepted at what people were telling her was a very prestigious college. It was the type of dream she and Jay's father always had for their son, even if, when they were raising him, they probably didn't even know there was a college named Tufts. Jay picked up the envelope but didn't open it. It should have been one of the happiest days of his life, but his emotions were tempered. First, it wasn't a total surprise because most of the suspense had been taken out of waiting for acceptance, because the football coach had told him he was a virtual lock. Apparently, one of their other quarterback recruits had decided to go to Brown. But the letter made it official, he was getting into a great school because he was a football player, and Tammy was being rejected at Wellesley because she didn't have a coach pulling for her. It wasn't fair, he had thought several times, but then he was also grateful that he was a football player. He thought about calling Tammy, but it didn't seem right for him to be so happy. So, he took the envelope, put it on the kitchen table so his mother could see it when she came home, and headed upstairs to finish writing the weekly report for Kiley's class.

NEW YORK TIMES, APRIL 2, 1964

> SAIGON, South Vietnam – South Vietnam has reached an understanding with the leader of right-wing forces in Laos that will enable Vietnamese troops to strike inside Laos against Communist guerrilla bases and supply routes, informed sources reported.

The phone rang just as Jay was about to leave the house for the drive to school on Thursday morning. He was already a few minutes later than usual leaving to pick up Tony, so he was thinking about not answering. But maybe it was his mother who had forgotten something and was calling from work.

"Hello," he yelled into the phone.

"So did you get anything?" he heard Tammy's voice asking without even saying hello.

Defensively, he replied, "Oh, yeah, I got accepted at Tufts."

"Why didn't you call me?" she bellowed.

Now he was really feeling defensive.

"I don't know. I got home late from practice, and I didn't want to bother you," he said.

The feeble excuses didn't fool her.

"What did you think? Because I didn't get accepted at Wellesley, I'm going to be mad at you for getting into Tufts? Come on, give me more credit than that," she said.

Now Jay felt bad that he hadn't called her. He would have loved to have shared the good news with her last night, but he was worried it might make her feel bad. He knew she would never say anything, but he wanted to spare her even a few minutes of anxiety.

"It's just not fair," he said. "I know the only reason I got in was because of football. You are smarter than I am. You should have gotten into every college you applied to."

The blond wasn't going to let him diminish the significance of his acceptance.

"First of all, I'm not smarter than you, and besides, I'm not sure, even if I had gotten into Wellesley, that it would have been the place for me. It's a little stuffy," she said.

"I know that's how I feel about Tufts," he said. "Hey, I'd better get going. I'm already late picking up Tony."

"Yeah, I'll see you in school," she said.

Jay was starting to hang up the phone, but he heard Tammy was still on the line, so he didn't put the phone down.

"Oh, by the way, I got into Connecticut College," she said in a low tone.

Jay quickly put the phone completely back to his ear.

"What?" he shouted into the phone. "You are making me feel bad about not telling you about Tufts, but you didn't tell me about that. You're a ball buster."

She was silent for a few seconds, but finally she said.

"Sorry, I was waiting for you to call me last night, and when you didn't, I was afraid something had gone wrong with Tufts at the last minute. Plus, I'm still surprised I got in. I guess my mother's friend had more influence with the admission office than I thought."

Jay jumped on her self-deprecation.

"You got in on your own," he declared without hesitation. "You didn't need a coach pushing for you like I did. So, are you going to go to Conn?"

"I don't know, we'll see. It's more expensive than UMass, and it might be a little stuffy for me. Now get going. I don't want Tony pissed at me for making you late. We'll talk about it."

"Oh yeah, we will talk about it," Jay declared.

NEW YORK TIMES, APRIL 9, 1964

> NEW YORK – Civil rights proponents are planning a dramatic demonstration for the first days of the World's Fair which opens April 12.

The Friday afternoon class was winding down when Kiley changed the subject from the debate of whether holding protests at the World's Fair would help or hurt the civil rights movement.

"I just want to mention something I saw in the Boston Globe this morning. It was about a speech Ted Kennedy gave on the Senate floor yesterday, trying to gain support for the civil rights bill. He said his brother was the first US President to state publicly that segregation was morally wrong. He said his brother's heart and soul are in this bill. That if President Kennedy's life and death had a meaning, it was that we should not hate but love one another. We should use our powers not to create conditions of oppression that lead to violence, but conditions of freedom that lead to peace. I know it's getting late in the school year, and as I have said, most of you are doing fine in this class. So, you don't need any extra credit. But I would be interested in what some of you think about what Senator Kennedy said about how much of President Kennedy's view of what America should be is in the Civil Rights Bill. It only needs to be a few hundred words of your thoughts. Give it to me on Monday. It's worth five extra points on your average."

Just then, the bell rang.

"Okay, have a good weekend," the teacher yelled, trying to be heard above the sound of thirty-plus students rushing for the door.

Tammy waited at the door for Jay to come from the other side of the room.

"Want to come over to my house and work on that report tonight?" she said to Jay as soon as they started walking down the corridor.

Jay looked over at the blond with a surprised expression.

"How do you know I'm going to do that report?" he asked. "You are the one always saying I already have an A in Kiley's class."

Tammy looked at him and, in a sarcastic tone, offered:

"Yeah, right, you not doing a report on Kennedy. That's a joke. Why don't you just come right over after your baseball game."

NEW YORK TIMES, APRIL 9, 1964

WASHINGTON -The House of Representatives gave President Johnson's legislative program a lift early today by passing an election-year farm bill and authorizing a nationwide food stamp plan to aid needy families.

"What did you write about Kennedy's view of what America would be in the Civil Rights Bill?" Tammy asked Jay as he sat at her kitchen table using her portable typewriter to write his paper for Kiley's class.

"I just wrote about how, in a college speech last spring, Kennedy said, 'All of us do not have equal talents, but all of us should have equal opportunity to develop those talents.' I think that's what he felt a Civil Rights law would do."

"What do you think?" he asked.

Tammy looked at him and, while flashing her easy smile, declared, "Your A in Kiley's class is safe."

ASSOCIATED PRESS, APRIL 14, 1964

HOLLYWOOD – Sidney Poitier, the hymn-singing Baptist, who helped nuns build a Catholic Church in "Lilies of the Field," won a best actor Oscar last night to become the first Negro to receive a top academy award.

Jay was hoping Tammy was still in the main lobby as he raced out of the locker room. He had left her there talking with some other kids about fifteen minutes earlier because, even though it had been raining all day, he figured Coach Horton would still have the pitchers do some throwing in the gym. But when he got to the gym, Horton said he thought a day off would be good for everybody. When he heard that, Jay didn't waste any time rushing out of the locker room and heading back up to the lobby. A smile came to his face when he saw Tammy standing with Karen Powers near the phone booth.

"Hey, we don't have practice," Jay yelled about ten yards before he was within normal speaking distance. "Do you want a ride home? It's still raining out."

Tammy turned with a smile.

"I know, Karen was just going to call her mother and see if she could pick us up. But we'll take a ride with you. You don't mind giving Karen a ride, do you?"

"Of course not, if she doesn't mind sitting in the middle next to the shift," Jay said, excited he had caught the blond before she left the school.

"I'll sit next to the shift. I'm used to it," Tammy said with a laugh.

NEW YORK TIMES, APRIL 14, 1964

NEW YORK – Henry Cabot Lodge has warned in a statement made public today that arguments being advanced for the neutralization of South Vietnam are "woolly and deceptive."

—

It had been raining all day, but it really started picking up intensity just as Jay and Tammy began driving away from Karen's house. It was only about twenty-five feet from the street where Jay parked his car to the back door of Tammy's house, but by the time they walked into the kitchen, they both were dripping wet.

"God, I can't believe how much it rained. My sweater is soaked," Tammy said.

"I know, my shirt and my pants are soaked," Jay added.

"I have to get out of these clothes," Tammy declared as she headed for the stairs.

"Go ahead, I'll wait here. I don't want to go into the living room and get everything wet," Jay said.

Tammy looked back toward Jay as she started up the stairs.

"Come with me," Tammy offered.

Jay's pulse suddenly jumped several beats, but he was tentative about accepting Tammy's offer.

"Where's your mother?" he asked.

"She's in the city, and my father is at work," the blond said without even looking back at Jay.

Jay didn't ask any more questions and quickly began following her up the stairs. When they reached the top of the stairs, she led the way into her bedroom. He had never actually been in a teenage girl's bedroom, but it looked a lot like what he had seen in some movies. There was a full-size bed in the middle of the room covered by a pink spread with two stuffed animals sitting on pillows at the head of the bed. He could feel his hands starting to tremble with excitement.

"Isn't that cute? You still love your stuffed animals," Jay said, trying to hide his nervousness with humor.

"That's my mother," Tammy said with a smirk. "I never make my bed before I go to school, but she never leaves the house without making sure all the beds in the house are made. She always puts those stuffed animals on my bed. I guess it makes her think

I'm still her little girl," Tammy said as she reached over, took the stuffed animals off the bed, and threw them on the chair in front of a dressing table on the far side of the room.

She then moved over to the front of a bureau. Jay figured she was going to take some clothes out of the bureau and head to the bathroom to change. Instead, she stood with her back toward Jay and began pulling her wet sweater over her head. Finally, she completely took it off and threw it on the floor beside her. The rain had soaked through her sweater, so her white blouse was also dripping wet. Once again, Jay thought the blond would reach into her bureau for a dry shirt and head to the bathroom to change, but instead she stayed in front of the dressing table and, without turning around, began methodically unbuttoning the front of the blouse. Then she unbuttoned the cuffs of the sleeves. When she finished, she slipped the wet garment off her shoulders and, like the sweater, threw it on the floor. Jay's nerves quickened as he stood looking at her bra strap across her bare back. His eyes then glanced down to her plaid skirt and brown knee socks. Her bold acts caught him by surprise, but he figured she definitely now would pull out a sweat-shirt and or something and put it on. Instead, still not turning to look at Jay, she unbuttoned the waistband of her skirt and let it fall to the floor. Suddenly, she turned. He tried to stay composed as he looked at her wearing nothing but a white bra, white panties, and brown knee socks.

"Why don't you get out of those wet clothes?" she said as she started moving toward him.

He wasn't sure what to think about her boldness, but he didn't hesitate to unbutton his short-sleeved madras shirt. By now, Tammy was standing in front of him as he took off the shirt and the white T-shirt he wore underneath.

"Aren't your pants wet too?" she said, while standing in front of him in her underwear.

Jay didn't need any more instructions. He unblocked his belt and the waistband on his chinos, letting the pants fall to the floor. Tammy moved close to him and put her arms around him while putting her head on his right shoulder. He hugged her, moved his face toward hers on his shoulder, and kissed her cheek. Then he worked his hands down to the two clasps on her bra and unhooked them. She moved her head up to his face as he slipped the loosened bra off her shoulders. They stood there in their nakedness to their waists, kissing for a few minutes, when Jay started working his hands down her back to the top of her panties. He slowly slid both hands inside down to her apple-cheeked ass. He held it firmly for a few seconds, but then moved his hands back up to the top of the panties. He put his hands on the thin wristband and slid it slightly down. But then he stopped and looked down into her eyes.

"It's okay," she said softly.

He bent his knees slightly and started pulling the panties down, moving his head down along the front of her naked body. When the panties reached the bottom of her thighs, he released his grip on them, and they fell to the ground on their own. As she stepped away from the panties lying on the floor, Jay pulled down his white jockey shorts and let them fall to the floor. She moved to him, and they stood there in a tight embrace, he totally naked; she naked except for her knee socks. They kissed and squeezed their bodies together for a few minutes before Tammy broke from his grasp.

"I don't need these," she said as she reached down, removed her knee socks one by one, before pulling back the spread on her bed and sliding her fully naked body onto the bed and under a sheet.

Jay followed, pulling back the sheet and moving on top of her.

NEW YORK TIMES, APRIL 15, 1964

WASHINGTON – The bipartisan floor managers of the civil rights bill said tonight that illegal and unruly demonstrations were hurting their efforts to get Senate passage of the bill.

—

"I went all the way with Jay," Tammy said as she and Marty were walking toward the parking lot after school on Wednesday.

Marty stopped suddenly, but she didn't look all that surprised.

"When?" she asked.

"Yesterday," Tammy offered as she stopped.

Marty fired back with another question.

"Where?"

"In my bedroom," Tammy said while not looking directly at her friend.

"Oh my God, you live dangerously," Marty declared.

Finally, Tammy turned directly toward her friend.

"No, I knew my mother was in the city to meet some friends for dinner, and it was right after school, so my father wasn't going to be home for a few hours," she said.

Marty looked at her friend and flashed a little laugh.

"Hey, when I asked you to be nice to him, I didn't mean that nice," Marty said, increasing her laugh.

Tammy started walking again, and Marty followed right next to her, not wanting to miss any of the retelling of the deed.

"I figured, why wait?" Tammy said. "Everybody is talking about doing it after the prom. What's the difference between now and two months from now? You want the first time to be with somebody you care about."

"Wait, it was your first time?" Marty said with a surprised look as she again stopped walking.

Tammy stopped and looked at her friend with a stern expression

"Yes, it was my first time. What did you think?" Tammy retorted.

"I didn't know, you never said," Marty said, shrugging her shoulders. "But I just figured between Dave and the guys down at the beach. You know, they were all older."

Tammy's face broke into a smile.

"Believe me, some of those guys might have gotten their hands in my pants, but they never got my pants off."

Marty hesitated a few seconds, but she had to ask.

"Well?" she said.

"Well, what?" Tammy asked, knowing exactly what her friend was asking.

"You know what?" Marty said, knowing her friend was now teasing her by holding out on a blow-by-blow description of her love-making with Jay.

"Let's just say your friend has either read a lot of books or he has done it before. He knew what he was doing. It was very, very nice," Tammy said with a sly smile as she turned and resumed walking toward the parking lot.

ASSOCIATED PRESS, APRIL 19, 1964

GO DEN, VIETNAM – Despite two and a half years of Intensive American economic and military support for South Vietnam, the Viet Cong enemy has gained steadily and dangerously in key areas.

"Hey, do you want to go to 11 o'clock mass, then take a ride to the beach?" Jay asked as soon as Tammy answered the phone.

He could detect a slight laugh on the other end of the phone.

"My parents have already left to go to my aunt's. You don't have to worry about trying to impress them with that taking me to church thing," she answered. "Let's just go right to the beach. It's nice out."

He actually did want to go to mass. He still possessed some of that "Catholics go to mass every Sunday" feeling he had grown up with, but he wasn't going to argue if she wanted to go right to the beach. Thirty minutes later, they were driving with the top down on the Healey and the sun shining on an abnormally warm mid-April day.

"Marty's going out with somebody," Tammy declared as she and Jay headed down the road toward the beach.

"With who?" he asked Tammy.

"All I know is his name is Ron. He's not from Jefferson, so I don't really know him. I just know she went to the movies with him Friday night."

"She has gone out with guys before," Jay said, feeling a little hurt that Marty hadn't even told him she had a date for Friday night.

"I know, but she called me yesterday morning to tell me about the date. She never calls me just to talk about a date."

ASSOCIATED PRESS, APRIL 22, 1964

WASHINGTON – Senate Republican leader Everett M. Dirksen of Illinois introduced his key amendment to the job section of the civil rights bill yesterday and said he believes it will help to pass the measure.

"Dirksen is a Republican, so why is he trying to help pass Johnson's Civil Rights Bill? Won't that make Democrats look good?" Kiley asked to start the Wednesday class discussion.

"He's a politician, and he thinks it will help him get reelected," Dan Aaronson offered. "He's from Illinois, and there are a lot of colored people in Chicago."

"That could be part of it," said Kiley. "But do you think he's also doing it because he really believes it's the morally right thing to do?"

NEW YORK TIMES, APRIL 26, 1964

WASHINGTON – President Johnson will send Congress tomorrow a plan to spend nearly a billion and two hundred million dollars in the coming year, to help the poverty-stricken Appalachia region, he announced yesterday.

—

Tammy was surprised when she received the Sunday morning phone call from Marty asking if she wanted to meet her at Sal's for breakfast. Sunday morning was usually the time Marty was with her family at church, but Marty explained she had gotten up early and actually had gone to seven o'clock mass by herself. Tammy couldn't help but worry that her friend had a problem, but she didn't want to probe her over the phone. So, she was sitting in a booth looking out the big front window at Sal's when she saw Marty walking up the street.

"Why did you walk? I could have picked you up." Tammy said as soon as Marty slid into the booth.

"I wanted to walk. It's a beautiful spring morning."

Tammy didn't waste any time trying to find out why Marty had wanted to meet on a Sunday morning.

"So, what's the problem?" Tammy asked.

Marty looked at her friend with an expression of surprise.

"There's no problem," Marty declared. "I don't know. I was just sitting there after my family left for mass, and I started thinking that without cheering, we don't talk as much as we used to. I mean, we see each other before school and in school, but with you spending so much time with Jay now, we just don't sit and talk like we did on the bus to games or after cheering practice. I guess I was feeling melancholy. Oh God, does this mean I'm getting old?"

Tammy just smiled.

"No, you have a long way to go before you start worrying about getting old.

"But you're right, since cheerleading ended, we haven't talked like we used to. I'm glad you called."

"So, have you decided where you are going yet?" Marty asked her friend about her college choice. "Time is getting short. You have to have a deposit somewhere by the end of this week, don't you?"

"Yeah, I'm going to Connecticut College," Tammy said. "Yesterday I told my father to send in the deposit."

"Wow, that kind of surprises me." Marty countered. "It doesn't seem like it's your kind of place. I kind of thought you would go to UMass. You know, someplace with football games and cheerleading and all that sort of stuff."

"Maybe this is what I need. Something that's totally different from anything I have ever done," Tammy said."

"Did you tell Jay?" Marty asked

"No, not yet," Tammy said with a perplexed look.

"Why, not?" Marty questioned.

"I don't know, maybe I'm still not sure if it is the right place for me. You are the first person I've told."

Two or three months ago, Marty wouldn't have been surprised if she had been the first person Tammy told about a major life decision. Recently, however, she had been getting the feeling she had been replaced by Jay as the person Tammy confided in the most, all of which was fine with Marty.

"Hasn't he been asking you what you are going to do?" Marty asked about Jay. "I know he has not sent in his deposit to Tufts yet."

"Yeah, he actually started talking about it last night when we were parking at the lake," Tammy offered with a perplexed look.

"What did you tell him?"

"I distracted him so we didn't have to talk about it. Do me a favor. If he calls you today for anything, don't tell him. I will tell him tonight. He's coming over to watch Arrest and Trial. Besides, it won't make any difference to him where I'm going to college."

"Yeah, right," Marty said in a sarcastic tone. "You know what he would do if you told him you were going to UMass."

"Yeah, I know," Tammy replied.

ASSOCIATED PRESS, APRIL 27, 1964

NEW ORLEANS – Gov. Nelson A. Rockefeller of New York has ordered his

> state's 17-member delegation to the annual conference of the Adjutant Generals Association of the United States to return home because the only Negro member was refused a room at the hotel convention site, it was disclosed last night.

Jay didn't waste any time starting the conversation once Tony got in the car and they headed off for the Monday morning ride to school.

"I'm going to Tufts," Jay declared without even looking over at his friend.

"Of course, you are," Tony said in a matter-of-fact tone.

The fact that his friend didn't seem the least bit surprised by the announcement caught Jay off guard, but he still felt he needed to explain his decision.

"I know we always talked about going to the same college, and I feel bad that I'm not going to be at UMass with you," Jay continued. "But it's just that, I didn't know this Tufts thing was going to happen and I—"

Tony immediately stopped his friend's feeble rambling.

"Stop, Tony said. "You don't owe me any explanation. Those were the dreams of little kids about going to college together. We are not little kids anymore. You have a chance to do something we never dreamed about. I knew from the day you told me the Tufts coach said he was interested in you that if you got in, you would go."

"I'm glad you always knew because I wasn't sure until last night," Jay said so quietly that Tony didn't really know he had said anything.

"So, does Tammy know?" Tony asked.

"Yeah, I told her last night after she told me she was going to Conn. College."

"Wow, she's going to Conn. College. That surprises me."

ASSOCIATED PRESS, APRIL 29, 1964

> MONTGOMERY, Ala. – A three-judge federal court yesterday ordered school authorities to put six Negro pupils back in class at Notasulga, where the high school was destroyed by fire 10 days ago.

My sister called from California last night, Tammy told Marty as they were sitting having coffee at Sal's on Wednesday morning before school.

"What did she want?" Marty inquired.

"She wanted to know what I'm doing about college."

"What did she say when you told her Connecticut College?"

"A lot of the same stuff you said. How she didn't think it was my type of school. She said I should come out, live with her, and go to college in California. She said California has great public universities, especially around the San Francisco area where she lives."

"What did you tell her?" Marty inquired.

"I said thanks, but no thanks. I'm not going to college in California. Girls from high schools in New England don't go to college in California."

THIRTEEN

ASSOCIATED PRESS, MAY 1, 1964

WASHINGTON – President Johnson told Democratic women last night that the day is coming when no office of the nation will be closed to women – "not even the office of President."

"See, even Johnson thinks a woman is going to be President someday," Jay said to Tammy as they headed down the corridor after leaving Kiley's Wednesday afternoon class.

"I don't think I'm ever going to see it in my lifetime," Tammy replied. "They won't even let us play high school sports like you guys do. If they won't let us play sports, what are the chances of men ever letting a woman be president?"

Jay just kept walking without saying a word.

ASSOCIATED PRESS, MAY 4, 1964

WASHINGTON – Sen. Russell B. Long, D-La, said yesterday there is a "real prospect" the Senate will pass the civil rights bill under a debate-limitation rule.

"Hey, I forgot to ask you this morning. Do you want to go into the city tomorrow afternoon and look for prom dresses?" Marty asked Tammy as they headed to their lockers following lunch. "My father said he would take the bus to work so I could use our car."

A sly smile came over Tammy's face.

"Does this mean you are going to the prom?" the blond asked.

"Yeah, I asked Ron Saturday night, and he said he would love to go," Marty offered.

"That's great," Tammy said with a big smile.

"It's just a date," Marty retorted, trying not to look excited.

But Tammy wasn't fooled by her friend's nonchalant reply.

"Now, who is the one afraid to admit her feelings?" Tammy said. "It's more than that, and you know it. It's the senior prom. You will only have one date in your life like this, and you asked Ron. That means something."

A few minutes later, the two girls walked into Kiley's classroom with the teacher standing at the door waiting to close it as soon as the second bell rang.

"Glad you could join us, ladies," Kiley quipped with a smile, then headed to the front of the room where he quickly delivered his opening salvo for the Monday class.

"So, a powerful southern senator says he thinks there is a real prospect the Civil Rights bill will pass. What do you think, Miss D'Errico?" he asked Joan D'Errico.

"I think he realizes people all over the country think it's the right thing to do. I'm not sure he agrees, but he knows it's a reality," said the girl who Jay had watched playing the lead role in the school play a few weeks ago.

NEW YORK TIMES, MAY 5, 1964

> WASHINGTON – The Supreme Court left standing yesterday a decision that school boards have no constitutional duty to end racial imbalance resulting from housing patterns. The action was a major setback for civil rights forces attacking what they call de facto segregation in Northern cities.

"So, what do you think?" Kiley said as the opening volley for the Tuesday class. "For months, we have been reading about how people are battling for equal educational opportunities in southern cities and towns, and here's a story about a form of education segregation in northern cities and the Supreme Court won't even do anything about it."

"That's why we need the civil rights bill to be passed," Marty immediately offered. "Then equal education will be the law and the Supreme Court won't have anything to do with it."

"Don't ever underestimate how much the Supreme Court can affect your life," Kiley replied.

NEW YORK TIMES, MAY 6, 1964

> WASHINGTON – President Johnson said today he might call Congress into special session after the political conventions if it did not soon end the civil rights debate and move on to other measures.

Jay was impatiently standing in Tammy's living room, waiting for her so they could go to HoJo's. He picked up the book sitting on the coffee table and read the title. "What is 'The Feminine Mystique'?" he asked the blond who was on the other side of the room, reading a note from her mother.

"Oh, it's a book that came out last year," she answered, "My sister sent it to me from California. She said I should read it."

"Have you?" Jay asked.

"No, I'll get to it sometime. Come on, let's go. I'm hungry."

NEW YORK TIMES, MAY 7, 1964

> WASHINGTON – On the first important vote on the Civil Rights bill, the bipartisan coalition won a hair-breadth victory last night when the Senate rejected 46-45 a jury trial amendment opposed by the Democratic and Republican leaders.

"Hello," Tammy said as she picked up the phone after getting up from the couch where she had been lying watching TV since she came home from school.

"You're home," the voice on the other end of the phone said without even identifying himself.

"Yeah, I'm home. Where are you?" Tammy asked, knowing it was Jay.

"I'm in the phone booth in the lobby at school. We had just started practice when it began raining really hard. So, Coach ended up calling off practice because the field was soaked."

"God, I didn't look out the window. I didn't realize it had started raining," Tammy said.

"What are you doing?" Jay asked.

"I'm watching General Hospital," she said in a matter-of-fact tone of voice.

"What is General Hospital?" Jay asked with a slight laugh.

"It's a new show that started last spring. I like it. Do you have a problem with that?" the blond shouted back in a good-natured tone.

"No, no, I don't have a problem with anything you do," Jay said.

"You are sucking up for something, and I know what it is," the blond said with a laugh. "Do you want to come over? My father is at work, and my mother will be at her women's club meeting until five or six."

"I'll be there in ten minutes," Jay declared.

NEW YORK TIMES, MAY 8, 1964

> WASHINGTON – The United States is urging its allies to step up their contributions to the war effort in South Vietnam as much for political and psychological reasons as to get extra technical help.

Jay was still thinking of Thursday afternoon at Tammy's house when he saw her walking through the front door of the school on Friday morning. So, he quickly moved through the lobby and intercepted her before she met up with some of the other girls at the far end of the lobby.

"Hey," he said with a big smile on his face. "Do you want to go to the movies tomorrow night to see *Dr. Strangelove*?"

"Sure," she said. "Should I ask Marty if she and Ron want to double?"

"I was kind of thinking of just you and me on a Saturday night," Jay said with a somewhat disappointed look. "But I guess I can live with Marty and her new boyfriend."

"Good, because sometimes you and I alone have the potential to get us into trouble," Tammy said with a sly smile as she headed toward the other girls.

ASSOCIATED PRESS, MAY 11, 1964

> WASHINGTON – The Rev. Martin Luther King Jr. said yesterday that massive demonstrations will be launched in Alabama by early June in a major assault against segregation in public places and restrictions on Negro voting.

"Do you have a game this afternoon?" Tammy asked Jay as they headed from the main lobby to their home rooms after the first bell sounded.

"No, just practice," Jay said.

"What time will you be finished?" she asked.

"I don't know about 4:30, I guess," Jay said, wondering what her questions were leading up to.

"Want to come over after practice? I will cook something for supper. My mother is meeting my father in the city for dinner. They won't be home until at least eight."

"I thought you and I being together alone had the potential to get us into trouble," said Jay with a smile.

"Sometimes a little trouble can be good," she said as she turned and walked through the door of her homeroom.

He stood in the hall watching her walk into her homeroom. How can she change that fast? he thought to himself. Saturday night, when he took her home after the double date with Marty and her new boyfriend, she just gave him a few kisses in the car and said she had to go in the house because it was late. Now, less than forty-eight hours later, she was asking him to come over to her house when her parents weren't going to be home with a not-so-subtle hint that a free dinner wasn't the only thing she was offering him.

UNITED PRESS INTERNATIONAL, MAY 14, 1964

SAIGON, Vietnam – Defense Secretary Robert S. McNamara ended a new mission to Saigon last night with the prediction that the anti-communist war in South Vietnam will be a long one.

The feel of spring was both in the air and in the minds of almost 600 Jefferson seniors, who only had a few more weeks of classes in their high school careers remaining. But while most of the seniors had given up being concerned with English, Math, and French, Kiley's classes were still alive with discussion.

"Mr. Kiley, I hate to admit it, but you might have been right back in September when you said this Vietnam thing would play a role in our lives. I'm starting to think this war, or whatever it is, will not be finished by the time we graduate from college," Mike Stone offered at the start of the Thursday morning class.

For once, Kiley seemed at a loss for words. He kept looking down at the morning paper as if he were reading the story about McNamara's prediction. Finally, he looked up at the class.

"Stone, let's hope we're both wrong."

NEW YORK TIMES, MAY 16, 1964

WASHINGTON – President Johnson alerted the congressional leaders of both parties yesterday that he would seek increased economic and military assistance for South Vietnam.

—

Jay and Tammy were silently walking down the hallway together after leaving Kiley's class, the last class of the day. Suddenly, Tammy declared.

"I know you're always saying it. But now I think more and more people of our generation are starting to understand that individuals can make a difference. That's why they are doing things like joining sit-ins and marching against discrimination."

Jay stopped walking, looked directly at the blond, flashed a smile, reached over, and gave her a kiss on the lips while the two were still standing in the middle of the hallway.

"Will you two get a room?" Tony joked as he walked past the pair.

NEW YORK TIMES, MAY 26, 1964

> WASHINGTON – The Supreme Court said yesterday that Prince Edward County, Va., must reopen its public schools, closed since 1959 to avoid desegregation.

"I'm not sure if my parents are going to go for Jay's idea of us sleeping overnight on the beach prom night," Tammy said to Marty as they were having coffee before school on Tuesday morning. "I kind of mentioned it to my mother last night, and she just looked at me with a strange look and said, 'We'll see.'"

"Do you think she's worried about her little girl losing her virginity on prom night?" Marty said with a laugh in a low tone as she moved closer to Tammy so nobody could hear her sarcastic reply.

"I don't know," Tammy offered. "I'm just not up to getting into an argument with her about it."

"That's okay," Marty said. "I asked Ron Saturday night if we could use his mother's Nash Rambler on prom night."

"Doesn't a Rambler have fold-down front seats that virtually turn into a bed?" Tammy asked.

"Yes, it does," Marty said with a smile.

"So, it's not just another date anymore," Tammy said with a smirk.

FOURTEEN

ASSOCIATED PRESS, JUNE 3, 1964

HONOLULU – Secretary of State Dean Rusk and Secretary of Defense Robert B. McNamara have not proposed any plan for Vietnam that would "enlarge the war to the north," U.S. officials said yesterday.

"Well, at least Rusk and McNamara don't have any plans to enlarge this Vietnam conflict," Kiley said with a measure of sarcasm shortly before the bell signaled the end of his Wednesday afternoon class.

A few minutes later, Jay saw Tammy still sitting at her desk when he was heading out of Kiley's class, even though everybody else was out of their seats and heading into the corridor. So, he turned and went down the aisle and stood next to her desk.

"Are you okay?" he asked.

"Yeah, just thinking of some things I have to do. Let's go." She said as she rose out of her chair and headed for the door. They left the room and silently walked about ten yards down the corridor when Jay finally broke the silence.

"Paul Reall said he could have the party after the prom at his house. It should be great. He has that huge basement, and you know his parents disappear when he has a party."

"I heard it should be fun," Tammy replied without showing much emotion.

"Do you want to talk to Marty about us and her and Ron sleeping on the beach after the party?"

"I don't know if that's going to happen, I'm not sure my parents will go for it," she replied.

"I didn't even think you were going to ask them," Jay said with a surprised look.

UNITED PRESS INTERNATIONAL, JUNE 7, 1964

> NEW YORK – President Johnson yesterday called upon the American people to look into their hearts and make the civil rights law, "a living reality."

Jay looked over at Marty and pointed to the empty desk while Kiley was still passing out the Monday N. Y. Times at the start of the second period.

"Where is she?" he mouthed without actually asking why Tammy wasn't in school.

Marty just shrugged her shoulders.

Jay immediately got out of his seat and asked Kiley for a library pass.

The phone rang four or five times without an answer, so Jay was about to hang up when suddenly Tammy's voice said, "Hello."

"Hey, are you okay?" he asked without even saying hello.

"Yeah, I'm okay," Tammy replied. "I guess I just got too much sun yesterday. I felt sick this morning, but I'm fine now."

"Remember, it was your idea to go to the beach so you could get a tan for the prom," Jay said with a laugh, relieved that Tammy was okay.

"I know," she replied. "Thanks for calling. Tell Marty to call me this afternoon. Now get back to class."

NEW YORK TIMES, JUNE 9, 1964

> ST. AUGUSTINE, Fla – A band of angry whites broke through police lines tonight and attacked nearly 300 racial demonstrators marching on downtown St. Augustine in the start of a massive integration drive.

—

"Okay, folks, settle down," Kiley yelled over the loud chatter of thirty-some teenagers who really didn't want to sit through any more classes, even Kiley's class.

"I know it's tough to keep your mind on school when it's seventy-five degrees outside and you all would rather be at the beach. But we still have some things to finish up here before you are official high school graduates," Kiley said with a broad smile. "In case you haven't checked the final exam schedule posted outside the guidance office, your final exam in this class is scheduled for next Tuesday morning. Officially, every teacher is required to give a final exam, but nothing in this class has gone by the book all year, and I see no reason to change now. So, your final exam will be a little different. There will be one question. You will have the whole test period to answer it, and nobody can get it wrong."

"Want to bet, Mr. Kiley? I guess you haven't been reading my weekly reports this year," Tony shouted out in self-mockery.

"Even you couldn't get this wrong, Gemma," Kiley said with a laugh. "Especially since I'm going to give you the question before the test."

"All right, Mr. Kiley, I've always said you are my favorite teacher," Tony said, continuing with his year-long humorous banter with the teacher.

"Coming from you, Gemma. I'm not sure if that's a compliment," Kiley said with another laugh.

Then Kiley's tone suddenly turned serious as he began talking about the details of their final exam.

"Each of you will be asked to list the five most significant events that have happened since the first day of your senior year. You have spent this school year reading about what is happening in this country. It has been a very interesting nine months since you first stepped into this classroom on Aug. 29th. Now tell me what you think were the five most significant events. I don't want just a list of five events. I want you to tell me why the event was significant to you. If you need to review, I gave Mrs. Brown in the library a copy of the Times every day, and she has kept them on file, but hopefully, most of you will not need to review. I suspect President Kennedy's assassination will be number one on many of your lists. That makes sense. You are the first high school students in sixty years to have their senior year mired by the assassination of this country's president. But don't just tell me President Kennedy's death was significant. Tell me why it was significant to you personally. Do the same thing with the other four events. I have tried to make you people think about why things are happening, not just that they are happening. This will be your last chance to show me you learned something. This class doesn't meet tomorrow, but if you want to talk about it, we can in our last two classes on Thursday and Friday, then exams start Monday."

He turned and began arranging some papers on his desk with his back to the class, obviously waiting for the bell to sound the end of the class. For a minute or so, you could have heard a pin drop in the class. There was none of the usual end-of-class banter just before the bell rang. It was as if Kiley had just delivered a declaration of stark reality. There were only two more days for him to open their eyes to what was happening in their world.

NEW YORK TIMES, JUNE 10, 1964

WASHINGTON – The Senate of the United States invoked closure on the civil rights bill today by a vote of 71-29, thus ending a 75-day filibuster.

"What color is your dress? "Jay asked Tammy as they walked down the corridor after the first bell on Wednesday morning.

"Why?" Tammy asked with a slight smile.

"I need to know so I can buy your flowers," Jay said sheepishly.

"I was wondering when you were going to ask," Tammy said, still flashing a smile.

"You could have just told me," Jay said defensively.

"That would have let you off too easy," she said now in full laughter. "So, what made you finally realize time is getting short?"

Jay hesitated, taking several steps without saying a word or looking at Tammy. Finally, he answered in a low tone, still without looking at the blond.

"My mother asked me this morning what color your dress was and if I had ordered your flowers."

"What did she say when you told her you hadn't even asked me what color my dress was?"

"I didn't tell her," he admitted.

"Wow, you lied to your mother," she said, knowing she had him squirming.

"I didn't lie, I just kind of said 'I have to get going' and rushed out the door. So what color is it?" he asked, trying to regain his verbal footing.

"Blue," she said as she started breaking away from him, heading toward her homeroom.

"Wait a minute," Jay yelled, attracting the attention of some people walking in the corridor. "What color blue—navy blue, sky blue—what?

"Blue like your eyes," she said in an elevated tone, causing the people walking nearby to turn and look at Jay, whose face was turning red.

ASSOCIATED PRESS, JUNE 11, 1964

WASHINGTON – President Johnson last night hailed the Senate vote to halt the civil rights filibuster as a "historic event – an action that demonstrated that the national will manifests itself in congressional action."

"So, what are your five events going to be for Kiley's exam?" Marty asked Jay as they walked up the stairs, heading toward Room 329 for their next-to-last regular Kiley class.

Jay had been giving the question serious thought, so he didn't need to do any review. The problem would be deciding what the five most significant events of the school year were.

"I'm still not sure," he said. "Kennedy's assassination definitely is number one, but after that, I'm not sure. King's speech the day before we started school will probably be two. The Beatles' first night on the Ed Sullivan Show might be number three. I think some of the stuff we have read about what's happening in Vietnam definitely is important; I just don't know what is the most important because I'm not sure which way that thing is going right now."

Marty offered her input without Jay asking,

"I think the killing of those little girls in the church bombing in September has to be one of them," she said.

"That's on my list of possibilities," Jay replied." It definitely made a lot of people sympathetic to the Civil Rights movement."

"I think Sidney Poitier winning an Oscar also was big," Marty said just as they were about to go into the room. "I mean, everybody goes to movies."

Tammy was already sitting at her desk talking to Karen Snow when Jay and Marty walked into the room, but Tammy didn't even look up to acknowledge their presence. But it didn't matter because Kiley came bursting into the room in one of his usual late entrances seconds before the bell sounded. He started talking as soon as the bell finished ringing.

"Yesterday certainly was an important day for everything we have been reading about all year," he offered. "The closure of the filibuster means President Johnson is going to get a vote on the Civil Rights Bill, and I think he knows he has the votes to win. A few months ago, I asked if you thought you would see a Civil Rights Bill before you graduated. I'm not sure if it is going to happen before you graduate from here in twelve days, but I think I can now say with confidence that you will see it before you start college."

They talked for nearly thirty minutes about how they had watched the progress of the Civil Rights Bill through Congress through the newspaper stories they read every school day. Mike Stone offered how he felt President Kennedy's death had helped the passage of the bill.

"I think you might have just given Gemma one of his exam answers," Kiley said with a laugh, obviously enjoying his final days with the class. Finally, the teacher had to cut off the discussion.

"Okay, one other thing before the bell rings," Kiley said. "The first day of class, I gave you a textbook and told you to take it home and put it someplace safe so you could return it on the last day of class. Well, folks, tomorrow is that last day, so hopefully you remember where you put that textbook." He turned and started heading to his desk to wait for the bell, but he suddenly stopped and turned back to the class. He stood just looking at the thirty-plus students for close to a minute before he finally spoke.

"In case I don't get a chance to say it tomorrow. I just want you to know that I have enjoyed this class more than any class I have ever taught. Mr. Lawson wasn't really sure when I told him what I wanted to do using the Times as a textbook. But I told him I thought there were some students in this school who were ready to do something different. You proved I was right, and I want to thank you."

"This country has changed a lot since the first day of this class, and I think it could change a lot more very quickly. I think some of you could play a role in those changes. If I can give you one piece of advice for your future, it would be to try to find your passion for your life's work."

There was stone silence throughout the classroom for at least thirty seconds, but then Tammy's voice broke the silence.

"THANK YOU, Mr. Kiley," she declared, and thirty-three heads nodded in agreement while also clapping.

NEW YORK TIMES, JUNE 12, 1964

PRETORIA, South Africa – Eight persons were sentenced to life imprisonment today on the grounds that they had plotted a "violent revolution" against South Africa's racial policies.

Nelson R. Mandela, Walter M. E. Sisulu, and the other defendants convicted under the anti-sabotage laws stood drawn and pensive before the Supreme Court here as sentence was pronounced. It ended one of South Africa's longest political trials.

The ball fell six inches inside the right field foul line. The Jefferson right fielder running at full speed picked up the ball and immediately fired toward home plate, but with two outs in the bottom of the eighth inning the Clinton runner on second had started running at the crack of the bat and by the time the throw one-hopped into the catcher's glove the Clinton runner had crossed the plate ending an exciting 3–2 extra-inning playoff game.

The thought struck Jay as he headed out of the dugout. His formal baseball career was finished. He had started playing Little League baseball when he was ten years old. It was the first team he had been on in any sport, and he had been on a baseball team every spring since then. He wouldn't play baseball at Tufts, so this was the last spring he would be on a real baseball team. He was thinking of calling Tammy when he got home and telling her his feelings about his baseball career ending, but he didn't. He figured she wouldn't understand.

ASSOCIATED PRESS, JUNE 16, 1964

WASHINGTON – The Senate voted repeatedly yesterday against last-minute attempts to amend the civil rights bill as it moved steadily toward a final vote on the measure.

When Jay saw Tammy get up and start walking up the aisle to put her exam paper on Kiley's desk, he rushed to the front and put his exam right on top of hers. He had actually finished writing five minutes earlier, but he sat there pretending to be proofreading, waiting for Tammy to finish. He hadn't talked to her for two days. They had gone together to a party at Russ Lawrence's house Saturday night. Russ had called it a pre-prom-grad party because it was a week before the prom and ten days before graduation. She had spent most of the night sitting with the other girls and getting people to sign her yearbook. When he took her home, he started kissing her in front of her house, but he could tell she really wasn't into it. So, he opened his door and walked around to open the passenger door. At least the chivalrous gesture brought a smile to her face. He didn't even try to give her a good night kiss at the door. Instead, he just tried to make plans for Sunday.

"I will give you a call tomorrow morning. Maybe we can just go for a ride tomorrow afternoon," he said.

But she quickly foiled his plans.

"No, I have to go down the beach and see about my waitressing job for this summer tomorrow. I will see you at school on Monday." But then she wasn't anywhere to be found Monday afternoon after exams, and she didn't answer the phone when he called Monday night. Her mother finally did answer the phone about 9 o'clock, but said she had come home and gone right to bed. So, he was desperate to talk to her on Tuesday after the exam. He caught up with her a few steps outside the door of Kiley's classroom.

"Hey, where were you yesterday?" he asked. "I looked for you in the lobby after the second exam, but Marty said you had already left."

"I had my mother's car because I had some things I had to take care of," she said in a rather stern voice. "I didn't know I needed to check with you."

"Okay," Jay said, trying to quickly change the mood. "Do you want to take a ride, maybe down to the beach? It's a beautiful day."

The offer didn't make the blond change her tone of voice.

"We can't always just take off to the beach to get away from our problems," she said.

"I didn't know we had any problems," Jay offered with a perplexed look. "Did I do something wrong?" he asked.

For the first time, Tammy looked directly into Jay's eyes and changed the stern expression on her face.

"No, you didn't do anything wrong. It's me, not you," she said. "It's just that I'm starting to wonder if Conn. College is the right place for me. Marty is going to New York City. Things happen in New York. I'm going to New London. What happens in New London?"

"A great education where you are not going to take a back seat to anybody just because you are a woman," Jay answered without hesitation.

"Yeah, I know," she said as she turned and started walking down the corridor alone.

UNITED PRESS INTERNATIONAL, JUNE 19, 1964

> WASHINGTON – Sen. Barry Goldwater announced yesterday that he will reluctantly vote against the civil rights bill.

"My sister is coming home for my graduation," Tammy said to Marty Friday afternoon as they drove to the big, old ballroom near the lake to join a few other girls putting up decorations for Saturday night's senior prom.

"Wow, that's nice. Did you know she was planning to come back from California just for your graduation?" Marty asked.

"No, but I called her Monday night to just talk about some things, and then Wednesday night she called back and said she and her husband were leaving on Thursday to drive back here for the graduation. She said she only has one little sister, so she wants to be here."

NEW YORK TIMES, JUNE 19, 1964

OXFORD, Ohio – The first phase of one of the most ambitious civil rights projects yet conceived has ended here in an atmosphere of mixed hope and doubt, fear and determination.

Some 200 college students, the vanguard of a volunteer force of 1,000, are drifting out of this quiet little college town to engage in a Negro voter registration drive in Mississippi.

"So are you bringing Ron to the party after the prom, or are you guys just going to take off in his mother's Rambler?" Tammy asked Marty as they drove back from decorating the ballroom.

Marty had a perplexed look.

"I don't know. I told Paul we would be there, but I'm not sure if it would be fair to Ron to put him in that position with just kids from Jefferson," Marty offered.

"So just go to the lake, I'm sure Ron will enjoy it," Tammy said with a big smile.

"We'll see how the night works out," Marty said as she tried to remove herself from being the center of the conversation. "So how about you and Jay? Do you have plans for some romantic evening, now that you are not worrying about it being the first time?"

"I don't know," Tammy replied. "He has tried to talk about going to the beach alone after the party, even if it isn't for the whole night. He said we could stay just long enough to see the sun rise in the morning. But I've avoided the subject."

"Anything wrong?" Marty asked,

"No, I just have a lot on my mind. Don't worry, I will make sure your friend has a memorable night," Tammy added.

ASSOCIATED PRESS, JUNE 20, 1964

WASHINGTON – The Senate last night passed the civil rights bill containing strong new barriers to racial bias in employment, public facilities, businesses and federal aid programs.

> The roll call vote was 73-27
>
> The measure now goes back to the House, which passed basically the same bill four months ago. Southerners there have vowed a last-ditch fight, but the odds appear heavily weighted against them.

Jay sat alone at the table, looking over at Tammy on the other side of the table with three other girls. For some reason, his mind drifted back to that first day of school when he asked Tony who that girl was. Now he's at the senior prom with her.

She was smiling and seemed happy, the way she had been so often until the past few weeks. He still didn't understand why she seemed so upset recently, but as Marty had said, "Give her a break. She has a lot on her mind." So, Jay tried to be upbeat, and tonight she seemed happy again. He hugged her tightly as they danced slowly to the band playing "Blue Velvet," "Surfer Girl," and "Put Your Head on My Shoulder." They both came off the dance floor sweating after a solid three minutes of "Louie, Louie" followed by several minutes of "Twist and Shout." It was approaching midnight when they stopped at Tammy's house after the prom so she could change out of her dress into a pair of Bermuda shorts and a blouse.

They were only a few feet inside the door of Paul's house when Russ Lawrence walked up to them carrying a bottle of Southern Comfort.

"Here, have a shot to get the night started," he said to the couple.

"No thanks," Jay said. "We'll just get a beer."

But Tammy surprised him.

"I'll have a shot," she said, taking one of the shot glasses. She gulped the liquor down without taking a breath.

Jay was stunned.

"What's that all about? You never drink like that," he said.

"Don't you want to have a good night. Doesn't every guy want his date to get drunk after the prom?" Tammy asked.

Jay didn't answer the question. He just looked at her with a perplexed stare.

"Let's get a beer," she said as she led Jay by the hand over to the big cooler at the far side of the room that was filled with beer and soda, but the beer cans outnumbered the soda cans almost two to one. Jay followed her to the cooler, and she reached in and grabbed two beers.

They sat on the couch, drinking a beer and talking to Jane Snow and Mike Stone. They hadn't been sitting there more than ten minutes when Tammy suddenly jumped up, declaring, "I need another one," and walked over to the cooler. She picked two cans out of the cooler and extended one in Jay's direction as if to ask, "Do you want one?" Jay shook his head. About fifteen minutes later, Russ walked by, still holding the bottle of Southern Comfort, which was now two-thirds empty.

"Last chance," he said, holding out the Southern Comfort bottle and a shot glass. Tammy didn't hesitate to grab the glass, but Jay waved his hand, signaling not to pour the liquor. Tammy suddenly became upset by Jay's attempt to keep her from having another drink.

"I know this is a man's world, but at least a woman can decide what she wants to drink," she said in a disgusted voice with a piercing look at Jay.

Jay lay back on the couch and watched her gulp down another shot of Southern Comfort. They were lying back on the couches with Jay's arm around Tammy's shoulder, both drinking beer and watching people dancing, when Marty and Ron came walking down the stairs. Tammy immediately jumped up, raced over, and threw a complete body hug around her friend.

Jay got off the couch and moved over to Marty and her date.

"I'm glad you two made it," he said to Marty.

"We're not staying long." Marty offered. "I just wanted to stop by because I told Paul we would be here."

Then she took her right arm away from Ron's shoulders and put both arms around Jay's neck, pulling herself close to his face, and gave him a kiss on the cheek. She then moved her mouth up closer to his ear.

"Is she okay?" she asked quietly, so only Jay could hear her inquiring about Tammy.

He looked down at her and moved closer to her ear.

"I don't know, we have only been here for thirty minutes, and she's already had four drinks. Did she say anything to you?"

Marty shook her head.

After Marty and Ron left, Tammy pulled Jay over to the corner of the room.

"Come on, let's get out of here," she said. "Do you have the blanket in your car?"

"Yeah, but I thought you said your parents didn't want you sleeping overnight on the beach," he replied.

"They don't, but we don't have to go to the beach. Jeanne Santos told me she and her boyfriend did it on that golf course over in Greenvale one night a few weeks ago. She said it was really exciting. She said the grass on the second green is really smooth."

Most teenage boys would have been up the stairs and out the door in a matter of seconds after an invitation like that from their prom date, but Jay didn't immediately move.

"Are you sure you're okay?" he asked. "You've had a lot to drink."

"I'm fine, let's go," she declared.

But as she started up the stairs, she stumbled, forcing Jay to grab her and literally carry her up the stairs and out the back door of Paul's house. He opened the passenger door of his car, and she slid inside, resting her head against the back of the seat as he rushed around to the driver's side and began driving away. She rolled her head toward Jay and threw her arms around him, making it almost impossible to drive.

"Are we going to the golf course?" she mumbled.

"No, we're going to the City Diner. It's open all night Saturday. You need some coffee."

When they arrived at the dinner, he told her to put her head back and rest while he went into the diner. By the time he returned, she had fallen asleep. So, he drove the few miles to the big parking lot behind the football stadium. It was dark and empty, out of the view of any passing cars on the road in front of the stadium. He woke her and told her to drink some of the coffee, which she did, but before long she had fallen asleep again. So, he sat there with her head resting on his shoulder. He sat for over an hour, hardly moving, with his legs stretched out over into the passenger side of the car. He seriously expected that at some point, a police car or someone would drive around the back of the stadium and see his car, but nobody drove past. He sat there just looking out at the clear sky, a slight warm breeze blowing through the window he had opened on the driver's side door. A half-moon on a clear night and some nearby street lights shed enough light to make the football field and the stands visible. At times, Jay would put his head back, close his eyes, and let his mind drift back to those fall Friday nights and Saturday afternoons when his life changed because of what happened on that field. It was warm, but he still reached behind the bucket seats, pulled out a blanket, and put it over Tammy, stretching it down to cover her bare legs to ward off any possible chill. Eventually, he looked at his watch and realized they had been in the parking lot for about two hours.

Finally, she awoke.

"How do you feel?" Jay asked as she began to stir.

"I feel like death warmed over," she said. "What time is it?"

"A little after three," he offered.

"Oh my God, how long have I been asleep?"

"Almost two hours."

"Shit, I have ruined your senior prom night," she declared as she sat up in the bucket seat. "I don't know what got into me. I'm sorry."

"You didn't ruin anything," he said.

"Yeah, just what every boy wants to do on his prom night. Spend three hours watching his date, sleep off a drunk."

Jay looked at her and smiled.

"It's not the first time I've bought your coffee at City Diner, trying to sober you up."

"What?" she said with a bewildered look. Then she remembered the night back in early October when he had picked up her and Marty after Debby Storti's wedding and sobered them up before driving them home.

"Boy, a lot has happened since then," she said.

"Yes, it has," Jay said, rubbing his hand along the side of her face. "I need to get you home. Your parents are going to be worried about you."

But the blond didn't want to leave, at least, not yet.

"My parents have been asleep for a long time. Remember, I have an older sister. They know about senior prom night. Don't worry," she said.

"Yeah, but if I don't get you home, they are going to be getting up for their morning coffee when you are walking in the door. Are you okay to go home?"

"I'm going to feel like shit all day Sunday, but I'm okay. I just wanted tonight to be special for you—a night you would never forget," she said.

"We are going to have a lot of other chances for special nights," he said with a smile and started the car.

NEW YORK TIMES, JUNE 22, 1964

PHILADEPHIA, Miss. – Three workers in a day-old civil rights campaign in Mississippi were reported missing today after their release from jail here last night.

> Leaders of the drive said they feared that the three men, two whites, both from New York, and one Negro had met with foul play.

Jay looked over at his mother, who was sitting in the passenger seat of her car as Jay drove toward the graduation ceremony being held at the football field. She was just looking out the side window, staring into the blue sky without saying a word. Jay was going to ask her what she was thinking about, but he suspected he already knew. This was a night she and Jay's father had worked for; dreamed about since that day in June 1946 when Jay was born. The day their son would graduate from high school and head off to college. Every day of their lives had been devoted to providing opportunities for their son so someday they would share a night like this together. But tonight, his father wasn't there.

"Are you okay, Mom? You're awfully quiet." Jay said as he drove toward the football field.

She turned and looked at her son with a soft smile.

"I'm fine. I'm just thinking of your father, he would have been very proud."

NEW YORK TIMES, JUNE 23, 1964

> WASHINGTON – A sharply divided Supreme Court reversed the convictions of 42 sit-in demonstrators, but without reaching the fundamental constitutional issue involved.
>
> The issue is whether the Constitution itself, without legislative action by Congress, prohibits the states from prosecuting for trespass persons who demand service without racial discrimination at privately owned places of business.

Jay knew he had called too early when Mrs. Clark answered the phone rather than Tammy. But he couldn't wait much longer after 8 o'clock Tuesday morning to make the call. He had already been awake for an hour, even though he didn't get home until one in the morning after going to three graduation parties on Monday night. He and Tammy had talked about going to the parties at graduation practice on Monday morning, but when they met up after the graduation ceremony on Monday night, she said she couldn't go to any parties because her parents wanted her to go out to dinner with her sister and brother-in-law. He even offered to come to her house later to pick her up after everybody returned from dinner, but she said that would be too late. He found that a little odd, but he didn't think too much about it because they had already made plans to go to the beach on Tuesday for what everybody said was going to be an all-day beach party.

"Hello, Mrs. Clark, this is Jay. I hope I didn't wake you up. I guess I didn't realize how early it was."

"Don't worry, Jay, I have been up for hours, unlike some people we know," Tammy's mother replied.

"Oh, she's not up yet. I'll call her back," Jay said, not wanting to upset the blond.

"No, Jay, it's time she gets up on a beautiful day like this. Hold the line, I will go wake her up. Oh, by the way, congratulations on your graduation. I'm sure your mother is proud."

"Thank you, I think she is," he said.

It was three or four minutes before Tammy finally came to the phone.

"Sorry to wake you, but what time do you want me to pick you up to go to the beach?" Jay asked before the blond could say a word.

There were several seconds of silence before Tammy finally spoke.

"Why don't you come over now?" she said.

"Now," Jay said in a surprised tone. "You just woke up. Don't you need some time to get ready? We probably will be at the beach until late tonight. Everybody is talking about this being our last big bash together."

"Come over now." Tammy reiterated without any further explanation.

Jay was puzzled, but he wasn't about to argue with the blond, once again remembering Marty's words, "Give her a break." So, he told her he would be there in fifteen or twenty minutes.

ASSOCIATED PRESS, JUNE 23, 1964

> ST. AUGUSTINE. Fla. – White gangs attacked Negro and white integrationists with fists and clubs twice today at a public beach in this racially torn city. The new outbreaks of violence came as a federal judge ordered Gov. Farris Bryant to show cause why he should not be held in contempt of court for banning after-dark demonstrations.

Tammy opened the back door only a few seconds after Jay knocked. She was barefoot and wearing a pair of jean shorts and the oversized Yale sweatshirt hanging off her bare shoulder, even though the temperature had already risen to the low 80s on one of the first days of official summer.

"Do you have your bathing suit on under that?" Jay asked, pointing to the sweatshirt.

"No, I don't. Let's go outside," she said.

Jay followed her to the picnic table in the backyard that they had sat at several times over the past few months, talking when Jay had stopped over after a baseball practice, and her parents were either in the kitchen or the living room. She sat at the end of one of the benches, but he remained standing.

"Sit down," she said.

He was hesitant because he was starting to sense tension, but he sat anyway with one leg on each side of the picnic table bench so he was looking directly at her. Their knees were touching, but their upper bodies were a few feet apart. She just looked at him without saying a word for a good minute, so he broke the silence.

"What's wrong?" he asked.

She tried to smile, but he could see the tears starting to well up in her eyes. So, he moved close to her and put both his arms around her and pulled her close to him. She stayed in the tight embrace for a couple of minutes without saying a word, but then she moved her upper body back away from him. Jay tried to move his face closer to hers and look into her eyes, but Tammy couldn't look straight into his eyes. So, she turned her face slightly as she spoke.

"I never planned on getting involved with anybody this year," she said, struggling for the words and still unable to look directly at Jay.

"But you did, didn't you?" Jay asked.

Finally, she looked straight at his face.

"Yes, I did, and it was wonderful," she said, "But, it's, it's time to end it."

Jay could feel his heart dropping into his stomach.

"What—you are breaking up with me?" he said, still trying to fathom what he had just heard.

"We are breaking up with each other," she said with a stern look, trying to hide any sign of emotion.

"But why?" he yelled.

"Because it's the right thing to do," she said, her eyes now looking down at her sweating hands.

"How do you know it's the right thing to do?" he offered in protest.

"I just do," she said, still trying to maintain her composure.

Jay couldn't find the words for an instant rebuttal, but finally, he asked.

"Why so sudden?"

"It's not that sudden," she said. "I have been thinking about it for a while."

Jay quickly started thinking of alternatives to a break-up.

"Look, maybe we are spending too much time together. We can take a little time away from each other. I have to go down to our beach and get everything ready to start life-guarding next week, and you are going to be starting your job waitressing, so we are going to be busy for a couple of days anyway. We both are going to be busy this summer, so it won't be like when we saw each other almost every day in school, but that doesn't mean we have to break up. I know we are going to be at different colleges in the fall, but we are not going to be that far apart. We could get together almost every weekend. I can take the train to New London, or you can take the train to Boston."

He looked at her for an answer, but she had her head down, just looking at her hands. He tried to move closer to her, but she got up off the picnic-table bench and walked a few feet away with her back to Jay. Finally, she turned around and looked at him.

"No, we couldn't," she said. "I've changed my mind. I'm not going to Conn. College."

The news caught Jay by surprise, but he had a quick solution.

"That's okay," he said. "UMass isn't that far from Boston. We can still be together a lot."

"I'm not going to UMass, either," she said.

Jay stood there with a totally bewildered look on his face.

"Where are you going?" he asked.

She walked back to the bench, sat down a few feet away from him, and calmly declared:

"I'm going to school in California,"

"What, where?" Jay shouted even though he was only a few feet away from her.

"I don't know yet, I'm going with my sister and her husband when they leave to go back to California this weekend. When we get there, I will look at schools. There are a lot of good colleges in California. I just think it's more of where I want my future to go."

He sat in total silence, just staring into space. Finally, he rose from the picnic table bench and stood looking down into her face, still without saying a word. Once again, she couldn't look him straight in the eye. Finally, she looked up at him.

"I'm sorry," she said. "I just think it is the best thing for both of us."

Jay's disposition had now turned to anger.

"Maybe it is for you," he said in a disgusted tone as he turned and walked out of the yard without looking back at the blond.

UNITED PRESS INTERNATIONAL, JUNE 26, 1964

PHILADEPHIA, Miss. – The first contingent of 200 sailors that President Johnson ordered into the search for three missing civil rights workers began beating their way into the dense Bogue Chitto Swamp yesterday.

Tammy opened the front door of her house on Friday afternoon and saw Marty standing there. The blond couldn't even get out a greeting before Marty went into a verbal rage.

"You asshole," Marty screamed while still standing on the top of Tammy's front steps.

"Oh, you talked to him," Tammy said, looking at her enraged friend.

"Yes, I talked to him this morning. Were you ever going to tell me yourself?" Marty said, her face still flush with anger.

"Well, I knew you would hear it from him, so I figured I would wait until you heard his side first. I'm surprised it took him three days to tell you."

"He has been down the beach ever since you two had your talk on Tuesday. Shit, I talked to you on Wednesday, and you never said anything about it. I thought we were friends."

"We are friends," Tammy declared. "I guess I thought you should hear it from him first."

Marty wasn't in any mood to extend her friend a sympathetic ear. Tammy had opened the screen door, but Marty made no effort to move inside the house.

"Why, because you were afraid to tell me what an asshole you are?" she shouted at the blond. "You said this was never going to happen. You promised me you would never hurt him. Never let it get to a point where he was going to be hurt when you decided you had had enough of him. Because you knew you were going to get tired of him, just like you got tired of all the other guys. He was fun to have around for senior year, but once we graduated, it only took you a day to get rid of him."

Tammy stood holding the screen door open, looking at Marty, but not offering a word of defense. Marty turned, walked down the stairs, and headed toward her parents' car, which was parked in front of the house. Suddenly, she turned and looked back at the blond, who was still standing holding the screen door open.

"Oh, enjoy California," she said in a loud, sarcastic tone. "I guess this kills the idea of you taking the train down to New York from New London once a month so we could still be together. But then again, I was just somebody who helped you pass the time in high school."

UNITED PRESS INTERNATIONAL, JUNE 29, 1964

> MINNEAPOLIS, Minn. – President Johnson said yesterday that the United States "must be prepared to risk war" in order to preserve its freedom and "when necessary, we will take the risk."

"Did you see her before she left?" Jay asked Marty as soon as she opened the door on Monday morning and signaled for Jay to walk into her living room. She didn't need to ask for an explanation to his question.

"Yeah, I saw her Friday," she said. "We kind of had a fight."

"About what?" Jay asked.

"You," she said, looking straight into Jay's face.

"Me, why would you fight about me?"

"Because we both care about you," Marty said.

Jay couldn't help but laugh at Marty's belief that Tammy cared about him.

"She certainly doesn't care too much about me, taking off like this without really explaining why," he said, walking away from Marty so she wouldn't see the hurt in his eyes.

"Believe me, she cares," Marty said.

"I don't think so," he said. "But anyway, I just stopped to say goodbye before I head down the beach to start lifeguarding tomorrow. I probably won't see you for a while."

He started heading out the door with a look of anger still evident on his face. Suddenly, Marty stopped him.

"Wait a minute, stay here," she said as she turned and headed up the stairs to her room. A few minutes later, she was back, carrying an envelope.

"I told you Tammy and I had a fight on Friday. I didn't tell you this was in my mailbox yesterday. She must have put it in the mailbox sometime yesterday morning before she left. She asked me not to show it to you, but I think you need to see it. But you have to promise me you are not going to go crazy trying to find out where she is or try to get a hold of her."

"Let me see it," Jay said as he reached for the envelope.

But Marty pulled it away before he could grab it.

"Not until you promise," she said, holding the letter close to her chest.

"Okay, okay, I promise," he said, finally taking the envelope from Marty's hands.

He took the letter out of the envelope and immediately recognized Tammy's handwriting on the same type of note paper that she had used in her letter to Dave in October.

Marty,

I know you are mad at me and I probably should leave it that way and head to California. But I can't. I don't care what anybody else thinks about me, but I care what you think. I don't think you understand how much your friendship has meant to me. You are the only person who understands who I really am. I know you think

I hurt Jay after I promised you I never would, but I want you to understand. I'm not doing this because I don't care about him. I'm doing it because I do care about him. If I stayed in New England for college, Jay would want to keep this thing between us going. Even if we are at different schools, we will only be a few hours away from each other. You know him. You know he wouldn't do some of the things he would have a chance to do in Boston because he was worrying about me. He needs to be free to meet new people, take advantage of every opportunity, so he can do the things he is dreaming about doing. He can get people to follow him; to care about the things he cares about, doing things that will help people. Look at you, a year ago, you didn't even know him. Now you hate me because you think I'm hurting him. I want to see him use all his time and all his talent doing things he feels will help people. He won't put all his efforts into doing those things if I'm still in the picture. I'm the one who needs to break this off and get away from here. I'm not giving up that much here. Maybe California is the perfect place for me right now.

Please don't show him this letter. It might get him thinking there is still hope for something between us and I don't want that.

Your friend (I hope)

Tammy

Jay finished reading and stood motionless, holding the letter. Marty watched him standing there, looking down at the letter, but no longer reading. Finally, she broke the silence.

"She's right, you know," Marty said.

Jay looked at her, but didn't say a word for a solid minute. Finally, a smile started creeping over his face.

"She always was," he said.

He foiled the letter, put it back in the envelope, and handed it back to Marty. Then he started heading out the door.

"Where are you going?" Marty asked.

"I think I will ride around a little, maybe out by the lake," he said.

"Want some company?" Marty asked.

Jay looked at her and smiled.

"If you don't mind, I think I want to do this ride by myself," he said.

She understood his desire for solitude, but she was concerned about him.

"You're not going to do anything stupid, are you?"

Jay laughed.

"Don't worry, I'm not going to hurt myself if that's what you mean," he said.

"Just making sure you are okay," Marty offered.

She reached up, put her arms around his neck, and gently gave him a kiss on his cheek. He wrapped his arms around her back and squeezed tightly.

"Thanks," he said.

"For what?" she said, flashing a sarcastic smirk, "a kiss on the cheek?"

"For being you," he said as he released his grip, turned away, and walked toward his car.

The top of the Healey was down, and the sun was shining brightly as Jay drove past the empty parking lot behind the high school.

NEW YORK TIMES, JULY 2, 1964

WASHINGTON – President Johnson signed the Civil Rights Act of 1964 tonight.

It is the most far-reaching civil rights law since Reconstruction days. The President announced steps to implement it and called on all Americans to help "eliminate the last vestiges of injustice in America."

JOHN GILOOLY is a former national award-winning sportswriter/columnist for the Providence Journal in Providence, Rhode Island. He is the recipient of an Associated Press Sports Editors national award for enterprising writing and a National Women's Sports Foundation "Billie" media award, along with several regional journalism awards. He is the author of two nonfiction books: *Pride on the Mount* and *Friday Night Thunderbolts*. *The Promise of the Class of '64* is Mr. Gillooly's first novel.

www.ingramcontent.com/pod-product-compliance
Lightning Source LLC
LaVergne TN
LVHW010648110826
845149LV00014B/2990

* 9 7 8 1 9 6 8 5 4 8 2 2 3 *